PENGUIN

EUGÉNIE GRANDET

Honoré de Balzac was born at Tours in 1799, the son of a civil servant. He spent nearly six years as a boarder in a Vendôme school, then went to live in Paris, working as a lawyer's clerk then as a hack-writer. Between 1820 and 1824 he wrote a number of novels under various pseudonyms, many of them in collaboration, after which he unsuccessfully tried his luck at publishing, printing and type-founding. At the age of thirty, heavily in debt, he returned to literature with a dedicated fury and wrote the first novel to appear under his own name, *The Chouans*. During the next twenty years he wrote about ninety novels and shorter stories, among them many masterpieces, to which he gave the comprehensive title *The Human Comedy*. He died in 1850, a few months after his marriage to Evelina Hanska, the Polish countess with whom he had maintained amorous relations for eighteen years.

Marion Ayton Crawford, who died in 1973, taught English Language and Literature in the Technical College at Limavady, Northern Ireland. She translated five volumes of Balzac for the Penguin Classics: *Cousin Bette*, *Domestic Peace and Other Stories*, *The Chouans* and *Old Goriot*.

CLASSICS

HONORÉ DE BALZAC

Eugénie Grandet

TRANSLATED BY
MARION AYTON CRAWFORD

PENGUIN BOOKS

PENGUIN BOOKS

Published by the Penguin Group
Penguin Books Ltd, 80 Strand, London WC2R 0RL, England
Penguin Putnam Inc., 375 Hudson Street, New York, New York 10014, USA
Penguin Books Australia Ltd, Ringwood, Victoria, Australia
Penguin Books Canada Ltd, 10 Alcorn Avenue, Toronto, Ontario, Canada M4V 3B2
Penguin Books India (P) Ltd, 11 Community Centre, Panchsheel Park, New Delhi – 110 017, India
Penguin Books (NZ) Ltd, Cnr Rosedale and Airborne Roads, Albany, Auckland, New Zealand
Penguin Books (South Africa) (Pty) Ltd, 24 Sturdee Avenue, Rosebank 2196 South Africa

Penguin Books Ltd, Registered Offices: 80 Strand, London WC2R 0RL, England

www.penguin.com

This translation first published 1955
23

Translation copyright © Marion Ayton Crawford, 1955
All rights reserved

Printed in England by Clays Ltd, St Ives plc
Set in Monotype Garamond

Except in the United States of America, this book is sold subject
to the condition that it shall not, by way of trade or otherwise, be lent,
re-sold, hired out, or otherwise circulated without the publisher's
prior consent in any form of binding or cover other than that in
which it is published and without a similar condition including this
condition being imposed on the subsequent purchaser

INTRODUCTION

WHEN Balzac as a young man of twenty was living and half-starving in a garret in Paris, given just sufficient time and money (two years and four francs a day), so his parents hoped, to prove that he could be as he asserted a literary man, or to cure him of the foolish fancy for ever and induce him to follow the lawyer's career which had been marked out for him, the work on which all his hopes and thoughts were fixed was a tragedy in the classical style, *Cromwell*. Posterity has endorsed the verdict passed on it by the professorial acquaintance of his brother-in-law's who was called on to consider it. He pronounced it to be completely lacking in any quality which might give hope of its success. But the play is important because of the models Balzac studied as he was writing it. He was trying with all his fabulous intellectual energy and powers of concentration to learn his chosen art, and his letters tell us of the passionate intensity of interest with which he was reading and analysing the works of the French classical theatre at that time. If Balzac had never read a play or seen one acted his strong dramatic sense would certainly still have found expression in the characters and scenes of his novels; and his romantic addiction to the sensational and the complex places him outside the main stream of the austere French tradition for both plays and novels. Yet it is possible to trace influences from, and affinities with, the plays he studied then, in his later novels; and of all the novels of the *Comédie humaine*, *Eugénie Grandet*, in 1883, one of the earliest, is generally considered the most classical.

All the characters of *Eugénie Grandet*, like the characters of 17th-century drama, and like so many of the characters of

Balzac's other novels, are drawn larger than life and appear simpler than real-life characters ever do, especially the character of Grandet, whose obsession dominates the book and gives rise to the tragedy. Balzac was intensely interested in psychological study, and his preoccupation with it is obvious in all his novels, but it is not the complexities and subtleties of men's minds, the discordant elements that fight for mastery in one human being, as the modern novelist sees them, that Balzac depicted. His characters are all of a piece, but represented with such power in their simplicity, or rather single-mindedness, that they become vehicles for the expression of universal truths, and the story of their lives has often an epic quality, or sometimes the direct working out of their apparently inevitable destiny seems to borrow from classical tragedy.

It is from comedy, however, that at first sight Grandet seems to have been taken. Balzac himself compared him to Molière's Harpagon. 'Molière created the miser, but I have created Avarice,' he remarked with his customary lack of proper modesty. In fact neither of the two characters is a mere abstraction, and of the two Balzac's is certainly the rounder figure, but their likeness is obvious. They are both studies in avarice, both broadly drawn with marked personal idiosyncrasies and tricks of speech which impose them on our minds. Both belong to the select band of the world's undying personalities. They are both seen by their creators in a blinding light which effaces all qualities but their dominant one, and illumines that one unforgettably.

The differences are clear enough too. Molière's purpose and the purpose of all those writers, like Jonson, who set living embodiments of human vices and follies in situations contrived to display them, was satirical, and the characters themselves do not alter in the course of the play. Balzac is only incidentally a satirist. He does not hate or despise his characters for their weakness or wickedness. He loves them, and displays all their qualities, good or bad, with enjoyment. The extreme unlovableness of some of the characters whom Balzac managed to sympathize with and find pleasure in considering is notorious.

A more important difference is that Balzac's chief characters are capable of development, and visibly change under the impact of circumstances in the course of the novel, as people alter in real life. It is even possible to say that this development of the characters is one of the principal things the novels, and especially this novel, are 'about'. And yet all these characters in all the vicissitudes and changes through which they pass hold fast to their dominant idea, to the inner dream by which they live. In Grandet it is gold, in Madame Grandet God, in Eugénie her love of Charles. For Nanon it is devotion to her master, for Charles social position.

When the dominant idea amounts to an obsession as it does in Grandet, and indeed this is true also of all the characters who hold a fixed idea so strongly, development can only be in a straight line. We find Grandet a miser and watch him grow into a maniac, indifferent to the unhappiness of the daughter he once cared for, robbing her of her inheritance from her mother, grasping on his death-bed at the precious metal of a crucifix, ready to demand an account of his fortune from beyond the grave. In this Grandet is less like Harpagon than he is like Othello or Macbeth, both destroyed by a developing weakness in their own nature, and spreading destruction round them because of it, or like Racine's heroes and heroines, or like the characters of the Greek dramatists, pursued for their crimes by inescapable avenging Furies. In fact an English reader would more readily accept the particular truth to life that Grandet represents if he met him on the stage. He is the kind of dramatic character whom we expect to see reveal himself in a plot which achieves its climax and end within a few hours; but Balzac has, perfectly successfully, set him in an action lasting years.

Unlike the characters of the great tragic dramatists, Greek, French, English, Balzac's characters are not set apart from the mass of mankind by noble blood and high social position, but only by the intensity of their passion.

When, within three days, with the coming of New Year's Day 1819, Grandet was bound to discover that Eugénie's gold coins were gone, Balzac says, 'In three days a terrible drama would begin, a bourgeois tragedy undignified by poison, dagger or bloodshed, but to the protagonists more cruel than any of the tragedies endured by the members of the noble house of Atreus.' Such a comparison is characteristic of him, not only because he loved allusions to classical literature, but because he was very consciously the first novelist to show that bourgeois tragedies *were* tragic, as tragic as any drama of classical tragedy to those concerned, and having a comparably destructive effect upon the fabric of society. The comparison too serves to heighten the tension and prepare for the dramatic scene which is to come. It is not less characteristic of Balzac that immediately after making this comparison he should note that Madame Grandet had not completed the woollen sleeves she was knitting, and that for want of them she caught a chill. He is never afraid of bathos.

In spite of the way in which Grandet's figure bestrides it like a colossus the novel is called not *Old Grandet* but *Eugénie Grandet*, and the greater and psychologically more interesting tragedy is hers. It is a tragedy of the development of her immature character under the pressure of passion, which immediately brings her into collision with her father's passion and later with a similar passion which has developed in Charles.

In this novel, perhaps more urgently than in any of the others, we are driven to ask ourselves what Balzac meant by Fate, and to what extent he sees the tragedy in his characters' lives as preordained. There is no simple answer to that question. Perhaps consideration of other aspects of the book may shed some

8

light on it. It is worth noting here, however, that the plot follows the rule for French classical tragedy: the incidents are determined solely by the characters of the actors, and are linked together in a solid chain of causal sequence. Balzac goes to great pains to establish each link in the chain of cause and effect. For example, even the apparent accident that Charles Grandet fails to realize that his uncle is a wealthy man is shown in a perfectly natural conversation between Charles and Eugénie to be an inevitable consequence not only of Grandet's mode of life, but of the ignorance of his affairs in which he had kept his daughter. The psychological development of each character, too, is made absolutely clear.

Balzac was writing the story of his own times in all his novels, and although *Eugénie Grandet* was written in 1833, before he had consciously conceived the idea of linking all the novels together, and although the few main characters are living quiet lives, buried in the depths of a narrow provincial town, he never lets us forget that they are living in the post-Revolutionary age, and in fact he is writing about them partly in order to show the working of the ideas and forces of that age.

Avarice is a vice we have always had with us, but the word had a new meaning in Balzac's time when, with the restraining force of the Church and a rigid social order gone, dazzling dreams of power strongly reinforced the natural hoarding instincts of the peasant, dreams which, with Napoleon's example before his eyes, he had every hope of realizing. Balzac notes, and does not think it fantastic, that Grandet, a former cooper, if his ambitions had been aimed higher, might have been a delegate to the congresses that decide international affairs and served France well, although he concludes by reflecting that it is probably only in his own environment that Grandet can exert his genius.

Intrigue, once confined to the Court at Versailles, had become widespread throughout the country, since almost anyone could aspire to any position, provided he had money and could get to know the right people. Everyone was greedy to grab power, and money meant power. Money in the early 19th century had become in a greater degree than ever before something achievable by the use of men's brains in being more ready than their neighbours to see and seize the new opportunities thrown in their way. Finance was beginning to assume the part it plays in the modern world. Society was taking on the fiercely competitive aspect that is a feature of modern life. Modern scientific theory was beginning to reveal to man his place in the world as but one of the higher animals who had reached his position of supremacy by the use of superior weapons in the general fight for survival. Balzac, chronicling in the *Comédie humaine* this society in eruption, was the first to study many aspects of the modern world.

The struggle to amass money and to achieve power is notoriously a grand theme of the *Comédie humaine*. The books are packed with ambitious men and adventurers, careerists and speculators, bankers, financiers, and misers of every conceivable kind, and many that would be inconceivable if he had not made living human beings of them. His success in portraying modern types of unscrupulous rascal led to his being accused of bringing them into being, nature imitating art; and the enormous popularity of his novels, which set unprincipled people in the limelight and gave them a certain prestige, has been blamed for the cynical outlook of the modern Frenchman, and the mania for social climbing and fortune-hunting which he was the first to record.

Balzac always declares his moral aim: he is concerned to show what damage these people do to themselves, to the State and to the fabric of society, but generally he enjoys himself so much, has so much sympathy with powerful and ambitious men, relates the doings of his villains with such gusto, that his moral aims are inclined to be overlooked by his readers. Money-making is a sordid business, and he spares us no detail of the sordidness and the callousness it engenders in human beings, but to him all the modern ways of building up a fortune were just as romantic (and ruthlessness was an element in the romance) as Charles Grandet's adventures half across the world in search of gold. It was in no spirit of cold scientific investigation, as a modern social inquirer might fill his notebooks and set down the result of his survey, that Balzac carried out his avowed purpose of documenting his age: the power of money and men's struggles in pursuit of it set his brain on fire. And to his misers, almost symbolic figures, gold has the magic, the romantic fascination which its name alone, its yellow glitter, held for the Conquistadores, and its devotees are known to one another by signs that betray their passion, and the cold metallic glitter of their eyes.

The tides that are sweeping France send their wash into the remote provincial town of Saumur. We watch the forces and passions that are changing the entire social scene in action in this backwater.

The foundation of Grandet's fortune was laid by the breaking up of the aristocratic estates and the expropriation of land after the Revolution. He increases it by selling wine to the Republican armies, and he ends by learning and putting into practice the lesson, strange and new to a country cooper, that money invested breeds money, and that this return is not dependent on the vagaries of the weather, like the crops grown on his land. His wife's grandfather and his own grandmother had been misers too, and they had kept their money in their stockings, thinking that money invested was money thrown away, since they were not free to handle and gloat over the stuff, but Grandet, while sharing their passion, is a man of the new age.

Gold, the actual precious metal, is constantly present before our mind's eye as we read *Eugénie Grandet*, piled up and gloated over in Grandet's strongroom, or taken at dead of night to Nantes to be sold in secret, part of Charles Grandet's equipment as a young exquisite in jewellery and toilet fittings, in Eugénie's store of beautiful coins whose names are an incantation which Grandet loves to recite, evoking for the reader the atmosphere of times when all trade was a glorious adventure, money was beautiful, and money transactions romantic. This is the 19th century, but the spacious piratical days of the 18th are not yet only a memory. These are still the days when a young man can set out for the East Indies with the scantiest of capital and return in a few years with a fortune, acquired with cold-blooded ruthlessness in the course of a highly romantic and adventurous life. It is entirely in keeping that Charles should bring his fortune home in the form of gold dust 'packed in three casks strongly bound with iron'. It strikes a more modern note that he should hope to do a profitable deal in the gold, and use the proceeds, by way of a successful marriage, by intrigue and knowing the right people, to rise to one or other of the highest positions in the state.

The love of money and passionate pursuit of it, studied in detail in the person of Grandet, are seen also in this book as a dynamic force in society, driving other characters and groups of characters, the Cruchots and des Grassins in Saumur, the whole business world and the world of fashion in Paris, as well as Charles Grandet.

Grandet's lonely wife and daughter in their gloomy home are isolated still further by the web of intrigue that surrounds them, woven by the rival parties who with their allies and plans of campaign are all busily working for the prize of the hand of the rich heiress, and the next step in first social, and then political, advancement. When Monsieur de Bonfons is in the end victorious, his rise is rapid. Charles Grandet, when he at last learns how rich is the prize he has thrown away, is quick to master his shock, and ready at once to try to take advantage of his acquaintance with the future husband of his wealthy cousin. 'We shall be able to push each other on in the world,' he says. De Bonfons rises to the top of his profession, and he is only waiting for a general election to make him a deputy, when death snatches him from his prizes. No sooner is de Bonfons out of the way than a new campaign is started: it is the Froidfond family this time whose nets are spread for the heiress. At the end of the novel we are told, and it is a large part of her tragedy, that Eugénie was fated to find that others approached her only with self-interested motives, that the pale cold glitter of gold was destined to take the place of all warmth and colour in her life. To the acquaintances who came to her drawing-room to play cards and to flatter her she was not a human being at all, but a figure set on a pedestal made of money-bags. Early in the book Balzac speaks of 'the only god that anyone believes in nowadays – Money, in all its power', and from one point of view the novel might almost be taken as a sermon on that text. It is dominated by the pale cold glitter of gold. Only simple people like Nanon and her husband who are not awake to what is going on in the world can be sincere in their affections.

The drama enacted in Grandet's house takes place, as it were, on a remote island surrounded by stormy seas. The Grandets are cut off, not only by the fact that they have no real friends among the Cruchot and des Grassins factions, but by Grandet's ceaseless intrigues to get the better of his neighbours and the fear and awe he is held in locally, with reason. The sharp eyes and busy tongues in Saumur that incessantly watch and comment form an isolating ring of gossip. Yet we are not allowed to forget that all these onlookers have busy lives of their own in which gossip and speculation, for example on Eugénie's possible husband, are only an ingredient, and what really matters is the price paid for the vintage. There are hints too that stories as dramatic and tragic as Eugénie Grandet's might be revealed if we watched other people as closely as we watch the Grandets. When Madame des Grassins invites Charles to dinner she says she will ask the du Hautoys and their lovely daughter, and remarks that she hopes the girl will be presentably dressed for once, as her mother is jealous of her and turns her out badly. It is just a casual remark, revelatory of Madame des Grassins' catty nature, but it gives a sudden glimpse of what could be another Balzacian tragedy, a sense of human passions and human frustrations that can be guessed at, and are only one instance of many that we know nothing of. Madame des Grassins' own life is a tragedy too, sketched in without emphasis or underlining in her various appearances in the Grandet drawing-room.

In Paris the business world and the world of fashion go busily about their own concerns, and we are kept aware of them through the coming and going of Charles and des Grassins and later de Bonfons, and through the letters that pass between Paris and Saumur, from Charles's father, from Charles to his friend and his mistress, from des Grassins to Grandet, from Charles in Paris to Eugénie, and finally from des Grassins to his wife about his interview with Charles.

This wealth of lives lived in various places and social groups, with the complexity of the way in which they meet and touch each other, is one of the things that make us ready to accept the suggestion that the *Comédie humaine* is in fact a chronicle of the actual world as it existed.

We are made aware of the many generations of forbears of Balzac's characters. The old houses of Saumur are part of the history of France, not because the town played any very striking or distinguished part in history, but because for hundreds of years the citizens in the houses, by merely living and sharing in the passions of their day, writing on the walls slogans that mean nothing to anyone now, subjecting strangers to a running fire of gibes as they passed down the streets, developing their own idiosyncrasies and twists of character, have impressed their stamp upon the houses they built and lived in, which in turn mould and influence their descendants who live there. When Eugénie's sensibility is quickened by her love for Charles, and the shock of hearing that her father would rather see her dead than married to him, she becomes aware of the heavy time-laden atmosphere of the ancient street. This is only one occasion of many when the reader is reminded of it, and of the curious eyes of the present inhabitants that peer from the houses.

The characters are set in families, very conscious of family ties, counting on fortunes to be inherited, surrounded by heirlooms valuable or tawdry, an old Sèvres sugar-bowl or a red plush purse, with portraits of grandparents and great-aunts hanging on the walls.

The influence of heredity has its part to play in their development, as it had in the development of Racine's tragic heroes and heroines, and the reappearance of family character-istics is pointed out to us, when the latent weaknesses of his Grandet blood show themselves at last in Charles, and Eugénie in a phrase recalls her father's method of dealing with a situation. The characters are rooted in the past.

In Scott's novels Balzac had studied life as exhibiting man's relation to his historic past, but he goes very much further than Scott did in the degree to which he made the past condition the present.

Since in reading the novel we feel that we already know everything material concerning the past of the Grandet family, it seems superfluous to find a possible ancestry for it in real life. It has been noted, however, that in Saumur Balzac must have heard talk of a certain Jean Nivelleau, a miser and money-lender in the town, of humble origin, who having built up a fortune had bought a fine estate just outside Saumur, and married his beautiful daughter to the Baron de Grandmaison, a former officer of Charles X's life-guards. Their grand-nephew and heir, Georges de Grand-maison, declared that Balzac wrote *Eugénie Grandet* in revenge for Nivelleau's refusal of him as a son-in-law. However that may be, and we have to note too that the dedication of the book does more than hint that Eugénie is studied from life, from the mysterious Maria about whom nothing factual is known, though Grandet's story may be founded on fact, as they say, the words seem ridiculous as we say them because Grandet's story *is* fact, a different sort of fact, and Grandet is not Jean Nivelleau. How could he be when the factors that have made him what he is include, as well as the generations of his ancestors and the buildings and furniture he has lived in and surrounded himself with, the shape of his head, the length of his nose and the wen on it, and even his name, as Balzac believed?

In the same way it is hardly of the first importance that, though the old Saumur which Balzac describes has partly disappeared, the vestiges remaining are said to bear witness to Balzac's exactness. Archaeological correctness, though he insisted that that was what he was giving us, and though it makes his books fascinating and sometimes wearisome storehouses of historical information, matters as little in Balzac's novels as it does in Dickens's. Dickens's London and Balzac's Paris and his country towns have their own kind of authenticity. They are alive like the characters with the essential vitality given them in the first place by the novelist's creative imagination, and are recreated ever afterwards by every reader in his own mind. It is in trying to achieve this sort of authenticity that films fall down so badly, because studio reconstructions, or even photographs taken 'on location', have so little power, compared with a novelist's vision, to set the imagination to work. At first sight some of Balzac's plots and many of his characters look like a godsend to the film industry, but films could do nothing but leave out a great deal that is vital to Balzac. They can photograph characters against a background exactly as Balzac described them: it is more difficult to convey the relationship between them, a product often not of years but of generations of life in the same place.

The ancient main street of Saumur leading to the market-place and Grandet's fields by the Loire form the wider setting of the story, but the heart of it is of course the gloomy old echoing house overshadowed by the ramparts, where the scene shifts from the dingy parlour where Madame Grandet and Eugénie spend so many hours in tedious needlework, and where so many grim social evenings are passed, up the rickety, worm-eaten staircase to Grandet's strongroom and Charles's attic bedroom, along the passage to Nanon's kitchen, and out under the draughty archway. The atmosphere of the house is all-pervasive, dominating the actors. Even Charles, whose incredulous astonishment at first sight of it serves to throw its peculiarities into vivid relief, succumbs to its influence and the qualities of his aunt and cousin, grows fond of the old house, and no longer finds the household ways so ridiculous.

The romantic garden where so many of the important scenes of the story are set recalls Amiel's dictum 'A landscape is a frame of mind'. It both echoes and evokes the emotional feelings of the characters. It literally echoes to the sound of everything that happens in the Grandet household: the light dry sound of autumn leaves falling to the ground as Eugénie watches from her window early in the morning after Charles's arrival, and later as she watches by her mother's deathbed, Charles's heart-broken sobs, the excited voice of Nanon, announcing a letter from Paris. Eugénie finds in it the expression of her feelings, and through her response to it we gain an insight into the nature of her feelings that we could acquire in no other way. Charles was to remember it all his life as it was when Grandet gave him the news of his father's suicide there. House and garden are a great deal more than merely a setting.

Sombre and lonely though her home is, when her mother and father die Eugénie has only additional reasons for clinging to it. She is bound to it by unbreakable ties. It has conditioned her whole existence, and in the end is to be a symbol of it.

To show the various influences affecting the characters, a

enormous period of time has to be covered in the novel. In his preoccupation with time, and the use he makes of it to give us a succession of portraits of his characters, Balzac looks forward to Proust. He manipulates the flow of time for the purposes of his plot, and makes the reader conscious of its passage, with great skill in *Eugénie Grandet*.

In starting his novel with a description of Saumur's main street Balzac is really plunging straight into his subject: *in medias res*, as he would probably say himself. He follows his usual custom in devoting a good many pages at the beginning to description and exposition, which set the characters in their environment and circumstances and cover their entire lives until the moment we meet them. This essential illumination of the reader is achieved here with great economy and clarity.

Then on one particular evening in the middle of November 1819 which supplies a dramatically effective opening scene, the reader is introduced into the Grandet family circle. It is the first day a fire has been lit in the parlour that autumn. It is Eugénie's twenty-third birthday, and the fact that it is time to arrange her marriage has been mentioned at supper. After supper the rival parties who are contending for the heiress's hand come to bring their birthday good wishes, and while the comedy of their false friendliness to the heiress and embittered jealousy of each other is in full swing over a game of cards there suddenly arrives the dazzling young stranger from Paris, whose coming supplies the inevitable spark that lights the train already laid for tragedy.

Once the action begins it moves extremely rapidly. During the four days that follow the plot is wound up, and the rest of the book is simply the narrative of the consequences, spread over years, of the events of those four days.

Eugénie is dazzled by her cousin at first sight. Next morning comes the stunning blow of her father's violent rejection of Cruchot's suggestion that she is to marry Charles, followed immediately by the news of his father's bankruptcy and suicide, which by reducing the romantic dandy to a penniless and heart-broken boy makes him even more irresistibly the object of all her tenderness.

Balzac here employs a device which he constantly and most successfully uses to give his characters depth and shed light upon two characters at once – he lets us see them with each other's eyes as well as with his. Nothing could be more effective than the way in which he lets us see what Charles and Eugénie find to love in each other, while making it plain that Charles's love will not last and that Eugénie is sowing the seeds of a passion that is to become a disease. Throughout the book too, we are forced to realize that the eyes with which Eugénie looks at her father see something quite different from what the reader sees; even when her picture of him changes as she develops, and as her passion sets her in opposition to him. Nanon, too, has a different picture of her master. The characters take on roundness when observed by different people from different points of view, and the points of view they hold illuminate the characters observing.

Within four days Charles has accepted his new situation and made his plans to seek his fortune in the East Indies. Eugénie has fallen irrevocably in love. Grandet has decided on the investment of his money, planned his game with his brother's creditors, and despatched des Grassins to Paris.

During these four days, the history of which fills more than a third of the book, we live with the characters hour by hour, in the usual routine of the Grandet household and the deviations from it occasioned by Charles's presence. Even when the day is over we are with the characters for a good part of the night, follow them into their dreams on the night of Charles's arrival, listen with Eugénie for Charles's cries and run up to his room on the second night, watch Grandet's midnight departure for Nantes with his gold, and see Eugénie read Charles's letters and give him her gold coins on the third.

On the fourth Grandet is tired so everyone goes to bed early.

After these four days the pace slackens a little. There is a little time given for Charles and the three women to grow into an intimate family group, for Eugénie to savour the poignancy of the love-affair soon to be cut short, and then Charles has gone. This brief spell of idyllic domestic happiness is important not only in deepening the ties between Eugénie and Charles, but in establishing the qualities of the women of the household, and forming an oasis which is to heighten the contrast of the wearisome desert of the years which follow.

At this stage of the story especially, Balzac neglects no means of making the reason for every thought and emotion that move the main characters absolutely clear, and the complete naturalness of their behaviour is very striking, especially at a time when contemporary writers were more concerned with what was romantic or picturesque than with psychological truth. To take one minor example, the tears which Eugénie and her mother shed as Grandet tells Charles of his father's death are *real* tears, not like the romantic tears of the heroines of the insipid romances of the end of the 18th century. To a modern taste, developed in the modern British (not French) convention of keeping a stiff upper lip in time of grief, Charles sheds too many tears and his loud sobbing is of course quite inexcusable. Balzac forestalls our criticism ... 'he was still just a boy, still at the age when feelings express themselves spontaneously'. We are constantly reminded that Charles and Eugénie are both rapidly changing at this period, and they are to change still further.

When Charles has gone we return to the Grandet household and the three women, saddened by his departure but bound closer together by their new interest and secret. 'Two months passed in this fashion.' And we have lived so intimately, day-long and day by day, with the three Grandets and Nanon that we know exactly how they have passed. And then with New

Year's Day 1819 comes Grandet's sensational discovery of the loss of Eugénie's gold. Under the pressure of her passion Eugénie's nature has developed its latent Grandet force and strength, and Grandet's passion and his daughter's confront each other with Eugénie's refusal to say what she has done with her coins. Months later, in an even more melodramatic scene, father and daughter are face to face with Charles Grandet's dressing-case between them, each armed with a knife, the one to prise the gold from the case, the other to kill herself if he should dare attempt it.

It is certain that Balzac had a good deal of sympathy with Grandet in his astonishment and rage at his daughter's defiance of him. To Balzac one of the worst results of the Revolution was the disintegration of the ordered groups of society, of which the family is the unit, into a mob of mutually suspicious individuals, all striving against each other to achieve selfish and fundamentally anti-social ambitions. The loss of parental authority meant the loss of a major element in national unity, and some of his novels show the disastrous consequences of this. And here was a daughter invoking the Code against her father, saying that she could do what she liked with her own money. Even if her father is Grandet this is deplorable. The passions of both father and daughter are anti-social in their results, and their opposition stimulates the growth of both.

Eugénie's is such a natural passion and so much more sympathetic to us than her father's, its influence to begin with is so entirely beneficial to Eugénie, extending and deepening her perceptions, giving her independence in thought and action, that its potential destructive force is revealed to us only slowly, when it is turned in upon itself and she spends her days dreaming of Charles on the mossy bench in the memory-filled garden, while Charles, as we have been carefully prepared by the earlier analysis of the flaws in his character to feel, must inevitably have forgotten her. But so similarly in one respect,

Grandet's passion has had a beneficial effect on his powers, developing his talent for making money into something like genius.

There follow long years, marked by Madame Grandet's death and Eugénie's gradual initiation into her father's secrets. Then, 'Five years went by in this way, and no event occurred to distinguish one day from another in the monotonous life that Eugénie and her father led.' Monsieur Grandet dies. The des Grassins are out of the running, but the Cruchots renew their campaign, and Madame des Grassins does her best to trouble their complacency by urging the claims to consideration as a suitor of the Marquis de Froidfond. Eugénie makes no comment, and says only to Nanon, one evening, as she goes to bed, 'How can it be, Nanon, that he hasn't written to me once in seven years?'

From the beginning to the end of the book every event is given its date and the lapse of time between the events is exactly noted. This last section of it, which covers years in the characters' lives, covers comparatively few pages (less than a third of the book, from Charles's departure to the end), but reading it we have a sense of time slowly, monotonously passing, marked by the ticking of the old parlour clock, making Grandet's faculties decline while his obsession grows, turning Eugénie's love to an obsession that feeds on itself, bringing changes and losses to the Cruchot and des Grassins families, making Charles develop along the lines that we have foreseen.

At last comes the fatal letter from Charles, and the instant decisive action taken by the strong-willed independent woman that we have watched Eugénie become, so different from the girl that Charles remembers, yet appealing and pathetic in her lonely isolation. To heap coals of fire on Charles's head by paying his father's creditors in full is consistent with what we know of her impulsive uncalculating generosity, and a beautifully neat and dramatic way for Balzac to finish off together at one stroke her relations with Charles and the business of Grandet's game with the creditors, incidentally providing a nicely comic scene between Charles and de Bonfons which puts the finishing touch to the portrait of her cousin. In Balzac's own words 'the *dénouement* of the drama begun nine years before' comes with her request to de Bonfons which amounts to a declaration that she wishes him to be her husband. Eugénie looks her destiny squarely in the face. She has no illusions about what the future holds for her, or what it is that de Bonfons finds attractive in her, although there is a rather pathetic trust in his honour and his power and willingness to be her shield and protector. He is 'a staunch friend and a man of honour', a man whom she had known so long that they were almost relatives. She makes her decisions and acts at once, and only when these steps are irretrievably taken, and de Bonfons sent post-haste to Paris and promised his reward, does she give way to tears. We have seen her grow in stature and rise to the height of her tragedy. The end of the story finds her turning to the other dream that had shared her thoughts with Charles – her dream of God, and spending Grandet's gold in public and private benefaction, painfully aware of what she misses in human warmth through the barrier that her great wealth opposes to all contact with her neighbours, a stiff old maid, observing the narrow and penurious ways that are by now as much a part of her nature as they had been of her father's. In time, we have reached what was the present day when Balzac was writing.

For Eugénie and for her mother religion is an obvious means of sublimating their unwanted powers of love and devotion (Balzac can never have heard the term used in this sense, but seems to have understood the process), but Balzac clearly intends us to see it as being much more. Their religion is apparently a matter of narrow observance of the laws of the Church, of blind obedience to its priests, no matter how unworthy, and good works, yet they are recipients of divine grace which has the power to transfigure human beings, to make them saints on earth, and to enable the soul to shine through the body as the hour of death approaches, and be seen to be in the act of taking flight for heaven.

The representatives of the Church in *Eugénie Grandet*, the Abbé Cruchot, the Talleyrand of his party, and the despicable creature sent by him to persuade Eugénie, whose confessor he is, in the very hour of her distress that it is her duty to marry, are by no means unique in the *Comédie humaine* in their worldliness, and, especially the Abbé, are very convincing portraits. They are balanced in other novels by a number of 'good' priests, yet quite often, as in *Eugénie Grandet*, the priests are much further from heaven than their parishioners.

Balzac had observed the power of the spiritual force often possessed by gentle, pious, unintellectual women, and he was interested in it as he was interested in all forces, especially in those that work powerfully to change and develop the nature of the people driven by them. The near approach of death and her concern for her daughter increase Madame Grandet's spiritual strength, and give her courage to stand up to her terrible husband where she thinks he is morally wrong, but, long before, her religion has enabled her to support the life she leads with dignity. Balzac characteristically notes and deplores the narrowness of her outlook, and the innocence, like Eugénie's, founded on ignorance, and he makes everything she says emphasize this narrowness, yet it is clear that in her pride and delicacy of feeling that made it impossible for her to ask her husband for money, she was of finer clay than Grandet, and that Balzac whole-heartedly sympathizes with her and approves of her. Such women are the cement that hold the family and so society together, and however they may suffer, and he does not underestimate their suffering, they can only endure and find their strength in God. Where his virtuous women were concerned Balzac appears to have held the sterling domestic moral views usually thought of as being the prerogative of the English Victorian middle class. Perhaps that does something to explain their lack of popularity with Balzac's critics, who find them too simple to be interesting. We have swallowed so much lush sentiment and false pathos about simple goodness in 19th-century novels (especially Dickens's) that simple goodness, especially in a pathetic situation, is apt to afflict us with nausea. Balzac's pathos is not usually false, however. It is inherent in the situation, and not mere tear-jerking for the sake of jerking tears. Nor are his innocent young girls mere wax dolls. He has an almost disconcertingly sharp eye for their defects in face and figure. When he lapses into rhapsody in his portraits of them, the rhapsody is part of the portrait which would not be complete without it. He is concerned with the expression of the spirit shining through the flesh in them, sometimes as seen by the Italian painters, especially Raphael, in their visions of the Virgin, and shown as a quality of light, light as if shed from a halo in the case of Victorine Taillefer in *Old Goriot*, the translucent quality of a half-open flower in the case of Eugénie Grandet. This is rhapsodical but not sentimental. There are many of these girls and young women in the *Comédie humaine*, and in the pot-boiling novels which preceded it, with a family resemblance, but with their own individuality. He has a tender feeling for them which strikes us as sincere, and his portraits of them are often graceful and charming. Their circumstances are nearly always narrow and restricting: Victorine is like a shrub with yellowing leaves, newly transplanted to an adverse soil, Eugénie spends her days in the dingy parlour, toiling at the household mending; and Balzac is not a person to find ignorance of the world romantic. Many of them, inexperienced and unsophisticated when we first meet them, are ready to fall in love for the first time, and when they do, seek their lovers' happiness at any cost to themselves. Like Eugénie, many of them are capable of showing a surprising fire and initiative when their circumstances change. They are not complex, but it seems a little unkind to blame Balzac for the whiteness or greyness of some strands in his pattern, when he has so often been reproached with the black and lurid red ones; since all his characters are simplified.

It is a more serious accusation against him that his pleasant likable characters are so invariably the victims of his wicked ones, though it may be thought that this is not really too great a simplification of what is true in life. Mauriac speaks of 'the fundamental manichaeism of Balzac, for whom darkness and light divide the kingdom between them': and it is true that Balzac's wicked characters go to and fro upon the earth unchecked, like incarnations of Satan, and the virtuous characters have no defences against them. The self-abnegation which these virtuous characters nearly always practise has a spiritual significance, as well as a social one, though because Balzac was less interested in this aspect than he was in the power of the evil forces opposed to them, the radiance and grandeur of their 'sublimity' is not so overwhelmingly revealed to us that we forget the crippling restrictions imposed on their earthly development and happiness, which Balzac, in fact, takes care to emphasize. And these restrictions are, of course, their tragedy. Not for Balzac's heroines the terrible splendour of Desdemona's tragedy, nor the crashing finality of Tess of the D'Urbervilles' catastrophic end, but the continued narrow colourless existence of a wealthy ageing woman in a provincial town, which we see prolonged into the future beyond the confines of the book.

Near the beginning of the book, when Balzac has drawn Madame Grandet's portrait and related her history, he exclaims, 'Have philosophers who meet with such women as Nanon, Madame Grandet, and Eugénie, not some grounds for their conclusion that Fate is, at bottom, ironical?' Near the end, when the forces of intrigue have triumphed and de Bonfons has won the prize of Eugénie's millions, we note that their victory is to be a barren one which de Bonfons will not live to enjoy. Balzac says, 'Heaven exacted vengeance ...' and in the next breath, '... but Eugénie was left, God's prisoner, and God poured quantities of gold into her lap, although gold meant nothing to her.' For a moment we think of Hardy ('The President of the Immortals ... had ended his sport with Tess'). Eugénie like Tess is an innocent and amiable person who after a life of unmerited misfortune comes to disaster. Was Balzac, like Hardy, indicting a Providence that plays a long-drawn-out game of cat and mouse with unoffending human beings? And where does the Heaven which punished de Bonfons for his wickedness come in?

De Bonfons' death has something a little too providential about it. It is not the inevitable result of all that has gone before, like the other events of the book. It was dramatically necessary in order to round off Eugénie's tragedy that she should marry him, that the marriage should be an empty farce, and that she should be left alone again to be the focus of new intrigue. But the God who kills de Bonfons has rather the air of a *deus ex machina*.

Balzac's comments on the irony of Fate, in curious contrast to his carefully planned demonstration of the fatality of the passions, have an oddly impromptu air, as if he was communicating what he has just discovered as he reflects afterwards on the events he is relating. These remarks reinforce the verisimilitude of events and persons, since it is clear that we are not watching puppets moved by the author, and give the book the character of an attempt through observation and analysis first of all to discover, and only secondly to show, not only the motives that actuate social behaviour, but the principles that would explain the universe, and the genuine power of man's sense of God, for those who possess it. It is both a strength and a weakness of Balzac's novels that they are very far from revealing any consistent system of thought. They are not simply, like Hardy's, an illustration of one central conflict – between man on the one hand and an omnipotent and indifferent or retributive Fate on the other. *Eugénie Grandet* shows more than one of the solutions that Balzac found to the questions that perpetually exercised his mind and stirred his strongest feelings. He found many others, which he tests in other novels, and many contradictory and mutually exclusive ideas which he was able to hold at the same time. His strength was that his complex and fabulously receptive mind was able not only to contain them all but to impose them on the picture of his world that he has given us, with tremendous force and conviction, so that impossible as it may be to accept all his varying solutions one cannot but feel the strong urge to examine his various creatures by the light he has turned on them. Hence the libraries of critical books that have been written about Balzac. Hence too the length of this essay which I must now conclude, I hope before I have quite exhausted the patience of my readers.

It has been an interesting experience to translate *Eugénie Grandet* after having translated *Old Goriot*. The two novels, *Eugénie Grandet* completed in 1833, *Old Goriot* in 1834, are in certain respects companion pieces, alike in being among their author's best work, yet very unlike in many ways.

As *Eugénie Grandet* was the earlier creation it would seem only natural that it should be much the simpler in plot, number and social range of characters, and variety of incident, if we did not remember the mass of other material that Balzac was writing contemporaneously with both of them, and the early pot-boiling novels, which were of the greatest possible complexity and crammed with characters and exciting incident. It is, I think, clear that in *Eugénie Grandet* Balzac has curbed his natural exuberance to meet the needs of a novel deliberately composed so far as possible in the classical tradition. His self-control is rewarded by the shapeliness of the novel. It is difficult to know whether to admire more the skill that in *Eugénie Grandet*, concentrating on a single simple drama, yet keeps us aware of the stir and movement of the world outside and incorporates it into the pattern, or that in *Old Goriot* succeeds in imposing unity on such a varied and complex scene.

Balzac's restraint in the composition of the novel is matched by restraint in the style. His portraits of the chief characters and descriptions of the setting are extremely economical, especially given the mass of material which his theories obliged him to include in them, and not only the major but the minor characters are presented with even more than his usual power and precision – for example the delicious portraits of Madame d'Aubrion and her daughter at the very end of the book, whose sparkling malice is in striking contrast to the tender compassion shown to such a character as big Nanon. The psychological comments are to the point, and effective in their object of showing the cause of every action, and reaction, of the persons concerned. Balzac does not here, as so often elsewhere, rush off at a tangent to give us a lecture on any subject that happens to be suggested to him by what he is saying. In the same way he refrains from calling on the astonishing wealth of image and metaphor, culled from every field of human experience, that he had at his command, and that he usually delights in inlaying his elucidations with. This, to those who enjoy what Balzac's critics agree was the badness of Balzac's style, makes the texture of *Eugénie Grandet* less rich and highly-coloured than that of *Old Goriot*, and it lacks the impetuosity and dash which in *Old Goriot* carries Balzac on from paragraph to paragraph with the onward rush of a waterfall, though it has its own spontaneous flow. Because the characters are much fewer, and on the whole simpler, and because in what they say Balzac is so vitally concerned to drive the individuality of the speaker home to the reader by every possible means, including the repetition of characteristic idiosyncrasies of speech, the dialogue generally is less amusing and varied, though always skilfully handled to achieve what Balzac aimed at doing through it.

The novel, in fact, has some of the defects of its great qualities: but because it is free from many of the faults that mars other among Balzac's finest novels, because it is comparatively stripped and bare of all inessentials, it is, I think, easier to see in it what some of Balzac's great qualities are.

M. A. C.

TO MARIA

May your name be set on this book,
whose fairest ornament is your portrait, like the branch of box set on the
door of a house to protect it against all
harm – the tree it comes from is unknown, but it is sprinkled with holy
water, blessed by the Church, and pious
hands ever renew it and keep it green.

De Balzac

Eugénie Grandet

In some country towns there exist houses whose appearance weighs as heavily upon the spirits as the gloomiest cloister, the most dismal ruin, or the dreariest stretch of barren land. These houses may combine the cloister's silence with the arid desolation of the waste and the sepulchral melancholy of ruins. Life makes so little stir in them that a stranger believes them to be uninhabited until he suddenly meets the cold list-less gaze of some motionless human being, whose face, austere as a monk's, peers from above the window-sill at the sound of a stranger's footfall.

One particular house front in Saumur possesses all these gloomy characteristics. It stands at the end of the hilly street leading to the castle, in the upper part of the town. This street, which is little used nowadays, is hot in summer, cold in winter, and in some places dark and overshadowed. One's footsteps ring curiously loudly on its flinty cobble-stones, which are always clean and dry; and its narrowness and crookedness and the silence of its houses, which form part of the old town and are looked down upon by the ramparts, make an unusual impression on the mind. There are houses there which were built three hundred years ago, and built of wood, yet are still sound. Each has a character of its own, and their diversity contributes to the essential strangeness of the place, which attracts antiquaries and artists to this quarter of Saumur.

It is difficult to pass by these houses without stopping to wonder at the enormous beams, whose projecting ends, carved with grotesque figures, crown the ground floor of most of them with a black bas-relief. In some places the cross beams are protected by slates which draw blue lines across the crumbling walls of a house which is topped by a high-pitched roof, which has bowed and bent under the weight of years, and whose decayed shingles have been warped by the long-continued action of alternate sunshine and rain. Worn blackened window-ledges catch the eye, whose delicate carving can scarcely be distinguished, and which seem too slight a support for the brown flower-pot full of pinks or roses, set there by some poor working woman. Further along the street one notes the doors, studded with huge nails, on which our ancestors recorded the passions of the age in hieroglyphs, once understood in every household, the meaning of which no one will now ever again unravel. In these symbols a Protestant declared his faith, or a Leaguer cursed Henri IV, or some civic dignitary traced the insignia of his office, celebrating the long-forgotten glory of his temporary high estate as alderman or sheriff. The history of France lies written in these houses.

Beside the ramshackle, rough-walled hovel, where the artisan has set up a glorified plane, the emblem of his craft, stands a nobleman's mansion. Above the round arch of the stone gateway some relics of his coat of arms may still be seen, scarred and broken in the many revolutions that have shaken the country since 1789.

They do business in the ground floors of the houses in this street, but you could not call these low-ceilinged rooms, innocent of glass window and display case, cavernous, dark, bare within and without, shops. Lovers of the medieval would recognize in them our ancestors' workshops in all their primitive simplicity. Their stout doors, heavily barred with iron, are divided into two parts, the upper of which is folded back during the daytime, and the lower, fitted with a bell, swings to and fro continually. Air and daylight filter into the damp cavern behind through the upper part of the door, or through the space left between the ceiling and the low wall which forms the shop-front, when the solid shutters, set at elbow level and held in place by heavy iron bolts, are removed every morning. This wall serves as a place on which to set out goods, as an indication of the nature of the business carried on.

There are no cheap-jack attractions there. The samples displayed consist of two or three tubs of salt and salt codfish, or a few bales of sailcloth or coils of rope, copper wire hanging from the rafters, cask hoops along the walls, or some lengths of cloth on the shelves. If you go inside, a neat and well-kept girl with the fresh good looks of youth, white-neckerchiefed, red-armed, lays down her knitting and goes to call her father or mother, who comes to attend you and supply your want, stolidly, pleasantly, or with an independent air, according to his temperament or hers, be it for two sous' worth of merchandise or for twenty thousand francs' worth.

You will see a dealer in barrel staves sitting at his door twiddling his thumbs as he gossips with a neighbour: to all appearances he possesses nothing more than some rickety bottle racks and two or three bundles of laths, yet his well-stocked timber-yard on the quay supplies all the coopers in Anjou. He knows, to a stave, how many casks he can *do* for you, if the vintage is good. A few scorching days make his fortune. A spell of rainy weather ruins him. In a single morning the price of a puncheon may rise to eleven francs or fall to six.

Here, as in Touraine, the business done in the district is dependent on the weather's vagaries. Vinegrowers, land-owners, timber-merchants, coopers, innkeepers, lightermen are all on the watch for a ray of sunshine. They go to bed in a state of dread, fearing they may hear next morning that there has been frost in the night. They dread rain, and wind and drought as well: they would like the weather arranged to suit them, and humidity, warmth, and cloud laid on according to their requirements. There is a perpetual duel in progress between celestial forces and terrestrial interests. Faces lengthen or deck themselves with smiles as the barometer falls or rises.

You may hear the words 'This is golden weather!' passed from mouth to mouth, or the remark 'It's raining gold louis!' exchanged between neighbours, from one end to the other of this street, the old High Street of Saumur; and everyone knows to a sou just how much profit a sunbeam or a timely shower is bringing him, and is mentally engaged in setting down figures accordingly on the credit side of his ledger. After about twelve o'clock on a Saturday in the summer you will not be able to do a sou's worth of business with these fine businessmen. Each of them has his vineyard, his own little bit of land, and goes there for the week-end.

Since all are dependent on the same conditions for their business they have no secrets from one another. Everything – expenses, purchases, and sales, to the very profit each will make, is known in advance, and so these people find themselves free for ten hours out of twelve to pass the time in happy diversion, in observation of their neighbours, comment on their affairs, and constant spying on their comings and goings. A housewife cannot buy a partridge without the neighbours asking her husband if the bird was cooked to a turn. A girl cannot put her head out of the window without being observed by all the groups of idlers. Consciences are clear there, or at least open for inspection, and the apparently impenetrable, dark, and silent houses are completely lacking in secrecy.

Life is lived almost entirely in the open air. The members of every family spend the day sitting by the door, and have all their meals and quarrels in public. No passer-by escapes being looked over by sharp eyes, and this scrutiny is the modern equivalent of the running fire of jeers and gibes a stranger arriving in a country town was subjected to in former days. Many good stories survive to remind us of that old custom, and the nickname 'lingo-slingers' applied to the natives of Angers, who excelled in that provincial sport.

The former mansions of the old town, which at one time

housed the noblemen of the region, are all situated at the upper part of this street, and among them the sombre dwelling which is the scene of the events of this story. These houses are venerable relics of an age when men and manners had that character of simplicity which it becomes more and more difficult to find in modern France. When you have followed the windings of this impressive street whose every turn awakens memories of the past, and whose atmosphere plunges you irresistibly into a kind of dream, you notice a gloomy recess in the middle of which you may dimly discern the door of Monsieur Grandet's house. Monsieur Grandet's house! You cannot possibly understand what these words convey to the provincial mind unless you have heard the story of Monsieur Grandet's life.

The nature of the reputation Monsieur Grandet enjoyed in Saumur, its causes and its effects, will not be fully grasped by anyone who has not lived for a time, however short, in a country town. Monsieur Grandet, who was still in 1819 called 'honest Grandet' by certain old people, though their number was noticeably declining, was in 1789 a master cooper in a very good way of business, who could read, write, and keep accounts. When the French Republic put the confiscated lands of the Church in the Saumur district up for sale, the cooper, then aged forty, had just married the daughter of a rich timber merchant. With all his own available money and his wife's dowry in hand, a sum amounting to two thousand gold louis, Grandet went to the office of the authority for the district, and there, with the help of his father-in-law who offered two hundred double louis to grease the palm of the rough-hewn Republican who was in charge of the sale of the public estates, he bought for the price of a crust of bread, in a deal legally, if not morally, unassailable, the finest vineyards in the neighbourhood, an old abbey, and some small farms.

As the inhabitants of Saumur were not very revolutionary-minded, honest Grandet passed for a daring fellow, a Republican, a patriot, a man interested in advanced ideas, whereas the cooper's interests and ideas were solely concerned with vines. He was nominated a member of the district administration of Saumur, and exercised a pacific influence in both politics and commerce. Politically, he befriended the fallen aristocracy and did his best to prevent the sale of the property of the Royalists who had fled; commercially, he supplied the Republican armies with one or two thousand hogsheads of white wine, and took in payment for them some meadowland of first-class quality, the property of a community of nuns, which had been held back from the first sales.

Under the Consulate the worthy Grandet became Mayor, carried out his public duties soberly and discreetly, and lined his purse more discreetly still. When Napoleon became Emperor his status was established, and he was from that time forward known as *Monsieur* Grandet. But Napoleon had no love for Republicans, and he replaced Monsieur Grandet, who had been looked upon as a red Republican, by a large landowner, a man with the aristocratic *de* before his name, and hopes of becoming a baron of the Empire. Monsieur Grandet said goodbye to his civic honours without regret. In the interests of the town he had seen to it that excellent roads were constructed, passing by his lands. The taxes he paid, on the extremely moderate assessment of his house and property, were not heavy. Since his various vineyards had been assessed, moreover, the unremitting care and attention he had given to his vines had resulted in their becoming classed as *la tête du pays*, a technical term applied to vineyards producing wine of the finest quality. He could reasonably claim the cross of the Legion of Honour, and he was awarded it in 1806.

In that year Monsieur Grandet was fifty-seven years old, and his wife about thirty-six. They had one child, a little girl of ten. Providence no doubt wished to console Monsieur Grandet for his fall from office, for in the course of the year he inherited three fortunes, two through his wife, from her mother Madame de la Gaudinière, *née* de la Bertellière, and her grandfather old Monsieur de la Bertellière, and one from his own grandmother on his mother's side, Madame Gentillet. Nobody knew just how much these inheritances were worth, for the three old people had been such impassioned misers that for years they had hoarded their money in order to gloat over it in secret. Old Monsieur de la Bertellière used to call investments 'throwing money away', finding more profit in the contemplation of his gold than in any interest on a loan. The town of Saumur, therefore, assessed the value of the estate according to an estimate of the amount that could have been saved of the yearly income, and Monsieur Grandet found himself the possessor of a new title to nobility, and one that our present passion for equality will never abolish – he paid more taxes than anyone else in the whole district.

He now cultivated one hundred acres of vineyard, which in good years would yield him seven or eight hundred puncheons of wine. He owned thirteen small farms, an old abbey, in which he had prudently walled up the windows in order to preserve the stained glass and the traceries, and one hundred and twenty-seven acres of grazing land, on which three thousand poplars, planted in 1793, grew and flourished. Finally, the house in which he lived was his own. This was evidence of his prosperity that lay visible to everyone's eye. As for his capital, only two persons were in a position to make even a rough estimate of its magnitude. One of these was Monsieur Cruchot, the notary, who did all the business connected with Monsieur Grandet's investments, and the other was Monsieur des Grassins, the wealthiest banker in Saumur, whose services the winegrower made use of secretly, at his own convenience, on many occasions of which nothing was known locally. Although both old Cruchot and Monsieur des Grassins possessed that closeness of mouth and cautiousness which in provincial towns engender trust and are conducive to money-making, they addressed Monsieur Grandet in public with such marked deference that observers could draw their own conclusions, and estimate their late mayor's fortune at a figure proportionate to the obsequiousness of the attention shown him.

There was not a person in Saumur who was not convinced that Monsieur Grandet had a treasure hoard, a secret hiding-place full of louis, and indulged himself nightly with the ineffable pleasures that the spectacle of a great pile of gold can give. The misers among them had a kind of certainty of it, as they watched the old fellow's eyes, to which contemplation of the yellow metal seemed to have communicated a yellow, metallic glitter. The glance of a man accustomed to drawing huge sums as interest on his capital, like the glance of the sensualist, the gambler, or the toady, necessarily contracts certain indefinable characteristics, a furtive, greedy, secret flicker, which do not pass unnoticed by his fellows who worship at the same shrine. This language of secret signs which they alone can interpret forms, as it were, a freemasonry among people of like passions.

Monsieur Grandet, then, inspired the respectful esteem which was the due of a man who never owed a penny to anyone, who, astute old cooper and winegrower that he was, habitually forecast with an astronomer's certainty when a thousand puncheons would be needed for his vintage, and when five hundred would be enough; who never lost by any speculation that he made, had always casks to sell when casks were worth more than their contents, was in a position to put his wine in his cellars and bide his time until the moment when a puncheon fetched ten louis, while lesser men were forced to sell early at half the price. His famous vintage in 1811, providently withheld and sold little by little as opportunity offered, had brought him in more than two hundred and forty thousand livres.

In matters of finance, Monsieur Grandet combined the characteristics of the tiger and the boa constrictor. Like a tiger he waited for his prey, lurking concealed until the long foreseen moment when it was at his mercy and he pounced; then the jaws of his purse opened to engulf a plenitude of coins, and he lay down again peacefully, like the gorged python, to digest; impassible, emotionless, methodical. No one could see him pass without experiencing a thrill of admiration, mingled with respect and terror. Had not everyone in Saumur felt his claws of steel rip the flesh, while he smiled politely? For one man Maître Cruchot had procured the money he needed to buy some land – at an interest of eleven per cent. For another Monsieur des Grassins had discounted bills, but at a ruinous rate.

Few days ran their course without Monsieur Grandet's name coming up in conversation, among men doing business in the market, or convivial groups in the evening, in the gossip of the town. There were some who felt a patriotic pride in the old winegrower's wealth. More than one merchant, more than one innkeeper, was in the habit of remarking to strangers, with a certain complacency, 'We have two or three millionaire firms here, sir; but Monsieur Grandet doesn't know himself how much money he has!'

In 1816 Saumur's ablest mathematicians reckoned the value of the cooper's landed property at nearly four millions; but as he must have drawn, on an average, something like a hundred thousand francs a year from his property between 1793 and 1817, it stood to reason that the money he possessed was nearly equal to the value of the land. And so, whenever Monsieur Grandet's name was mentioned over a game of boston or some discussion about vines, knowing fellows always used to say, 'Old Grandet? – the old man must have between five and six millions.'

'You are cleverer than I am – I have never been able to find out the exact figure,' Monsieur Cruchot or Monsieur des Grassins would remark, if one of them chanced to overhear what was said.

If someone from Paris happened to mention the Rothschilds or Monsieur Laffitte, Saumur people would ask if they were as rich as Monsieur Grandet. And when the Parisian answered the question, with a pitying smile, in the affirmative, they would look at one another incredulously and shake their heads.

A fortune so large enfolded every action of its owner in a cloak of gold. Certain eccentricities in his way of life may, at one time, have given rise to ridicule and mockery, but ridicule and mockery had died away, and now his most trivial acts had the weight of judicial decisions. His remarks, the clothing he wore, his gestures, the way he blinked his eyes were regarded as signs from an oracle, had been studied by the entire neighbourhood with the care a naturalist gives to the study of the workings of instinct in animals, and recognized by everyone to be the outward manifestations of a profound dumb wisdom.

'It will be a hard winter,' one man would say to another; 'old Grandet has put on his fur gloves. We ought to pick the grapes.' Or 'Grandet is laying in a lot of cask staves; there will be plenty of wine this year.'

Monsieur Grandet never bought either meat or bread. His tenant farmers paid their rent partly in kind, and brought him all the poultry, eggs, butter, and corn he needed every week. He owned a mill, and the miller was obliged, over and above paying his rent, to fetch a certain quantity of grain, and send back the bran and flour. Big Nanon, the one servant in his house, although she was no longer young, herself baked all the bread every Saturday. Some of his tenants were market gardeners, and Monsieur Grandet had arranged that they should supply him with vegetables. As for fruit, his own land yielded so much that he sent the greater part of it to market. His firewood was gathered from the hedges, or taken from the old half-decayed stumps of trees which he was clearing from the sides of his fields, and his tenants chopped it for him, carted it to town, stacked it obligingly in his outhouse, and in return received – his thanks. The only things for which he was known to spend money were consecrated bread, sittings in church for his wife and daughter, and their dress; candles, big Nanon's wages, and the relining of her saucepans; the payment of taxes, the repair of his buildings, and the costs of cultivation of his land. He had recently acquired nine hundred acres of woodland, which he had persuaded a neighbour's keeper to look after for him, with a promise that he should find it worth his while. Game had appeared on Grandet's table for the first time after the acquisition of this property.

Grandet's manners were plain and unadorned. He had little to say. Generally his ideas were expressed in brief sententious phrases, spoken in a low voice. Since the time of the Revolution, when he had been something of a public figure, the old fellow stammered in a tiresome way whenever he had to speak at any length or take part in a discussion. This stammer, the incoherence of what he said, the torrent of words in which he drowned his thought, his striking inability to produce a logical argument, were all ascribed to deficiencies in his education, but were all affected, for reasons that will be made sufficiently clear in the course of this story. He had four phrases, moreover, like algebraic formulae, which met every situation and solved every problem of daily life and business – 'I do not know.' 'I cannot do so.' 'I do not intend to have anything to do with it.' 'We shall see.' He never said in plain words either 'yes' or 'no', and put nothing down in writing. He listened impassively, chin in hand, when he was spoken to, his elbow supported on the back of his other hand, and whatever the business under discussion, when once his opinion was formed he never reconsidered it. His smallest transactions were carried through and completed only after prolonged reflection. When his adversary, after conducting the conversation in a masterly fashion, thought that he held him in the hollow of his hand, and had himself disclosed to Grandet what his intentions were, Grandet would say, 'I can decide nothing until I have consulted my wife.' His wife, whom he had reduced to a state of complete subjection, was a most convenient smoke-screen for him in business affairs.

He never paid visits, or dined away from home, wishing neither to offer nor receive hospitality. He was so unobtrusive and noiseless in his comings and goings that he seemed to be trying to economize his expenditure even of muscular energy. So consistent was he in his respect for ownership that he took care not to disturb or displace anything belonging to someone else. Yet in spite of his low voice and careful and discreet behaviour, his speech and habits were those of a cooper, especially when he was at home, where he was less guarded than elsewhere.

Physically, Grandet was five feet in height, thickset and squarely built, with legs measuring twelve inches round the calf, knees gnarled like tree-trunks, and broad shoulders. He had a round sun-burnt face, marked by smallpox, a firm chin, uncurving lips, white teeth. His eyes had the calm and deadly gaze vulgarly attributed to the basilisk. His forehead, which was deeply furrowed, bulged in a fashion not without significance for the physiognomist. His sandy hair, now turning grey, was silver and golden, according to certain young people who did not realize what a serious matter it was to make a joke about Monsieur Grandet. His nose, which was thick at the end, had a veined knob on it which was popularly said, with some reason, to be full of malice. In this face were written a dangerous craftiness, a calculated rectitude, the selfishness of a man who, day by day, concentrated all his emotions on saving money, and on the only being in the world who meant anything to him, his daughter and sole heiress, Eugénie. Everything about him, too, bearing, manner, carriage, evinced the self-confidence that unbroken success in all one's enterprises breeds. Pliant and smooth-spoken though he might appear to be, Monsieur Grandet had a nature hard as bronze.

He was always dressed in the same fashion: to see him today was to see him as he had been since 1791. His heavy shoes were tied with leather laces. Winter and summer he wore thick woollen stockings, knee-breeches of coarse chestnut-coloured homespun, with silver buckles, a velvet waistcoat, striped yellow and purplish-brown, buttoned up to the throat, a loose chestnut-coloured coat with full skirts, a black neckcloth, and a Quaker hat. His gloves, made like a gendarme's for hard wear, lasted him nearly two years, and to keep them clean he was in the habit of placing them tidily, always on the same spot, on the brim of his hat. So much, and no more, was known in Saumur about Monsieur Grandet.

Only six townspeople had the right of entry to Grandet's house, and they were divided into two camps. The most important member of the first of these was Monsieur Cruchot's nephew. This young man was president of the court of first instance in Saumur, and ever since his appointment he had added the important words 'de Bonfons' to his name, and was doing his best to make Bonfons efface and replace Cruchot in the public mind. He already signed himself C. de Bonfons. Any litigant ill-advised enough to call him 'Monsieur Cruchot' soon found out, in court, what a blunder he had made. The magistrate was indulgent to those who called him 'Monsieur le Président', but he favoured the flatterers who addressed him as 'Monsieur de Bonfons' with his most gracious smiles.

Monsieur le Président was thirty-three years old, and owned the estate of Bonfons (*Boni Fontis*), worth seven thousand livres a year. He had expectations from his uncle the notary, and another uncle, the Abbé Cruchot, a dignitary of the Chapter of Saint-Martin de Tours, who were both reputed to be very well-off. These three Cruchots, supported by a considerable number of cousins, and connected by marriage with twenty families in the town, formed a party as the Medici family used to do in Florence long ago, and as the Medici had their Pazzi, so the Cruchots, too, had their deadly rivals.

Madame des Grassins, the mother of a twenty-three-year-old son, came constantly to Grandet's house, and assiduously played cards with Madame Grandet, in the hope of obtaining the hand of Mademoiselle Eugénie for her dear Adolphe. Her husband, the banker, energetically seconded his wife in her campaign by the secret services which he was for ever rendering to the old miser, and he never failed to bring up his reinforcements to the battlefield at the right moment. The three des Grassins had their adherents too, their cousins and their trusty allies. On the Cruchot side, the abbé, the Talleyrand of the party, ably supported by his brother, the notary, hotly disputed the terrain with the banker's wife, and strove to secure the wealthy heiress for his nephew, the president.

This underground struggle between the Cruchots and the des Grassins for the prize of Eugénie Grandet's hand was watched with passionate interest by all the citizens of Saumur of every degree. Would Mademoiselle Grandet marry Monsieur le Président or Adolphe des Grassins? That was a burning question. Some solved the problem by saying that Monsieur Grandet had no intention of giving his daughter to either of them. The former cooper, they said, was eaten up with ambition, and was on the look-out for some peer of France for his son-in-law, a nobleman who would find that an income of three hundred thousand livres made all the Grandet casks, past, present, and to come, acceptable. In reply to this others argued that Monsieur and Madame des Grassins were both of good family and exceedingly well off, that Adolphe was a very nice-mannered and pleasant young man, and that unless the Grandets had a pope's nephew up their sleeves, a match so suitable should be good enough for a family of nobodies, and especially for a man whom all Saumur had seen with a cooper's adze in his hand, and who, moreover, had once worn the red cap of liberty. The more astute observers pointed out that Monsieur Cruchot de Bonfons was free to visit the Grandets whenever he pleased, while his rival was received only on Sundays. Some maintained that Madame des Grassins, as she was on more intimate terms with the women of the family than the Cruchots were, had opportunities of inculcating certain ideas which could not fail to win the campaign for her sooner or later. Others retorted that there wasn't a person in the world with greater powers of insinuation than the Abbé Cruchot, and that with a woman on one side and a churchman on the other there wasn't a pin to chose between the parties.

'When Greek meets Greek –' said a local wit.

Those who were more experienced and wiser in the ways of the world declared that the Grandets knew too well what they were about to let all that money pass out of the hands of their own family. Mademoiselle Eugénie Grandet of Saumur would be married, so they said, to her cousin, the son of the other Monsieur Grandet of Paris, a rich wholesale wine merchant. But to this both the Cruchot party and the Grassinists had an answer:

'In the first place, the two brothers have not met twice in the last thirty years. Moreover, Monsieur Grandet of Paris aims high for his son. He is not Mayor of his district, deputy, colonel of the National Guard, a judge of the tribunal of commerce, for nothing. He does not acknowledge the Grandets of Saumur as relatives of his, and intends his son for a daughter of one of Napoleon's dukes.'

There was little indeed that could be said about an heiress that was left unsaid, when tongues were wagging for fifty miles round, and even in the very public vehicles, from Angers in the west to Blois in the east!

At the beginning of the year 1811 the Cruchot party won a signal victory over the Grassinists. The estate of Froidfond, celebrated for its park and fine château, with its farms, rivers, fishponds, and forest, valued at three millions altogether, was put up for sale by the young Marquis de Froidfond, who was obliged to realize his capital. Maître Cruchot, President Cruchot, and the Abbé Cruchot, with some help from their allies, managed to prevent its being sold in small lots. The notary made an excellent bargain for his client. He successfully represented to the young man that he would have endless trouble suing defaulting purchasers of small lots before he could collect the purchase money; it would suit his interests better to sell to Monsieur Grandet, a man whose credit was good and who moreover could pay for the property in hard coin. In this way the fair marquisate of Froidfond was edged towards Monsieur Grandet's gullet, and he, to the great astonishment of Saumur, paid for it in cash, with discount deducted, after all the formalities had been completed. The news of this transaction caused a stir in places as far away as Nantes and Orléans.

Monsieur Grandet went to see his château, making use of the free transport provided by a farm cart which was returning there, and having cast a proprietorial eye over his estate he came back to Saumur, satisfied that this investment would bring him in five per cent, and fired with a magnificent ambition: he would complete and round off the marquisate of Froidfond by adding all his own property to it. Meanwhile, to replenish his almost empty coffers, he would cut down every stick in his woods and forests, and sell the poplars in his meadows.

With all this in mind, one may now realize the import of the words 'Monsieur Grandet's house' – that grey, cold, silent house at the upper end of the town, under the shadow of the ruined ramparts.

The two pillars and arch that framed the doorway, and the house itself, were built of a white stone peculiar to the Loire valley, a tufa which is so soft that its average life is barely two hundred years. It had weathered fantastically. The stone was irregularly pitted with a multitude of holes of various sizes, so that it looked like the vermiculated stone often used in French architecture, and piers and voussoirs gave the entrance the appearance of an entrance to a jail. Above the arch there was a long bas-relief carved in harder stone, four worn and blackened figures representing the four seasons. The bas-relief was surmounted by a projecting stringcourse on which several chance-sown plants had found space to grow; yellow pellitory, convolvulus and other bindweed, plantain, and a flourishing little cherry-tree.

The massive door of dark oak was warped and cracked, split in every direction and apparently falling to pieces, but a pattern of long iron pins with large heads, symmetrically placed, strengthened and held it firmly together. A square grating, quite small but filled with close-set rusty bars, was set in the middle like a geometrical ornament, behind a knocker which hung there from a ring, and knocked on the rueful-looking head of an immense iron bolt. The knocker, oblong in shape, and of the kind our ancestors called 'jaquemart', was like a huge exclamation mark. An antiquary scrutinizing it closely would have discovered traces of the typical clown's face once carved upon it, but long since effaced by use.

Curious eyes peering through the little grating, designed for the recognition of friends in times of civil war, could make out in the greenish light of a gloomy archway a flight of broken steps which led up to a garden picturesquely enclosed by thick walls, down which moisture damply trickled and in which grew tufts of sickly-looking shrubs. These walls were part of the old fortifications, and beyond, on the ramparts, the gardens of several neighbouring houses could be seen.

The principal room on the ground floor of the house was a parlour, which was entered by a door under the arch of the gateway. Few people know how important a part this room plays in the life of the small towns in Anjou, Touraine, and Berri. The parlour is hall, drawing-room, study, boudoir, and dining-room, all in one; it is the theatre of family life, the centre of the home. It was to this room the local hairdresser came twice a year to cut Monsieur Grandet's hair. The tenant farmers, the parish priest, the sub-prefect, the miller's boy, all found their way in here. The two windows of the room, which had a floor of wooden boards, gave on the street. Wooden panelling, topped with antique moulding and painted grey, lined the walls from floor to ceiling. The naked beams of the ceiling were also painted grey, and the spaces between showed yellowing plaster.

An old brass clock case, inlaid with arabesques in tortoise-shell, adorned the clumsily-carved, white stone chimney-piece, above which stood a mirror of greenish glass, whose edges, bevelled to show its thickness, reflected a thin streak of light along another antiquated mirror of Damascus steel.

The two branched candlesticks of gilded copper which decorated each end of the chimney-piece gave double service; if one removed the branch roses which served as candle-sockets, the main stem of roses set in a pedestal of bluish marble with antique copper fittings could be used as a candle-stick for ordinary occasions.

The old-fashioned chairs were covered with tapestry, depict-ing scenes from La Fontaine's fables; but anyone unaware of this would have had difficulty in making out what the subjects were, the colours were so faded, and the figures so much darned and mended as to be almost indistinguishable from the background.

In each corner of the room stood a corner-cupboard, or rather a kind of sideboard topped by a tier of dirty shelves. An old inlaid card-table with a chess-board top was placed be-tween the two windows. On the wall above this table hung an oval barometer set in a black frame decorated with a carved knot of ribbons, once gilt, on which the flies had frolicked so wantonly that the existence of gilding could now only be guessed at. Two portraits in pastel hung on the wall opposite the fireplace, representing, so it was said, Madame Grandet's grandfather, old Monsieur de la Bertellière, as a lieutenant in the Guards, and the late Madame Gentillet as a shepherdess.

Crimson curtains of silk material manufactured in Tours

hung in the windows, and were looped back with silk cords and immense tassels. These luxurious hangings, so little in accord with Grandet's mode of life, together with the pier-glass, the clock, the tapestry-covered chairs, and the rosewood corner sideboards, had been included in the bargain when the house was bought.

In the window nearest to the door stood a straw-bottomed chair, raised on blocks of wood so that Madame Grandet as she sat could look out at passers-by in the street. A work-table of bleached cherry wood filled the other window recess, and Eugénie Grandet's little armchair was set close by. Day after day, from April to November, for the last fifteen years, time had passed peacefully for mother and daughter here, in constant work. On the first day of November they were at liberty to take up their winter position by the fireplace. Only on that day did Grandet allow a fire to be lit in the parlour, and he forbade it after the 31st of March, no matter how chilly the early days of spring and autumn might be. A little brazier, which big Nanon managed surreptitiously to keep full of live embers from the kitchen fire, helped Madame and Mademoiselle Grandet to get through the coldest mornings and evenings in April and October. The mother and daughter kept all the household linen in repair, and devoted their days so conscientiously to this extremely laborious task that if Eugénie wanted to embroider a collar for her mother, the time she needed had to be borrowed from her sleep, and she was forced to deceive her father in order to have light to sew by. It was a long-established custom of the miser's to dole out candles to his daughter and big Nanon, just as he doled out the bread and provisions for the day's meals each morning.

Big Nanon was perhaps the only human creature in existence who could have put up with her master's tyranny. The whole town envied Monsieur and Madame Grandet her services. Big Nanon, so called on account of her height of five feet eight inches, had worked for Grandet for the last thirty-five years. Although she earned only sixty livres a year, she was reputed to be one of the richest servant girls in Saumur. Sixty livres a year, accumulating through thirty-five years, had given her some capital, and she had recently placed four thousand livres in Maître Cruchot's hands for the purchase of an annuity. This result of her long and unremitting thrift loomed enormous in the eyes of the local servants. They were all jealous of the poor woman, who would be sixty in a few years, seeing her with provision made for her old age, and with no thought of how hard she had worked to make it, and under what harsh conditions.

At twenty-two years of age Nanon had been quite unable to find a situation anywhere, her grim appearance had been so much against her. Poor girl, this general distaste for her homely features was very unfair. Set on the shoulders of a grenadier her head would have been greatly admired. But suitability to its purpose is necessary in all things, so they say. When a fire at the farm where she had herded cows obliged her to seek work elsewhere she had come to Saumur to look for a place in service, full of a robust courage and ready to tackle anything. Monsieur Grandet was at that time thinking of getting married, and already considering his housekeeping arrangements. He took note of this girl, who had been rebuffed at door after door. As a cooper he was a judge of physical strength, and he foresaw the use that might be made of a female built like Hercules, planted as solidly on her feet as a sixty-year-old oak tree on its roots, wide-hipped, broad of back, with a carter's hands and a sturdy honesty as unquestionable as her virtue. Neither the warts which disfigured Nanon's warrior-like face nor her brick-red complexion, neither her muscular arms nor her rags and tatters, dismayed the cooper, who was then young enough to be still sensitive to misery. And so he clothed and shod and fed the poor girl, paid her wages and worked her hard, without using her too harshly. Finding herself accepted in this way big Nanon secretly wept for joy, and became sincerely attached to the cooper, who for his part exploited her in feudal fashion.

Nanon did everything. She cooked and washed, taking the dirty linen down to the Loire to wash it and bringing it back on her shoulders. She rose at dawn and went to bed late. She prepared the meals for all the grape-gatherers at the vintage, and kept a sharp eye on the market-folk. She guarded her master's possessions like a faithful dog, and trusting him blindly, obeyed his most unreasonable commands, treating his whim as law without a murmur.

In the year 1811, the year of the famous vintage which cost unheard-of toil and trouble to gather in, when Nanon had been in his service for twenty years, Grandet made up his mind to give her his old watch, the only present she ever received from him. It is true that he handed on his old shoes to her (for they fitted), but the quarterly reversion of Grandet's shoes could not possibly be considered a present, they were so worn. Sheer necessity had made the poor girl so miserly that Grandet had come to feel the affection for her a man feels for his dog, and Nanon for her part had let a collar of servitude be put round her neck, and had ceased to feel its spikes. Though Grandet might be rather too niggardly with the bread, she did not grumble. She cheerfully remarked that a lean diet was good for the health. In that household no one was ever ill.

And then Nanon was one of the family. She shared Grandet's jokes and his fits of depression, was warmed by the same sun and nipped by the same frosts as he was, and in his enterprises she was a fellow-worker. What sweet compensations there were in this equality! And never had her master said a grumbling word to her about apricots or peaches, plums or nectarines eaten under the trees, out in the vineyards where they were planted between the rows of vines.

'Go on, help yourself, Nanon!' he would say in the years when the branches were bent beneath the weight of fruit, and the farmers had so much they had to feed it to the pigs.

To a peasant girl, who had worked in the fields, who from her childhood had met with nothing but unkindness, to a girl whom only charity had saved from having nowhere to lay her head, old Grandet's equivocal mirth was as grateful as sunshine. Besides, Nanon's single heart and simple mind had room for only one feeling and one thought. For thirty-five years she had held a picture in her mind of herself, bare-foot and in rags, standing at the gate of Monsieur Grandet's timber-yard and hearing the cooper say 'What is it, my dear?', and her gratitude to him was perennially fresh in her heart.

Sometimes as Grandet watched her and reflected that she had never heard a word of compliment addressed to her, that she knew nothing whatever of the tender feelings women have power to stir, and might well appear before God one day as chaste as the Virgin Mary herself, he was seized with pity, and would say, 'Poor Nanon!' This exclamation was always followed by an indescribable look from the old servant. These words, repeated in this way from time to time over many years, formed links in an unbroken chain of friendship. Pity had taken root in Grandet's heart and the lonely girl found it entirely acceptable, but there was something revolting in it. It was a vile miser's pity which cost the old cooper nothing and warmed his heart agreeably, while it was Nanon's whole sum of human happiness. Who can refrain from repeating 'Poor Nanon'? God will know his angels by the tones of their voices and the sadness hidden in their hearts.

There were many households in Saumur where the servants were better treated, but where the masters did not fare very well for all their kindness. And so people asked, 'What can the Grandets do to that big Nanon of theirs, to make her so devoted to them? She would walk through fire for them!'

Her kitchen, with its iron-barred windows looking out into the yard, was always clean, neat, cold, a true miser's kitchen where nothing was allowed to be wasted. When Nanon had washed up, locked what was left over from dinner in the safe, raked out the fire, she left her kitchen, crossed the passage that separated kitchen from parlour, and sat down to spin hemp in the company of her employers. A single candle had to meet the needs of the whole family in the evening.

The servant slept at the end of the passage, in a closet with no direct lighting. Thanks to her robust health she came to no harm in this hole, in which in the deep silence that brooded night and day over the house she could hear the slightest sound. It was part of her duty to sleep with one eye open, like a watch-dog, and keep guard even while she rested.

What the other rooms in the house were like will be revealed in the course of the story, but, in any case, this sketch of the parlour, where all the splendour and luxury that the household could lay claim to were concentrated, gives some idea of the bareness of the rooms above.

One day in the middle of November in the year 1819, as evening was falling, big Nanon lit the fire for the first time. The autumn had been very fine that year. The day was an anniversary well known to the Cruchot and Grassinist parties, and the six antagonists were preparing to sally forth, armed to the teeth, for an encounter in the parlour, there to vie with one another in demonstrations of friendship.

In the morning all Saumur had seen Madame and Mademoiselle Grandet, with big Nanon, on their way to the parish church to hear mass, and everyone had remembered that today was Mademoiselle Eugénie's birthday.

And so, choosing a time when they judged that dinner would be just over, Maître Cruchot, the Abbé Cruchot, and Monsieur C. de Bonfons hastened to arrive to do honour to Mademoiselle Grandet, before the des Grassins. They all three carried huge bunches of flowers, which they had gathered in their small hot-houses, but the stalks of the magistrate's flowers were elaborately tied, and wrapped in a white satin ribbon with a gold fringe.

That morning Monsieur Grandet had followed his usual custom on the red letter days of Eugénie's birthday and saint's day. He had come to her room before she was up to give her a surprise and solemnly offer his present, which for the last thirteen years had been a rare gold coin. Madame Grandet on these occasions usually gave her daughter a winter or summer dress, according to the season. These two dresses and the gold coins which she received on New Year's Day and her father's birthday as well, gave her a little income worth about a hundred crowns; and Grandet took great pleasure in watching her accumulate the money, for did it not mean simply pouring his money from one box to another, and at the same time, as it were, cherishing and fostering his heiress's avarice? From time to time he demanded an account of her wealth, which at one time had been added to by the la Bertellières, and he always told her as he looked at it, 'This will be your wedding *dozen*.'

The *dozen* is an ancient custom still adhered to and reverently preserved in a few districts in the centre of France. In Berri or Anjou, when a girl gets married, her family, or her future husband's, must give her a purse with twelve gold or silver coins, or twelve dozen, or twelve hundred, according to the circumstances of the family concerned. The poorest herd-girl would not dream of marrying without her *dozen*, even if it were only of twelve pence. They still talk in Issoudun of a fabulous dozen given to a rich heiress, which consisted of a hundred and forty-four Portuguese moidores; and when the Pope Clement VII gave his niece Catharine de Medici in marriage to Henry II, he presented her with a dozen priceless antique gold medals.

At dinner Mademoiselle Grandet had worn her new dress, and her father, pleased to see his Eugénie looking her best, had exclaimed in high good humour, 'As it's Eugénie's birthday, let's have a fire! It will be a good omen.'

'Mademoiselle will be married within the year, that's cer-

tain,' said big Nanon, as she carried away the remains of a
goose, that poor-man's-pheasant of the coopers.

'So far as I can see, there's no possible husband for her in
Saumur,' observed Madame Grandet, with a timid glance at
her husband, which in a woman of her age was a sign of complete matrimonial subjection, and revealed how thoroughly
her spirit was broken.

Grandet looked at his daughter, and said gaily, 'The child is
twenty-three years old today! We shall soon have to see about
doing something for her.'

Eugénie and her mother silently exchanged a glance that
showed the close understanding between them.

Madame Grandet was a thin, desiccated-looking woman, as
yellow as a quince, awkward and slow in her movements, one
of those women who seem born to be tyrannized over. She had
a large frame, a big nose, a high forehead, great eyes, and at the
first glance vaguely recalled those cotton-textured fruits that
have lost all their flavour and juice. Her teeth were few and
discoloured, her mouth deeply lined, her chin of the nut-
cracker type. She was an excellent woman, a la Bertellière to
the backbone. The Abbé Cruchot managed to find occasional
opportunities for telling her that she had been rather good-
looking once, and she did not disagree. An angelic sweetness
of nature, helpless resignation like that of an insect in the hands
of tormenting children, unusual devotion to her religion, unvarying evenness of temper, a kind heart, had won for her
universal pity and respect. Her husband never gave her more
than six francs at a time for pocket money. Although she
appeared to be well-off, this woman who had brought Monsieur Grandet more than three hundred thousand francs in her
dowry and the fortunes she had inherited, had always felt so
profoundly humiliated by her state of dependence and subjection, although the gentleness of her nature prevented any
revolt against it, that she had never asked her husband for a
sou, nor had she made any comment about the documents

which Maître Cruchot presented for her signature from time to time. In everything she did she was actuated by this unreasoning secret pride, which Grandet was constantly wounding, this magnanimity which he was incapable of understanding.

Her dress never varied. She always wore a gown of greenish levantine silk, which she made last her for nearly a year, a wide white cotton neckerchief, a straw bonnet, and was seldom seen without a black silk apron. She went out so rarely that her shoes suffered little wear and tear. Indeed she needed little, and never wanted anything for herself. Grandet's conscience sometimes pricked him a little when it occurred to him that a long time had elapsed since he last gave his wife six francs, and after the vintage when he sold his wine he always stipulated that his customer should provide pin-money for her into the bargain. These four or five louis from Dutch or Belgian buyers formed the part of Madame Grandet's annual income that she could count on most surely. But when she had received her five louis her husband often used to say to her, as if they shared a common purse, 'Can you let me have a few sous?' And the poor woman, only too pleased to be able to do something for the man whom her confessor represented to her as her lord and master, gave him back more than one crown from her little store in the course of the winter. Whenever Grandet disbursed the five-franc piece which was the monthly allowance for petty expenses of dress for his daughter, and for needles and thread, he never failed to ask his wife, after he had buttoned up his pocket again, 'And what about you, mother? Do you want anything?' 'We will talk about that later, my dear,' Madame Grandet would reply, with maternal dignity.

It was an unworldly attitude of mind, completely thrown away upon Grandet, who thought he treated his wife handsomely. Have philosophers who meet with such women as Nanon, Madame Grandet, and Eugénie not some grounds for conclusion that Fate is, at bottom, ironical?

After dinner, when the question of Eugénie's marriage had

been raised for the first time, Nanon went to fetch a bottle of blackcurrant cordial from Monsieur Grandet's room, and stumbled and nearly fell as she was coming downstairs again.

'Clumsy creature! Are *you* going to start coming croppers?' asked her master.

'It's that rickety step, sir. It gives way under your feet.'

'She's quite right,' said Madame Grandet. 'You should have had it mended long ago. Eugénie nearly sprained her ankle on it yesterday.'

'Here,' said Grandet, noticing that Nanon looked very pale. 'As it's Eugénie's birthday, and you nearly had a fall, take a drop of cordial. That'll set you on your feet.'

'Upon my word, I deserve it too,' cried Nanon. 'Many a one in my place would have broke the bottle, but I would sooner break my elbow, holding it up out of harm's way.'

'Poor Nanon!' muttered Grandet, as he poured out the cordial.

'Did you hurt yourself?' asked Eugénie, looking at her with concern.

'No. I plumped down on my back and brought myself sharp up.'

'Well, as it's Eugénie's birthday, I'll mend your step for you,' said Grandet. 'I suppose it's too much to ask of you women, to put your foot down in the corner where it is still firm.'

Grandet took the candle, leaving his wife, daughter, and servant with only the dancing firelight for illumination, and went to look for his tools, a piece of board, and some nails, in the bakehouse.

'Do you want any help?' Nanon shouted to him, when she heard the sound of his hammer.

'No! No! I'm an old hand at this kind of job,' answered the cooper.

At this very moment, while Grandet was repairing his worm-eaten staircase with his own hands, and whistling with all his might as he called to mind the work he had done in his youth, the three Cruchots knocked at the door.

'Oh, is that you, Monsieur Cruchot?' inquired Nanon, looking through the little grille.

'Yes,' the magistrate replied.

Nanon opened the door, and the three Cruchots groped their way to where the firelight shining out into the dark passage revealed the parlour door to be.

'Oh, you've come to help us keep her birthday!' said Nanon, as she caught the scent of flowers.

'Excuse me, gentlemen,' cried Grandet, recognizing his friends' voices. 'I'll be with you in a moment! No one can say there's any false pride about me; I'm mending a broken tread in my stairs here myself.'

'Go on, by all means, Monsieur Grandet! The charcoal-burner is mayor in his own house,' said the magistrate sententiously, and then laughed at his allusion, which remained a private joke of his own, for no one else understood it.

Madame and Mademoiselle Grandet rose to greet the visitors. The magistrate took advantage of the screening darkness to say to Eugénie: 'Will you permit me, Mademoiselle, to wish you, on the occasion of your birthday, a long succession of prosperous years, and may you long continue to enjoy your present good health!'

He proffered a big bunch of flowers of a kind rarely seen in Saumur, and then taking the heiress by the arms he kissed her on both sides of her throat with a complacent warmth that made Eugénie blush, looking as he did so like a great rusty nail. This was his idea of how a courtship should be conducted.

'Don't stand on ceremony,' said Grandet, coming into the room. 'How you do go it on high days and holidays, Monsieur le Président!'

'With Mademoiselle Eugénie at his side every day would be a high day for my nephew,' answered the Abbé Cruchot, who was also armed with a bouquet. He kissed Eugénie's hand. As for Maître Cruchot, he kissed her without formality on both cheeks, and said,

'This sort of thing makes us feel that we're getting on, eh? Twelve months older every year!'

Grandet, who could never have too much of a good thing and repeated every joke till it was worn to shreds, now said as he set down the candle in front of the clock,

'As it's Eugénie's birthday, let's have an illumination!'

He carefully removed the branches from the two candelabra, set a socket in each pedestal, took a fresh candle wrapped in a twist of paper from Nanon's hands, placed it in the socket and fixed it firmly, lighted it, and then went over to his wife and sat down beside her, looking as he did so from his friends to his daughter, and then turning his gaze upon the two lighted candles.

The Abbé Cruchot, a plump tubby little man, with a well-worn reddish wig, and a face like a card-playing old lady's, stretched out his well-shod feet with their silver buckles as he remarked questioningly,

'The des Grassins have not come?'

'Not yet,' answered Grandet.

'But you expect them?' asked the old notary, screwing up a face as full of holes as a colander.

'Oh, yes. I think they will come,' said Madame Grandet.

'Is the vintage over? Are all your grapes in?' Président de Bonfons inquired of Grandet.

'Yes, everywhere!' replied the old winegrower, springing to his feet and striding up and down the room, his chest inflated with the conscious pride of his announcement, 'everywhere!'

As he passed the door into the passage, he caught sight of big Nanon sitting by her fire in the kitchen, with a light, preparing to spin there, to be out of the way of the birthday party.

'Nanon,' he said, walking out into the passage, 'will you kindly put out your fire and candle and come and join us? Heavens above, the room is surely big enough to hold us all!'

'But you're expecting grand folk, sir.'

'Aren't you as good as they are? They sprang from Adam's rib like yourself.'

Grandet rejoined the president, and continued the conversation.

'Have you sold your wine?' he inquired.

'No, I am going to hold it. If the wine is good now it will be better still in two years' time. The growers, as of course you know, have sworn to stick to the prices we've agreed on, and the Belgians won't get the better of us this year. If they go away, well, in the end they'll come back again.'

'Yes, but we must stand firm,' said Grandet, in a voice that filled the president with foreboding.

'Can he be driving a bargain behind our backs?' he thought.

Just then a knock announced the des Grassins family, and their arrival put an end to a conversation between Madame Grandet and the abbé.

Madame des Grassins was one of those plump, lively, pink and white little women who are still young at forty, thanks to a regular and well-ordered existence in the claustral seclusion of life in the country. They are like the last roses in autumn, which are delightful to the eye, but whose petals have something chilly and pinched about them, and whose scent is fading. She dressed rather well, sent to Paris for the latest fashions, led society in Saumur, and held receptions on certain evenings. Her husband, who had once been a quartermaster in the Imperial Guard, but had been badly wounded at Austerlitz and had then retired on a pension, still treated everyone, in spite of his consideration for Grandet, with a soldier's breezy bluntness.

'Good day, Grandet,' he said, holding out his hand to the winegrower with an air of conscious superiority to the other visitors, with which he always crushed the Cruchots. And then, after a bow to Madame Grandet, 'Mademoiselle,' he said to Eugénie, 'You are always charming, always good and fair, and indeed I do not know what more one can wish you.'

Then he presented her with a little box which his servant carried in, which contained a Cape heath, a plant only recently introduced into Europe, and very rare.

Madame des Grassins kissed Eugénie very affectionately, pressed her hand, and said,

'Adolphe has made it *his* business to give you my little remembrance.'

At this a tall fair young man, who looked rather pale and fragile, moved forward. His manners were passably good but he seemed to be rather shy, in spite of the fact that in Paris, where he was studying law, he had just overspent his allowance by eight or ten thousand francs. He kissed Eugénie on both cheeks and offered her a workbox with fittings of silver-gilt. It was a trumpery enough piece of goods, in spite of the little shield bearing the initials E. G. carefully engraved in Gothic characters, a detail which made the whole thing appear more imposing and better finished than it in fact was. Eugénie opened the box with a thrill of pleasure. She was suddenly filled with a sensation of overwhelming happiness, as complete as it was unexpected, a surge of emotion characteristic of girls of her age, which made her cheeks turn pink and her hands tremble with delight. Her eyes turned to her father as if to ask if she might accept it, and Monsieur Grandet said, 'Take it, my girl!' in tones that would have made the reputation of an actor. The three Cruchots stood aghast at the sight of the happy, elated look the heiress, apparently dazzled by such undreamed of splendours, turned on Adolphe des Grassins.

Monsieur des Grassins held out his snuff-box to Grandet, took a pinch of snuff himself, shook off a few specks of the powder that had fallen on his blue coat and the ribbon of the Legion of Honour in his buttonhole, then glanced at the Cruchots with an expression that said, 'Parry that thrust if you can!' Madame des Grassins looked about her with polite interest in search of the Cruchots' presents, and let her eyes linger on the blue glass jars in which their bouquets had been set with a malicious woman's mocking admiration.

Faced with this delicate situation, the Abbé Cruchot left the company to seat itself in a semi-circle round the fire while he walked with Grandet to the back of the room. When these two elders had reached the window recess at the greatest distance from the des Grassins party, the priest whispered in the miser's ear, 'Those people yonder don't mind throwing money out of the windows.'

'What does it matter, if it falls into my cellars?' the old winegrower answered.

'If you felt inclined to give your daughter gold scissors, you could well afford to do so,' said the abbé.

'I am going to give her something better than a pair of scissors,' replied Grandet.

'My nephew is a blockhead,' the abbé thought as he looked at the magistrate, whose tousled hair did nothing to enhance the charms of his ill-favoured dark face. 'Why couldn't *he* have hit upon some expensive piece of nonsense?'

'We're ready for your game of cards, Madame Grandet,' said Madame des Grassins.

'As we're all here, we can make up two tables ...'

'As it's Eugénie's birthday,' said old Grandet, 'you should have one game of lotto for everybody. These two children can join in it.'

The former cooper, who never played any game whatever, pointed to his daughter and Adolphe.

'Come, Nanon, set the tables out.'

'We will help you, Mademoiselle Nanon,' said Madame des Grassins, cheerfully. She was in high spirits at the pleasure she had given Eugénie.

'I have never been so pleased with anything in my life,' the heiress told her. 'I have never seen anything so pretty anywhere.'

64

'It was Adolphe who chose it,' Madame des Grassins whispered in her ear; 'he brought it from Paris.'

'Go on, play your game, you damned interfering schemer!' muttered the president to himself. 'If you ever find yourself in a law court, either you or your husband, you'll find it will go hard with you.'

The notary, sitting in his corner, watched the abbé placidly, as he thought,

'The des Grassins may do what they like. My fortune and my brother's and my nephew's amount altogether to eleven hundred thousand francs. The des Grassins have at most half of that, and they have a daughter to provide for. They are welcome to give her whatever they like! The heiress and her presents will all be ours some day.'

By half-past eight, two tables had been arranged. The fascinating Madame des Grassins had succeeded in placing her son beside Eugénie. The actors in the scene, so commonplace in appearance, but full of interest to anyone who looked beneath the surface, had been provided with cards of various colours and blue glass counters, and were apparently listening to the jokes cracked by the old notary, who had some humorous comment to make with every number he drew, but the thoughts of everyone were fixed on Monsieur Grandet's millions. The old cooper himself complacently surveyed his guests, looking from Madame des Grassins' pink feathers and fresh gown and the soldierly head of the banker, to the faces of Adolphe, the magistrate, the abbé, and the notary, and said to himself with considerable self-satisfaction, 'They are all after my crowns. They have come here to spend a boring evening in hopes of winning my daughter. Ha! my daughter isn't for any of them, and these people are nothing but harpoons for my fishing!'

The gaiety of this family party, the laughter to the accompaniment of big Nanon's humming spinning-wheel, genuine only when it was Eugénie's or her mother's, the pettiness of the minds that were playing for such large stakes, the young girl herself, like one of those birds that are the innocent victims of the high value placed on them of which they know nothing, tracked down, taken in a net of false friendship which she accepted as sincere; everything combined to make the scene enacted in the dismal old parlour, ill-lighted by two candles, a scene of sorry comedy. But is it not, indeed, a scene played out in every country, in every age, shown here in its simplest form?

Old Grandet towered above the other actors in this drama, exploiting the false affection of the two families and drawing enormous profits from their pretence of friendship. He made its meaning clear. There, incarnate in a single man, revealed in the expression of a single face, did there not stand the only god that anyone believes in nowadays – Money, in all its power?

With Grandet the gentle emotions held only second place: in three pure hearts they were dominant – Nanon's, Eugénie's, and her mother's. Yet how much ignorance there was in their innocent simplicity! Eugénie and her mother knew nothing of Grandet's fortune. They saw life in the pale light of their dim conception of it, and neither prized money nor despised it, accustomed as they were to do without it. Their finer feelings, frustrated without their being aware of it, but keen, the fact that these existed, though in secret, made them strangely alien in this gathering of people whose life was purely material. How horrible is man's condition! He does not own one happiness whose source does not lie in ignorance of some kind.

Just as Madame Grandet won a stake of sixteen sous, the highest ever punted in that room, as big Nanon was chuckling with delight at the sight of Madame pocketing such a splendid sum, a knock on the front door echoed through the house, making such a din that the women started in their seats.

'No Saumur man would knock in that fashion,' said the notary.

'What do they thump on it like that for?' cried Nanon. 'Do they want to break our door down?'

'Who the devil is it?' exclaimed Grandet.

Nanon took one of the two candles and went to open the door, and Grandet followed her.

'Grandet! Grandet!' cried his wife, in sudden apprehension of she knew not what, and she impulsively hurried to the door of the room.

The card-players looked at one another.

'Perhaps we should go too?' suggested Monsieur des Grassins. 'That knock sounded to me as if someone was up to mischief.'

But Monsieur des Grassins had barely caught a glimpse of a young man and a porter from the coach-office who had two huge trunks and a variety of travelling-bags draped round his person, when Grandet turned on his wife, and said sharply,

'Go back to your lotto, Madame Grandet. Leave me to interview this gentleman.' And then he slammed the door.

The excited players sat down again, but did not go on with their game.

'Is it someone who lives in Saumur, Monsieur des Grassins?' inquired his wife.

'No, it's a traveller.'

'He must be from Paris, then.'

'As a matter of fact,' said the notary, pulling out his old turnip of a watch which was a couple of fingers thick, and as clumsy as a Dutch ship, 'it's nine by the clock. Bless me! the mail coach is always on the minute.'

'Did he look young?' asked the Abbé Cruchot.

'Yes, and he has luggage with him weighing three hundred kilos, at least,' Monsieur des Grassins replied.

'Nanon is still out there,' Eugénie remarked.

'It must be some relation of yours,' said the president.

'Let's put down our stakes,' said Madame Grandet gently. 'I know by his voice that Monsieur Grandet was vexed.

67

Perhaps he would not be pleased to find us talking about his affairs.'

'Mademoiselle,' said Adolphe to his neighbour, 'it's probably your cousin Grandet. He's a very good-looking young fellow. I saw him once at a ball at Monsieur de Nucingen's.'

Here Adolphe stopped short: his mother had stamped on his foot. She asked him for two sous for his stake, and added under her breath, 'Will you keep your mouth shut, you great goose!'

Just then Grandet returned to the room, and Nanon and the porter could be heard walking upstairs. Behind Grandet came the traveller who for the last few minutes had been the object of so much curiosity and had set the company's wits so excitingly to work. Indeed his arrival in this house, his descent upon this gathering, had produced much the same effect as a snail's invasion of a beehive, or the introduction of a peacock into some commonplace village farmyard.

'Take a seat near the fire,' said Grandet, addressing the stranger.

Before sitting down the young man bowed very courteously to the company. The men rose to their feet and bowed politely in reply, and the women made a ceremonious curtsy.

'I am sure you are cold, Monsieur,' said Madame Grandet. 'You have perhaps come from ...?'

'How like women!' the old winegrower interrupted her, looking up from the letter which he held in his hand. 'Let the gentleman have a little peace.'

'But, father, perhaps he needs something to eat or drink after his journey,' said Eugénie.

'He has a tongue,' replied the winegrower harshly.

Only the stranger was surprised at this scene. The others present were accustomed to the worthy fellow's overbearing manner. But after the two inquiries had been thus rudely cut short, the stranger got up, turned his back to the fire, raised one foot to warm the sole of his boot, and said to Eugénie,

'Thank you, cousin, I dined at Tours.' And glancing at Grandet, he added, 'I don't need anything. I am not in the least tired.'

'You have just come from Paris, I presume?' inquired Madame des Grassins.

Monsieur Charles – for that was the name of the son of Monsieur Grandet of Paris – when he found himself being catechized in this fashion, proceeded to take out an eyeglass which hung from a chain round his neck, applied it to his right eye, and examined both what was on the table and the persons sitting round it, stared very coolly at Madame des Grassins, and when he had completed his survey said to her, 'Yes, madam.'

'I see you are playing lotto, aunt,' he added. 'Please go on with your game. It is too entertaining to stop short in the middle ...'

'I knew it was the cousin,' thought Madame des Grassins, watching him out of the corner of her eye.

'Forty-seven,' called the old abbé. 'Keep count, Madame des Grassins. Isn't that your number?'

Monsieur des Grassins put a counter on his wife's card, while she, with a mind full of gloomy foreboding, looked from the cousin from Paris to Eugénie and back again, and had not a thought to spare for lotto. From time to time the young heiress stole a glance at her cousin, and it was easy for the banker's wife to note in her looks a *crescendo* of wonder or curiosity.

There was certainly a striking contrast between Monsieur Charles Grandet, a good-looking young man of twenty-two, and the worthy provincials, who were already fairly revolted by his aristocratic airs, and were all studying him with care with an eye to taking him off later. A word of explanation is required at this point.

At twenty-two young men are close enough to childhood to indulge sometimes in childish silliness. Perhaps ninety-nine out of a hundred of them would have behaved exactly as Charles Grandet did. A few days previously his father had told him that he was to go to spend a few months with his uncle in Saumur. Perhaps Monsieur Grandet of Paris had Eugénie in his mind. Charles's mind was busy with other thoughts. This was his first visit to the country, and he had made up his mind to cut a dash in provincial society as a young man of fashion. He would drive the neighbourhood distracted with his splendour, mark the date of his arrival as a red-letter day in its history, and introduce it to the latest refinements of Parisian luxury. In short, Charles was prepared to devote more time to manicuring his nails in Saumur than he would spend in Paris, and determined to appear there in full fig, with no concessions to the carelessness in his dress which an elegant young man does sometimes affect, and which is not without a charm of its own.

And so Charles had brought with him the most becoming shooting costume he possessed, the finest gun, the most decorative knife with the prettiest sheath in Paris. He had brought the most elaborate collection of waistcoats, grey, white, black, beetle-green, shot with gold, spangled, mottled, speckled, double-breasted, with roll collars and stand-up collars, collars turned back, and collars buttoned up to the throat with gold buttons. He had a specimen of every variety of tie and cravat in favour at the moment, two coats designed by Buisson, and his finest linen, the handsome gold-fitted dressing-case that his mother had given him; all the appurtenances of a young man about town, not forgetting a ravishing little writing-case, given him by the kindest of women, kind to him at least, who was making a tiresome boring journey in Scotland at the moment, in her husband's company, a victim of suspicions which demanded the sacrifice for the time being of her happiness; and plenty of dainty note-paper for writing a letter to her every fortnight.

In fact his cargo of Parisian frivolities was as complete as it was possible to make it, and no agricultural implement that a young idler needs, to cultivate the art of living, was missing, from the horse-whip which serves to start a duel to the pair of handsome, richly chased pistols that end it.

His father had told him to travel alone and modestly, so he had reserved the coupé of the diligence for himself, and was well enough pleased not to spoil the freshness of a delightful travelling carriage which he had ordered for his journey to meet Annette, the great lady who ..., etc., whom he was to rejoin next June at Baden.

Charles expected to meet crowds of people at his uncle's house, to hunt deer in his uncle's forests, in fact to live the life of a guest at a château. He did not think of looking for his uncle at Saumur at all. He had only made inquiries there in order to learn the road to Froidfond. And when he heard that his uncle was in town, he expected to find him in a large mansion.

His first appearance at his uncle's house, whether it were in Saumur or at Froidfond, must be made in suitable style, so Charles had put on his choicest travelling outfit, the smartest one he had which had the elegance of simplicity, the most *adorable*, to use the current epithet for perfection in man or thing. At Tours a hairdresser had been summoned to recurl his beautiful chestnut hair, and he had changed his linen and put on a black satin cravat and a round collar which framed his pale mocking face becomingly. A long overcoat, fitting tightly at the waist, was left half-unbuttoned to show a cashmere waistcoat with a roll collar, under which was a second, white, waistcoat. His watch was fastened to one of his buttonholes by a short gold chain, and negligently tucked into a pocket. His grey trousers were buttoned at the sides, and decorated at the seams with black silk embroidery. The freshness of his grey gloves had nothing to fear from contact with the gold-headed cane which he twirled with an easy grace. His travelling cap completed a picture in perfect taste. Only a

Parisian, and a Parisian from the highest spheres, could fit himself up in this style, and not only avoid looking ridiculous, but even give to all his affectations an air of being modishly right, carrying them off with a gallant swagger, the dash of a young man who possesses a fine pair of pistols, skill in their use, and Annette.

Now if you want to understand the mutual surprise of the Saumur citizens and the young Parisian as they looked at one another, and the striking effect the traveller's elegance achieved against the grey shadows of the gloomy room, among the figures which composed the family group, you must try to picture the Cruchots.

All three of them took snuff, and had long ceased to trouble about drops on the end of their noses and little black specks scattered over their shirt frills; and their shirts were discoloured, with dingy and crumpled collars. Their cravats, limp from long use, rolled themselves into a string as soon as they were put on. They possessed such an accumulation of linen that they need only launder it twice a year and could keep it, dirty, at the bottom of their presses, and so Time had stamped it with his grey and ancient colours. Every grace was lacking in them, and the lack was aggravated by an apathy more proper to senility. Their faces, as faded as their threadbare coats, as creased as their trousers, were worn, the skin toughened and shrivelled, a grimace their only expression.

In the country, people gradually cease to care about their appearance. They no longer dress to please others, and eventually become reluctant even to buy a new pair of gloves. The dress of the other guests was as slovenly, as unfinished-looking, as generally wanting in freshness as the Cruchots'. Indeed there was one point on which the Grassinists and Cruchotins were in complete agreement – horror of the fashionable.

When the Parisian raised his eyeglass again to examine the unusual features of the room, the rafters in the ceiling, the dingy colour of the panelling, with the marks like full-stops that the flies had imprinted on it, which were numerous enough to punctuate both the *Encyclopédie méthodique* and the *Moniteur*, then the lotto players immediately raised their noses to examine *him*, with as much curiosity as they would have shown if he had been a giraffe. Even Monsieur des Grassins and his son, who were not unfamiliar with the appearance of a man of fashion, joined in the company's astonishment, either because they were swayed by the general opinion, which is always incalculable in its influence, or because they shared it, and they demonstrated their agreement by satirical glances which seemed to say, 'You see how they do things in Paris!' They were all able to watch Charles at their leisure, too, without any fear of displeasing the master of the house. Grandet was absorbed in the long letter he held in his hand, and he had taken the only candle from the table to read it by, without concerning himself about his guests or their convenience.

It seemed to Eugénie, who had never in her life seen such a paragon of beauty, so wonderfully dressed, that her cousin was a seraph come from heaven. She breathed the perfume of that shining head of hair, so gracefully curled, with delight. She would have liked to touch the satiny skin of those enchanting, fine, gloves. She envied Charles his small hands, his complexion, and the freshness and delicacy of his features. In fact, if such a comparison can convey the emotions of an ignorant girl who spent all her time darning stockings and patching her father's clothes, who had passed her life by that window under the dirty wainscoting, looking in the silent street outside to see scarcely one passer-by in an hour, the sight of this exquisite youth gave Eugénie the sensations of aesthetic delight that a young man finds in looking at the fanciful portraits of women drawn by Westall for English *Keepsakes*, and engraved by the Findens with a burin so skilful that you hesitate to breathe on the vellum for fear the celestial vision should disappear.

Charles drew from his pocket a handkerchief embroidered by the great lady who was travelling in Scotland. When she saw this charming piece of work, which had been executed with love during the hours lost to love, Eugénie looked at her cousin to see if he was really going to use it. Charles's manners, his gestures, his way of raising his eyeglass, his supercilious pose, his scorn of the work-box which such a short time ago had given the young heiress so much pleasure, and which he obviously thought an absurd piece of rubbish, everything, in short, which scandalized the Cruchots and des Grassins, delighted her so much that before she went to sleep that night she could not but muse and ponder for long over this phoenix among cousins.

Meanwhile lotto numbers were being drawn very languidly, and the game was soon brought to an end. Big Nanon came into the room, and said for everyone to hear, 'You'll have to give me some sheets, Madame, to make the gentleman's bed.'

Madame Grandet rose and followed Nanon, and Madame des Grassins at once said in a low voice, 'Let us take our sous and give the game up.'

They all took their coins from the old chipped saucer the stakes had been placed in, and then the company with one accord turned their chairs towards the fire.

'Have you finished your game?' inquired Grandet, without looking up from his letter.

'Yes, yes,' replied Madame des Grassins, as she crossed the room to take a seat beside Charles.

Eugénie, prompted by a thought that came with the strange new feelings in her newly-awakened heart, left the room to help her mother and Nanon. If she had been questioned by a practised confessor she would no doubt have acknowledged that it was not of her mother or Nanon that she was thinking, but that an almost painfully sharp desire had seized her to go and look at her cousin's room, to arrange things with her own hand, to see that nothing was forgotten, that everything he might require was there, and the room as neat and pretty as it could possibly be made. Already Eugénie believed that only she held the key to her cousin's tastes and ideas. As a matter of fact she came very luckily, just in time. Her mother and Nanon were leaving the room, thinking that they had done everything, but she convinced them that everything was still to do. She suggested to Nanon that it would be a good idea to air the bed with a warming-pan of embers from the kitchen fire. She herself covered the old table with a clean white cloth and urged Nanon to be sure to change it every morning. Her mother was soon persuaded that it was absolutely necessary to light a good fire in the fireplace, and Nanon induced to carry up a big pile of firewood to the passage outside without saying a word to her father. She ran to one of the corner cupboards in the parlour to get an old japanned tray that had belonged to the late M. de la Bertellière, and found a hexagonal crystal glass as well, and a little gilt spoon with nearly all its gold rubbed off, and an old glass scent-bottle with cupids engraved on it, and placed them all in triumph on a corner of the mantelpiece. More sudden inspirations had crowded into her mind in a quarter of an hour than she had had in all the years since she was born.

'Oh, mamma,' she said, 'my cousin will never be able to bear the smell of a tallow candle. Suppose we bought a wax one?...'

She went, as light as a bird, to her purse for five francs that she had been given for the month's expenses.

'Here, Nanon,' she cried. 'Do run quick.'

'But what will your father say?'

This awful objection was raised by Madame Grandet, when she saw her daughter with an old Sèvres sugar-bowl that Grandet had brought from the château at Froidfond in her hand.

'And where will you get sugar from? Are you mad?'

'Nanon can easily buy sugar when she goes for the candle, mamma.'

'But what about your father?'

75

'Suppose his nephew couldn't drink a glass of sugar and water if he wanted it, would that be right? Besides, he won't notice it.'

'Your father notices everything,' said Madame Grandet, shaking her head.

Nanon was hesitating: she knew her master.

'Do go, Nanon; as it's my birthday today, you know!'

Nanon burst out laughing at this joke, the first she had ever heard her young mistress make, and did as she was told.

While Eugénie and her mother were doing their best to beautify the room Monsieur Grandet had allotted to his nephew, Charles, in the parlour, found himself the object of Madame des Grassins' seductive attentions.

'You are very brave,' she said, 'to leave the pleasures of the capital in winter to come and stay in Saumur. But if you don't find us too alarming you shall see that one can have a good time even here.' And she favoured him with a very provincial killing glance.

In the country, women are accustomed to behave so demurely, with such cautious reserve, that their eyes acquire an expression of furtive eagerness, like that sometimes seen in the eyes of the clergy, who regard all pleasure as something stolen or forbidden.

Charles felt so completely out of his element in this room, such leagues away from the vast château and sumptuous surroundings that he had credited his uncle with, that as he looked more closely at Madame des Grassins he saw a faded likeness in her face of the faces he was accustomed to see in Paris. He responded gracefully to the social invitation addressed to him, and they fell naturally into conversation.

As she spoke Madame des Grassins gradually lowered her voice to suit the confidential nature of her remarks. She and Charles were equally in need of an interchange of confidences. And so after a few moments of provocative chatter and jokes half-seriously intended, the guileful provincial lady was able to make some remarks intended for Charles's ear alone, without fear of being overheard by the others, who were talking about the sale of the vintage, the all-absorbing topic of conversation at the moment in Saumur.

'If you will honour us with a visit, Monsieur,' she said, 'both my husband and I will be very pleased to see you. Our *salon* is the only one in Saumur where you will meet both the wealthy business people and the gentry. We belong to both sets. Indeed they only mix in our house: they come to us because they find it amusing. Both circles, I am proud to say, think highly of my husband. In that way we will try to relieve the tedium of your stay here, for, good heavens! if you stay with Monsieur Grandet what's to become of you? Your uncle is a miser, and his whole mind is fixed on his vine cuttings; your aunt is a saint, and hasn't two ideas to knock against each other; and your cousin is a ninny, a common little thing with no education and no dowry, who spends all her time mending dish-cloths.'

'This woman seems a very good sort,' said Charles Grandet to himself. Madame des Grassins' wiles had not been exerted in vain.

'I'm beginning to think that you want to monopolize the gentleman, my dear,' said the big, solid-looking banker, laughing.

The notary and the president had both a more or less spiteful comment to make on this remark, but the abbé looked shrewdly at the pair and then, after taking a pinch of snuff and offering his box to the company, put what everyone was thinking into words. 'And who could do the honours of Saumur better than Madame des Grassins?' he said.

'Well, what do you mean by that, Monsieur l'Abbé?' asked Monsieur des Grassins.

'It is meant in a sense most flattering to you, sir, to Madame des Grassins, to the town of Saumur, and to this gentleman,' the astute ecclesiastic added, turning to Charles. Without

77

appearing to pay the slightest attention to their conversation he had managed to catch the drift of it.

'I don't know if you remember me at all, Monsieur,' said Adolphe, finding words at last, with what he hoped was an air of easy unconcern. 'I once had the pleasure of dancing in the same quadrille as you at a ball in Monsieur le Baron de Nucingen's house, and ...'

'Quite so, Monsieur. I remember it perfectly,' replied Charles, surprised to find everyone's attention focused upon him.

'Is this gentleman your son?' he asked Madame des Grassins.

The abbé favoured her with a malicious glance.

'You must have gone to Paris very young?' Charles went on, turning to Adolphe again.

'There's nothing to be done about it, Monsieur,' said the abbé. 'We send our children off to Babylon as soon as they are weaned!'

Madame des Grassins, with a look that failed to conceal astonishing depths of feeling, appeared to be asking the abbé what he meant.

'You must come to the country,' he went on, 'to find women of thirty, or a little more, with a son about to take his degree in law, who look as fresh and youthful as Madame des Grassins. It seems no time at all to me since the young men and the ladies stood on chairs at balls to see you dance, Madame,' the abbé added, turning to his fair adversary. 'Your triumphs are as unfaded in my memory as if it was only yesterday they happened ...'

'Oh! the old rascal!' said Madame des Grassins to herself. 'Can he have guessed? ...'

'It looks as though I can count on being a great success in Saumur,' Charles thought, and he unbuttoned his overcoat, thrust a hand into his waistcoat, and stood staring into space like Lord Byron in Chantrey's statue.

Grandet's inattention, or rather his absorption in his letter and state of preoccupied reflection, had not escaped notice. Both the notary and the magistrate were watching the old fellow's face, thrown into high relief by the light from the candle, for slight changes in his expression which might give them a clue to the contents of it. The winegrower as a matter of fact was hard put to it to maintain his customary composure, and indeed it is not difficult to imagine how his countenance changed, for here is the fatal letter:

MY BROTHER,

It is now nearly twenty-three years since we last saw each other. We met then to make arrangements for my marriage, and we parted in the happiest circumstances. Indeed I could hardly be blamed for not foreseeing, at that moment when you thought the prosperity of our family a matter for congratulation, that you would one day be its sole support and stay. When this letter reaches your hands I shall no longer be alive. A man in my position does not survive the disgrace of bankruptcy. I have held my head above water as long as I could, hoping to weather the storm, but now I am forced under. My stockbroker's failure, following on the failure of Roguin, my notary, swept away my last resources and has utterly ruined me. I am in the painful situation of owing nearly four millions, with assets amounting to no more than twenty-five per cent. My stock of wines is worth only a fraction of its value, since prices have fallen so calamitously in consequence of the abundance and good quality of your vintages. In three days' time all Paris will say 'Monsieur Grandet was a rogue!' and I, an honest man, shall lie in a shroud of infamy. My son I rob both of his good name, which I have tarnished, and of his mother's fortune. He knows nothing of it yet, poor idolized unhappy child. When we parted affectionately it was well he did not know that that farewell to him was to be one of the last actions of my life, that that affection was the last I should ever show him. Will he not live to curse me? Oh! my brother, my brother, our children's curse is a terrible thing! They may appeal against our curse, but there is no appeal against theirs. Grandet, you are my elder brother, I have a right to ask you to see that I am spared this. Do not let Charles cast bitter words upon my tomb. Oh, brother, if I wrote this letter in my blood and tears I should not suffer so much pain, for I should weep, should bleed, should be dead and should suffer no more; but now I suffer and face death with dry eyes.

So you are now Charles's father! He has no relatives on his mother's side, for reasons which you know. Why did I not allow myself to be led by social prejudice? Why did I yield to love and marry the natural daughter of a great nobleman? Charles is the last of his family; he is alone in the world. Oh, my poor boy! my unhappy son! ... See here, Grandet, I have not turned to you for any help for myself – in any case your fortune is perhaps hardly large enough to stand a claim amounting to three millions – but I am imploring you to help my son. God knows, brother, my hands are joined in supplication as I think of you. In dying, Grandet, I entrust Charles to you. I can look at my pistols without a pang, in the assurance that you will be a father to him.

Charles is very fond of me. I was so good to him; I never crossed him. He will not curse me. Besides, as you will see, he has a sweet nature; he takes after his mother. He will never give you any trouble. Poor boy! he is accustomed to luxury. He has never experienced any of the hardships you and I put up with in our early days, when we were poor ... And now he is left without a penny, and alone – for all his friends will cut him – and it is I who have brought these humiliations on him. Ah! I wish I had the strength to send him here and now to heaven, to his mother! But this is madness.

To return to the subject of my misfortunes and Charles's part in them. I have sent him to you for you to break the news of my death, and his own future prospects. Be a father to him, but be an *indulgent* father. Do not ask him to give up his idle way of living all at once; it would kill him. I beg him on my knees to renounce his claim to his mother's fortune: but I don't need to beg him – he is honourable, and will feel that he must not add himself to the number of my creditors. See that he duly renounces his claim to my succession at the proper moment. Keep nothing from him of the struggle he must face, and the hard conditions of the life I leave him to; and if he has any affection left for me, tell him in my name that all is not lost for him. For it is true that hard work, which was our salvation, can give him back the fortune I have lost; and if he will listen to his father's voice, which is anxious for his sake to speak from beyond the grave, let him leave this country and go to the Indies. And, brother, Charles is an honest and enterprising young man: you will give him a start in life, some stock for trading – he would die rather than not repay it. I know you will do that for him, Grandet. If you did not you would pay for it in remorse! Ah! if my boy found no help or kindness in you I would pray to God for vengeance throughout eternity for your hardheartedness!

If I had been able to withhold a few payments it would have been quite legitimate to send him a small sum, because of his mother's fortune, but my end of month payments took all I had. I would die with an easier mind if I knew my boy's future were settled; I wish I could feel your warm handshake warm my heart with its solemn promise; but I have no time. While Charles is on his way to you I am obliged to file my schedule of assets and liabilities. My affairs are all in order. I am trying in my final arrangement to demonstrate the good faith in which I acted, and show that my misfortunes were due to no fault or dishonesty of my own. In doing this do I not work for Charles?

Farewell, brother. May all God's blessings be yours for the generosity – I have no doubt of it – with which you accept this trust! There will be one voice which will pray for you unceasingly in that world where we must all go one day, where I already am.

VICTOR-ANGE-GUILLAUME GRANDET

'You're having a chat, eh?' said old Grandet, as he folded up the letter carefully in its original creases and put it in his waistcoat pocket.

He looked at his nephew in an ingratiating, embarrassed way, trying to dissimulate his feelings and calculations.

'Are you warmer now?'

'I'm very comfortable, my dear uncle.'

'Well, where have the women gone to?' his uncle went on, forgetting for the moment that his nephew was to sleep under his roof. Eugénie and Madame Grandet came in as he spoke.

'Is everything in order upstairs?' the worthy man asked them, recovering his self-possession.

'Yes, father.'

'Well, nephew, if you are tired, Nanon will show you to your room. Bless me! there's nothing very fancy about it, but you will make allowances for poor winegrowers who never have a sou to their name. The taxes swallow up everything we've got.'

'We don't want to be in the way, Grandet,' said the banker. 'You may have matters to discuss with your nephew. So we will wish you good-evening. Goodbye till tomorrow.'

At this all the guests rose and took their leave, each in his own characteristic manner. The old notary went out to fetch his lantern which he had left under the archway, and came back to light it. Then he offered to escort the des Grassins home. Madame des Grassins had not foreseen the event which had brought the evening to a premature close, and her maid had not come.

'Will you honour me by taking my arm, Madame?' said the Abbé Cruchot.

'No, thank you, Monsieur l'Abbé. I have my son here,' Madame des Grassins replied stiffly.

'Ladies don't risk their reputations with me, you know,' the abbé continued.

'Why not take Monsieur Cruchot's arm?' said her husband.

The abbé conducted the charming lady briskly along until they were a short distance in front of the rest of the party.

'That's a good-looking young man, Madame,' he said, emphasizing his meaning with a pressure on her arm. 'That's the end of that story: the play is played out. You will have to say goodbye to Mademoiselle Grandet, Eugénie will go to the Parisian cousin. Unless the young man happens to have a fancy for some girl in Paris, your son Adolphe will have another rival, and the most ...'

'Nonsense, Monsieur l'Abbé. The young man will not be slow to see that Eugénie hasn't a word to say for herself. And her best days are over. Did you notice her this evening? She was as yellow as a quince.'

'Perhaps you pointed that out to her cousin?'

'Indeed, why should I trouble ...?'

'If you always sit beside Eugénie, Madame, you won't need to say much to the young man about his cousin. He will make his own comparisons ...'

'He promised without much urging to come and dine with us the day after tomorrow.'

'Ah, Madame, if you wished ...'

'And what would you have me do, Monsieur l'Abbé? Are you trying to put evil ideas into my head? I have not reached the age of thirty-nine and kept my reputation spotless, thank God, in order to compromise myself now, even if it were for the sake of the Grand Mogul's Empire. We are both old enough to know what such talk means. For a clergyman you have very odd ideas, I must say. For shame! Such a notion might have come out of *Faublas*.'

'So you have read *Faublas*?'

'No, Monsieur l'Abbé. I meant to say *Les Liaisons dangereuses.*'

'Ah, that's an infinitely more moral book,' said the abbé, laughing. 'But you are making me out to be as depraved as any modern fashionable young man! I only meant to ...'

'Can you dare to tell me that you were not thinking of giving me some shocking advice? Isn't it clear enough? If this young man, who is a very good-looking young fellow, I grant you that, paid court to me he would have no further interest in his cousin. In Paris, I know, there are some devoted mothers who sacrifice themselves in that way for the sake of their children's happiness and welfare, but this is not Paris, Monsieur l'Abbé.'

'No, Madame.'

'And besides,' she went on, 'I would not want, and Adolphe himself would not want, a hundred millions bought at such a price.'

'I said nothing about a hundred millions, Madame. That might perhaps be too much for your powers of resisting temptation, and mine too. Still, I believe that an honest woman may indulge in a little harmless flirtation with the best and most praiseworthy of motives. Indeed it's practically a social duty, and part of ...'

'You think so?'

'Isn't it our duty to try to be as pleasant as we can to other people? Excuse me a moment while I blow my nose – Believe me, Madame,' he went on, 'he gave you a rather more flattering scrutiny through that eyeglass of his than he favoured me with. But then I forgive him for preferring to honour beauty rather than old age.'

'It's plain,' said the president's gruff voice, 'that Monsieur Grandet of Paris sends his son to Saumur with extremely matrimonial intentions.'

'But in that case, why should the cousin descend upon us like a bombshell?' the notary answered.

'That doesn't mean anything,' observed Monsieur des Grassins. 'Old Grandet is close-mouthed.'

'Des Grassins, my dear,' said his wife, 'I have invited the young man to dinner. You must go and ask Monsieur and Madame de Larsonnière to come too, and the du Hautoys, and their lovely daughter, of course. Let's hope she is presentably dressed for the occasion! Her mother is jealous of her, and gets her up so badly! – I hope that you gentlemen will honour us with your company too?' she added, stopping the procession as she turned to address the two Cruchots behind her.

'Here you are, at your own door, Madame,' said the notary.

When they had said good-bye to the three des Grassins and turned their steps homeward, the three Cruchots put their wits to work, applying the genius country people have for minute analysis to the examination in all its bearings of the great event of that evening, which had made a change in the positions of the Cruchotins and the Grassinists in regard to one another. The admirable common sense which governed all the actions of these longheaded schemers made both parties feel the necessity of a temporary alliance against the common foe. For were both parties not concerned to prevent Eugénie from falling in love with Charles, and Charles from thinking of Eugénie? What resistance could the Parisian offer to the web of smooth insinuations, falsely sweet slanders, damning praises, naïvely revealing vindications, which would be ceaselessly spun around him for his deceiving?

When the four relatives were left alone in the living-room Monsieur Grandet spoke to his nephew:

'We must go to bed,' he said. 'It is too late to start talking about the business which brings you here, now; we will find time for that tomorrow. We breakfast at eight o'clock here, and we have a midday snack of fruit, a crust of bread, a glass of white wine; then we dine, like Parisians, at five o'clock. That is the way of it. If you would like to explore the town or have a look at the country round about, you are free as air to do so. You will excuse me if I am usually too busy to go with you. People here will very likely tell you that I'm a wealthy man. They can't keep their tongues still – it's Monsieur Grandet this! and Monsieur Grandet that! I let them talk. Their chatter does my credit no harm at all. But I haven't a sou and, old as I am, I work like any young fellow who has nothing in the world but an indifferent plane and two stout arms. You may perhaps find out for yourself soon enough what a crown costs when you earn it by the sweat of your brow. – Here, Nanon, where are the candles?'

'I hope you will find everything you need, nephew,' said Madame Grandet. 'But if you want anything, you should call Nanon.'

'That is not very likely, my dear aunt. I believe I have brought all my requirements with me! May I wish you and my young cousin good night?'

Charles took a lighted wax candle from Nanon, a very yellow and old wax candle, of local manufacture, that had lain long in an Anjou shop, and was so like a tallow candle that Monsieur Grandet, who in any case was quite incapable of suspecting that such a thing could be in his house, did not notice its magnificence.

'I'll show you the way,' the worthy cooper said.

Instead of going out directly by the door to the archway, Grandet, in compliment to his guest, led the way along the passage that separated the kitchen from the parlour. A folding door with a large oval pane of glass set in it closed off this passage near the staircase, as a means of keeping out the chill gusts of cold air which swept in from the archway. But the north wind whistled none the less rudely there in winter for all that, and the living-room, in spite of strips of list nailed round the doors, was barely kept even passably warm.

Nanon went out to bolt the entrance gate, and then shut up the living-room. She crossed to the stable to unchain a wolf-dog, whose cracked bark sounded as if he suffered from laryngitis. The savage temper of this animal was well known; he recognized only Nanon as a friend. A bond of sympathy existed between these two creatures of the fields.

Charles looked round him at the dingy smoke-discoloured walls and the worm-eaten staircase, now shaking under his uncle's heavy tread, with dismay and growing disillusionment. The place struck him as being like a hen-roost. He looked back over his shoulder with a questioning glance at the faces of his aunt and cousin, but this staircase was so familiar to them that they saw no reason for astonishment, and taking his glance for an expression of friendly interest they responded with a pleasant smile that drove his heart into his boots.

'What on earth induced my father to send me here?' he said to himself.

When he reached the first landing he saw three doors, painted a dark brownish-red, set without mouldings and almost unnoticeably in the dusty walls. They were embellished, however, with very conspicuous heavy iron bars, running across their width and ending in a streamer-shaped ornamental pattern with tongues of metal like flames, which matched the pattern of the iron plates set on either side of the long keyholes.

A door at the top of the stairs, giving access to the room above the kitchen, was evidently blocked up. It could only be reached, in fact, through Grandet's bedroom, and he used it as his private retreat. The single window that lighted it, on the courtyard side, was guarded by a grating of massive iron bars. Grandet allowed nobody, not even his wife, to set foot inside: he required that he should be left alone there, and undisturbed, like an alchemist among his crucibles. No doubt there was some secret hiding-place ingeniously concealed in the room, for the title-deeds of his estates were stored here and here he kept the balances he needed for weighing gold louis. Here, by night and secretly, receipts were made out, sums received were acknowledged, and plans were laid, to such effect that other businessmen, seeing Grandet always ready and prepared in every business matter, might be excused for imagining that he had a fairy at his beck and call, or perhaps a fiend. Here, no doubt, while Nanon's snoring shook the floor-boards, while the wolf-dog watched and yawned in the courtyard, while Madame and Mademoiselle Grandet soundly slept, the old cooper would come to commune with his gold, to caress and worship, fondle and gloat over his gold. The walls were thick, the shutters close. He alone had the key of this laboratory where, so it was said, he pored over plans on which every fruit tree he possessed was plotted, and calculated his yield to the last shoot in his vineyards, to the last faggot of his timber.

Eugénie's room was opposite this blocked door. Then at the far end of the landing, the rooms occupied by Monsieur and Madame Grandet ran the length of the entire front of the house. Madame Grandet had a bedroom beside Eugénie's, with a glass door between. Her husband's room was separated from hers by a partition, and from the mysterious workroom by a thick wall. Old Grandet had lodged his nephew on the second floor, in a high-ceilinged garret above his own room, so that the young man would be heard if he took it into his head to prowl about.

When Eugénie and her mother reached the landing they kissed one another and said good night; then, after a few parting words to Charles, which sounded formal and indifferent enough but came warmly indeed from the girl's heart, they went to their rooms.

'This is your room, nephew,' said Grandet, opening the door. 'If you want to go out you will have to call Nanon. Without her – goodbye to you! The dog will gobble you up without a with your leave or by your leave. Good night. Sleep well. Aha! the ladies have given you a fire in your room,' he went on.

As he said this big Nanon appeared, armed with a warming-pan.

'Upon my word, just look at this!' said Monsieur Grandet. 'Do you take my nephew for a woman in a delicate state of health? Be off with you, Nanon, and your pan of embers!'

'But the sheets are damp, sir. And the gentleman really is as dainty as a woman.'

'Well, let it be, since you have taken it into your head,' said Grandet, giving her shoulder a push; 'but mind you don't set the place on fire.' And the miser made his way downstairs again, grumbling to himself as he went.

Charles stood aghast amid his trunks. His glance took in the sloping walls of an attic room hung with the kind of paper, yellow and strewn with bouquets of flowers, favoured by country inns, a mantelpiece of rough cracked stone that struck chill even to the eye, crazy yellow wooden chairs with cane seats, an open night-table large enough to hold a fair-sized sergeant of light infantry, a meagre strip of rag carpet beside a canopied bed whose curtains visibly trembled as if the whole worm-eaten contraption were about to crumble into dust. He looked soberly at big Nanon, and said,

'Tell me, my good girl, is it true that I'm in Monsieur Grandet's house? Monsieur Grandet, formerly the Mayor of Saumur, and the brother of Monsieur Grandet of Paris?'

'Yes, you are, sir. In the house of a very kind, very amiable, very perfect gentleman. Am I to help you to unpack your trunks?'

'Yes, indeed, I wish you would, old soldier! Did you ever serve in the Horse Marines?'

'Ho! ho! ho! ho!' was Nanon's reply. 'Who may the Horse Marines be? Are they salt water men? Do they go to sea?'

'Look, get my dressing-gown out of that bag. Here's the key.'

Nanon was wonderstruck at the sight of a green silk dressing-gown, brocaded with gold flowers in an antique design.

'You're going to put on that to go to bed?' she exclaimed.

'Yes.'

'Holy Virgin! The altar cloth that that would make for the parish church! Dear, darling young gentleman, give it to the Church and you will save your soul, for it's fit to make you lose it. Oh! how sweet you look in it! I'll go and call Mam'selle to come and look at you.'

'Nonsense, Nanon, since it's Nanon you're called! Do hold your tongue and let me go to bed. I will put my things in order in the morning. If you like my dressing-gown so much you can save your own soul with it. I am far too good a Christian to take it away from you when I go, and you can have it to do whatever you like with.'

Nanon stood stock still for a moment, staring incredulously at Charles, quite unable to believe him.

'Give *me* that finery!' she said as she went out. 'This gentleman's asleep on his feet and dreaming already. Good night.'

'Good night, Nanon. – What in the world am I doing here?' Charles said to himself as he fell asleep. 'My father is no fool: there must be some point in this journey. Oh, well! tomorrow's soon enough for serious business, as some Greek fogey or other said.'

Eugénie stopped in the middle of her prayers and said to herself, 'How nice my cousin is!' And her prayers were left unfinished that evening.

No particular thought crossed Madame Grandet's mind as she went to bed. Through the communicating door in the partition she could hear the miser walking to and fro in his room. Like all timid wives she had thoroughly studied the character of her lord and master. Signs imperceptible to other eyes had told her, as a gull foresees the approaching storm, of the tempest raging in Grandet's heart; and at such times she lay low, 'as still as death', to use her own expression.

Grandet stared at the door, lined with sheet iron on the inner side, that he had had fitted to his workroom, and muttered to himself: 'What an odd idea of my brother's to bequeath his son to me! A pretty legacy! I haven't twenty crowns to give away. And what would twenty crowns be to that dressed-up young puppy, who stared at my weather glass as if he thought a bonfire the proper place for it?' And, thinking over the probable consequences of this sad bequest, Grandet was perhaps more perturbed in spirit than his brother had been when he made it.

'*Me* have that golden gown!' Nanon was saying as she fell asleep, wrapped in fancy in her altar cloth, dreaming of flowers, brocade, figured silk, for the first time in her life, as Eugénie dreamed of love.

Into a girl's innocent and uneventful life there comes a day marked with delight, when the sun's rays seem to shine into her very soul, when a flower looks like the expression of her thoughts, when her heart beats more quickly and her quickened brain, in sympathy, ceases to think at all, but all ideas are dissolved in a feeling of undefined longing. It is a time of innocent sadness and vague joys that have no sharpness of edge. When babies first observe the things round them, they smile: when a girl first dimly perceives the existence of love, she smiles as she smiled when a child. If the light is the first thing we turn to with love, surely it is love that first brings light to the heart? This day had dawned for Eugénie. She had begun to see life clearly for the first time.

Eugénie, like all country girls, was accustomed to rise early in the morning. Next morning she got up earlier than usual, said her prayers, and then set about the business of dressing, an occupation that from that day on was to hold some interest for her. She first brushed her chestnut hair till it shone, twisted the heavy braids up on top of her head with the most scrupulous care to prevent stray hairs escaping, and pinned them with a prim tidiness that set off her face, the simple style harmonizing with its shy candour, and purity of line. Then as she washed her hands over and over again in cold spring water that roughened and reddened the skin, she looked at her beautiful round arms and wondered what her cousin did to have such soft white hands, such well-kept nails. She put on new stockings and her prettiest shoes. She laced herself right up, careful not to leave undone a single eyelet hole. For the first time in her life she wished to look her best, and felt how pleasant it was to have a new, well-made dress that suited her, to put on.

When she was dressed she heard the church clock strike, and was astonished to hear it strike only seven. She had got up too early because she was so anxious to have all the time she needed to dress carefully. As she knew nothing of the art that leads a woman to try placing a curl in a dozen different positions to study the effect, she simply crossed her arms, sat down at her window and looked out at the courtyard, the narrow garden, and the high terraced gardens up above on the ramparts. It was a rather gloomy view, shut in by the old walls, but one not without the strange beauty of solitary spots and places left to grow wild.

Close to the kitchen door there was a well with a stone coping round it and an iron framework above, supporting a pulley. This was overgrown by a vine, with leaves now withered and reddened by the chill air of late autumn, whose crooked stem had found its way to the house wall, and clinging against it, ran the length of the house and ended by a woodpile, where the logs were arranged as precisely as the books on a bibliophile's shelves. The flagstones of the courtyard were dark with age and lack of traffic, and stained with a growth of mosses and weeds. The massive walls were clothed with greenery, splashed here and there with long brown marks where water trickled. At the far end of the courtyard the eight dilapidated steps leading to the garden gate were half-buried under high-growing plants, and looked like the tombstone of some medieval knight, put there by his widow at the time of the Crusades, and neglected ever since. A low wall of crumbling stone supported a decrepit trellis whose wood was rotting and falling to pieces, but climbing plants wrapped friendly arms about it in unrestricted liberty. Two stunted apple trees raised their gnarled and knotty branches on either side of the wicket gate. The garden itself contained only narrow borders edged with box divided by three parallel straight gravelled walks, and ended at the foot of the ramparts in a thicket of limes. At the far end there were also raspberry canes, and near the house an immense walnut tree whose overhanging branches cast their shade over the window of the cooper's strongroom.

It was a fine morning, with the clear luminous sky characteristic of autumn in the Loire valley, and the sun was rapidly dispersing the light night frost that clung to the picturesque walls and stones and tangled foliage of this garden and the courtyard. Eugénie discovered a completely new charm in the scene before her, which on every previous day had seemed so ordinary and familiar. As the sunlight grew and filled the world outside, a host of confused thoughts rose in her mind. A vague inexplicable happiness filled her being, pervading and wrapping her round as completely as a cloud might envelop her body. All the objects that her eyes rested on in this curious old garden that was her world seemed to share her feelings and her thoughts, and she herself was one with her surroundings. When the sun's rays reached a corner of the wall from which fell fronds of maidenhair fern, and showed its thick stems and glossy foliage shot with colour like a pigeon's throat, rays of bright hope lit the future for Eugénie; and ever afterwards she was to take pleasure in looking at this bit of wall, whose pale flowers, harebells, and bleached grasses held associations as sweet as a childhood memory. The rustle of a leaf, as one fell from time to time to earth in this echoing court, seemed to answer the girl's secret questionings, and she might have sat there, musing, all day, without noticing the passing of the hours. But suddenly a surge of violent feeling took possession of her. She rose restlessly to her feet again and again, to go to her mirror and look at her face, in just the spirit of a conscientious writer reading his work through, criticizing it and saying hard things about it to himself.

'I am not good-looking enough for him!'

This was Eugénie's humble thought, a thought fertile in suffering. The poor child was unjust to herself; but humility, or rather a fear of being unworthy, is one of the first-awakened attributes of love.

Eugénie was robust and strongly made, in physique like many girls of the lower middle classes whose beauty is often rather coarse; but though Eugénie resembled the Venus de Milo in figure, she was refined by that sweetness of Christian feeling which gives a woman a dignity and distinction unknown to the classical sculptors. She had a very large head, the masculine but delicately chiselled forehead of Phidias's Jupiter, luminous grey eyes, in whose clear brightness her pure life was mirrored. An attack of smallpox, too mild to leave scars, had a little blurred the outlines of her features and brushed the rosy colour from her fair oval face. In spite of this loss of bloom her skin was still so soft and delicate that her mother's gentle kiss marked her cheek with a momentary tinge of red. Her nose was a little too big, but it was in keeping with the generous lines of her strikingly red mouth, with its full lips expressive of goodness and love. Her throat was round and flawless. The curve of her breast in a dress modestly buttoned to the throat caught the eye and stirred the imagination. No doubt she possessed little of the grace which is lent by well-made and fashionable clothes, put on with an eye to their effect, but to judges of beauty the firmness of her tall, well-knit figure must constitute a charm.

In short, Eugénie, so vigorous and built on such a generous scale, had nothing of the prettiness that pleases the crowd; but she was beautiful with that unmistakable beauty that only artists delight in. A painter, searching on this earth for a type of the celestial purity of Mary, requiring that all women's eyes should possess the proud humility that Raphael's vision gave them, demanding that purity of line whose creation is due often to the artist's chance inspiration, but which is kept or acquired in fact only by a virtuous and Christian life – a painter haunted by this ideal would have seen at once unconscious innate nobility of soul in Eugénie's face, a world of love in the calm forehead, and in the setting of the eyes, the fall of the eyelids, something divine. The serenity of her features, never spoiled or tired by the expression of pleasure, the turn of her head, made one think of vague still horizons beyond tranquil lakes. This calm, softly-coloured face, which seemed to diffuse light round it like a half-open flower, held the quality of restfulness, communicated the charm of the nature reflected in it and compelled the eye to linger on it. Eugénie was still on the brink of life, where a child's illusions bloom like flowers, and daisies are picked with a delight unknown in any pleasure of later years.

And so it came about that she looked at herself in her mirror, knowing nothing yet of love, and said,

'I am too ugly; he won't give me a thought!'

Then she opened her door and listened, crept out on to the landing and craned her neck over the stairs to hear what the household was doing.

'He is not up yet,' she thought when she heard Nanon bustling about, coughing as she always did in the morning, sweeping the living-room, lighting the kitchen fire, chaining up the dog and talking to her animal friends in the stable. And Eugénie ran downstairs and out to the stable, where Nanon was milking the cow.

'Nanon, Nanon, be a dear, and have cream for my cousin's coffee!'

'But, Mam'selle, you did ought to have thought about that yesterday,' said Nanon with a hearty laugh. 'I can't make cream for you off this morning's milk. Your cousin is a duck, a sweetheart, a perfect love of a man. You didn't see him in his gold and silk night wrap. I saw him with my own eyes. The linen he wears is as fine as M. le Curé's surplice.'

'Nanon, do make us some fancy bread.'

'And who will give me wood to heat the oven, and flour and butter?' demanded Nanon. In her capacity of Grandet's prime minister she took on an immense importance in Eugénie's eyes, and even in Eugénie's mother's eyes, sometimes. 'Are we to rob *himself* to feast your cousin? You ask him for the butter and flour and firewood, he's your father, he may give them to you. Look, here he is coming to see to the provisions ...'

Eugénie fled to the garden, terrified, as she heard the stairs creaking under her father's tread. Her sensitive modesty made her shrink from observation. She felt peculiarly conscious of her own sense of happiness, and was sure, as most of us are in such circumstances, perhaps not without reason, that her thoughts were written on her face for anyone to read. Then, too, as she noticed for the first time the bleak bareness of her father's house, the poor girl felt a sort of vexation at her inability to make it a more fitting setting for her cousin's elegance. She felt a passionate need to do something for her cousin – but what? She had no idea. She was so guileless and single-hearted that she was ready to act as her angelic nature prompted her without misgivings or any examination of her impressions and feelings. The first sight of her cousin had awakened a woman's natural instincts in her, with all the more force because she was twenty-three and mature in body and mind.

For the first time in her life the sight of her father struck terror into Eugénie's heart. She realized that he was master of her fate, and was conscious, with a sense of guilt, that she was concealing some of her thoughts from him. She began to walk hastily along, and was astonished to find herself breathing an air that seemed purer and more refreshing, warmed by a sun whose rays made her whole being glow with new vigour and fresh life.

While she was trying to think of some means of getting her teacake, a tiff was blowing up between big Nanon and Grandet – a thing as rare as swallows in winter. The cooper had come, armed with his keys, to dole out the day's rations.

'Is there any bread left from yesterday?' he asked Nanon.

'Not a crumb, sir.'

Grandet took up a big round floury loaf, shaped in one of the flat baskets they use for baking in Anjou, and was about to cut it when Nanon said,

'There are five of us today, sir.'

'That's true,' replied Grandet, 'but this loaf of yours weighs six pounds, you'll have some left over. Besides, I know these young fellows from Paris, they never touch bread. You'll soon see.'

'Do they eat *frippe* then?' asked Nanon.

In Anjou, *frippe*, a word from the popular dictionary, means anything that is eaten spread on bread, from butter, an ordinary everyday sort of *frippe*, to preserved nectarines, the very grandest *frippe* of all; and anyone who as a child has licked off the *frippe* and left the bread will understand Nanon's remark.

'No,' replied Grandet, 'they don't eat *frippe* either. They're like love-sick girls, as you might say.'

Now that he had sparingly provided for the day's meals, the miser was about to go to his fruit-loft, not forgetting, first of all, to lock his store-room cupboards, when Nanon stopped him, saying,

'Just give me a little flour and butter, and I'll make a cake for the children.'

'Do you want the house to be turned upside down for my nephew's sake? Is my nephew to eat me out of house and home?'

'The thought of your nephew never entered my head, any more than the thought of your dog, any more than it entered yours ... Here, you've only handed me out six lumps of sugar! I want eight.'

'What next, Nanon? I've never seen you act like this before. What's come over you? Are you mistress here? You shall have six lumps of sugar, and that's all.'

'Well, then, what is your nephew to sweeten his coffee with?'

'Two lumps. I'll do without.'

'You'll do without sugar, at your age! I'd sooner buy you some myself, out of my own pocket!'

'You mind your own business.'

In spite of the fall in price of sugar, it was still in the cooper's eyes the most precious of colonial products. To him it was still worth six francs a pound, as it had been in the time of the Empire. The economical use of it which had been a duty then, had now become an inveterate habit with him. But all women, even the simplest, can make shift to attain their ends. Nanon let the question of sugar drop, to make sure of the cake.

'Mam'selle,' she called through the window, 'don't you want some cake?'

'No, no,' answered Eugénie.

'Well, Nanon,' said Grandet, as he heard his daughter's voice, 'here you are.'

He opened the bin the flour was kept in, measured out some flour, and added a few ounces of butter to the piece he had already cut.

'I'll want firewood to heat the oven,' said the inexorable Nanon.

'Oh, well, take what you need,' he replied gloomily; 'but you will have to make a fruit tart at the same time, and cook the whole dinner in the oven, so that you won't have to light another fire.'

'Bless my soul!' cried Nanon. 'You don't need to tell me that.'

Grandet gave his trusty prime minister a look that was almost paternal.

'Mademoiselle,' the cook called, 'we're going [to make a] cake!'

Grandet came back again with his fruit, and set a first plate[?]ful on the kitchen table.

'Look, sir,' said Nanon, 'what lovely boots your nephew has! Just look at the leather. How nice it smells! What do you clean that with? Am I to use your egg polish on them?'

'No, Nanon, I'm afraid the egg would spoil that kind of leather. You had better tell him you don't know what to use to clean morocco ... yes, that's what it is, and he will buy you some polish himself in Saumur for his boots. I have heard that they put sugar into the polish to make it shinier.'

'Is it good to eat then?' the servant asked, raising the boots to her nose. 'Bless my soul, they smell of Madame's eau-de-Cologne! Oh, what a joke!'

'A joke!' said her master. 'You think it's a joke for boots to cost more than the man who wears them is worth?'

'Oh, sir,' Nanon began again when her master returned from a second visit to the fruit-loft, which he had carefully locked behind him. 'You will want to have broth once or twice a week, won't you, on account of your ...?'

'Yes.'

'I'll have to go to the butcher's.'

'You'll do nothing of the kind. You can make us some chicken broth, the tenants won't see you want for fowl. And I'll tell Cornoiller to kill some ravens for me. That's the game that makes the best broth on earth.'

'Is it true, sir, that they feed on dead things?'

'You're a fool, Nanon! Like every other creature they live on what they can pick up. Don't we all live on the dead? Where else do legacies come from?'

Having no further orders to give, Grandet pulled out his watch, and seeing that there was half an hour to spare before breakfast, he took up his hat, gave his daughter a kiss, and said to her,

o take a walk along the Loire to my
something I want to see to there.'

fetch her straw hat lined with rose-coloured
; then father and daughter walked down the
towards the market square.

you off to so early in the morning?' said the
ot, meeting them.

a look at something,' Grandet replied, under no
illusions as to the coincidence of his friend's morning walk.
When the miser went to take a look at something, the notary
knew by experience that there was always something to be
gained by going too. And so he joined the party.

'Come along, Cruchot,' Grandet said to him. 'You're one
of my friends; I'm going to demonstrate to you what a stupid
thing it is to plant poplars in good soil ...'

'You think the sixty thousand francs you pocketed for those
poplars in your meadows by the Loire not worth having,
then?' said Maître Cruchot in wide-eyed bewilderment. 'What
luck you had there! ... Felling your trees just when there was a
shortage of white wood at Nantes, and you could get thirty
francs each for them!'

Eugénie listened absent-mindedly, unconscious of the fact
that the most critical moment of her life was approaching,
that in answer to a question from the notary she was to
hear pronounced upon her her father's sovereign decree.
Grandet had reached the splendid meadow-land he owned by
the Loire, where thirty labourers were busy clearing away the
roots of the poplars that had stood there, filling in holes and
levelling the ground.

'See how much ground a poplar takes up, Maître Cruchot,'
he said to the notary. – 'Jean,' he called to a workman,
'm-m-measure round the s-s-space with your r-r-rule.'

'Four feet by eight,' the workman replied, when he had
done this.

'That's thirty-two feet lost,' Grandet said to Cruchot. 'I

had three hundred poplars in this row, hadn't I? Now three h-h-h-hundred times thirty-t-t-two f-f-feet eats up the space for f-f-f-f-five hundred trusses of hay. Allow twice as much again for the space on either side, that's fifteen hundred; and then there is the space in between. Say a thousand t-t-t-t-t-trusses of hay altogether.'

'Well,' said Cruchot, helping his friend out, 'a thousand trusses of hay would bring in about six hundred francs.'

'S-s-say twelve hundred, f-f-f-for the aftermath is worth three or four hundred. Well, now! r-r-r-r-reckon what twelve hundred f-f-francs per annum f-f-f-for f-f-f-forty years amounts to at c-c-c-compound interest at the ordinary r-r-r-ate.'

'I make it about sixty thousand francs,' said the notary.

'Fair enough! That's s-s-s-sixty thousand f-f-f-f-rancs. Well,' the winegrower went on, without stammering, 'two thousand forty-year-old poplars would not bring me in fifty thousand francs. There's a loss on them. I worked that out for myself,' he said complacently. 'Jean,' he continued, turning to the labourer, 'fill in all the holes except those down by the river, and plant those young poplars that I bought down there.' Then with a slight movement of the wen on his nose that looked exactly like a sardonic smile he looked round at Cruchot and added, 'If I set them along by the Loire they will find their food at Government expense.'

'Oh, that's clear: poplars should only be planted on poor soil,' said Cruchot, dazzled by Grandet's longheadedness.

'Q-q-quite so, sir,' replied the cooper laconically.

Eugénie, who was looking at the glorious expanse of the valley and the Loire that lay before her without heeding her father's calculations, suddenly gave all her attention to Cruchot's remarks when she heard him say to his client,

'So you have brought a son-in-law from Paris? All Saumur is talking about your nephew; they can think of nothing else. I shall soon have marriage settlements to draw up, eh, Grandet?'

'D-d-did y-y-you come out early t-t-to t-t-tell me that?'

retorted Grandet, accompanying the inquiry with a twitch of his wen. 'Well, you're an old friend, I'll be p-p-p-plain with y-y-you and t-t-tell you w-w-what you w-w-w-want t-t-to know. S-s-s-see here, I would r-r-rather throw my d-d-d-d-daughter into the L-l-loire than give her to her c-c-c-cousin: you c-c-can m-m-make a p-p-p-public announcement of that. Or no, just l-l-let them g-g-gossip.'

The scene swam before Eugénie's eyes as she heard him speak. The vague hopes of happiness far in the future which had begun to grow in her heart had suddenly sprung up and burst into perfect bloom, and now her treasure of flowers was cut down before her eyes and flung on the ground. Since the evening before she had felt herself being bound to Charles by all the ties of happiness that can unite two souls; and from that moment, it seemed, sorrow was to confirm and strengthen those ties, for is it not woman's noble destiny to be touched more deeply by the dignity of sorrow than by fortune's splendours? How could her father's affection for her have died in her father's heart? What crime could Charles be guilty of? They were questions to which she could find no answer. Her young love, itself so profound a mystery, was already wrapping itself in mysteries. When they turned to go home again she made her way back unsteadily, and as she reached the gloomy old street which she had lately walked down with such joy, she found its appearance sad, she inhaled the atmosphere of melancholy that time and long experience had steeped it in. Love was teaching her all its lessons.

When they drew near the house she walked quickly on ahead of her father and, after knocking, waited for him by the door. But Grandet, noticing a newspaper still in its wrapper in the notary's hand, had started a conversation with him.

'What figure does Government stock stand at now?' he said.

'I know you won't take my advice, Grandet,' answered Cruchot, 'but you should buy without delay. You can still make twenty per cent on it in two years. And there is the interest as well, which is pretty good – a return of five thousand livres on eighty thousand francs invested. You can buy now at eighty francs fifty centimes.'

'We shall see,' replied Grandet, rubbing his chin.

'Good God!' said the notary, who had by this time opened his newspaper.

'What's the matter?' exclaimed Grandet, and as he spoke Cruchot pushed the paper in front of his eyes and said, 'Read that!'

'Monsieur Grandet, one of the most respected businessmen in Paris, shot himself through the head yesterday, after making his appearance on 'Change as usual. He had previously sent in his resignation to the President of the Chamber of Deputies, and had also resigned his position as Judge of the Tribunal of Commerce. The failure of MM. Roguin and Souchet, his stockbroker and notary, had involved him in some financial embarrassment. Monsieur Grandet, who was greatly esteemed and whose credit stood high, would no doubt have found assistance in his difficulties on the market, and it is to be regretted that a man of such high character should have yielded to the first impulse of despair ... etc.'

'I knew about it,' the old winegrower said.

In spite of his professional imperturbability, Maître Cruchot felt his blood run cold when he heard this remark. He shuddered at the thought that perhaps Grandet of Paris had implored help from the millions of Grandet of Saumur, in vain.

'What about his son?' he asked. 'He was so light-hearted yesterday.'

'He knows nothing at all yet,' replied Grandet, with the same absence of emotion.

'Good-bye, Monsieur Grandet,' said Cruchot. He now understood the position, and went off to reassure Monsieur de Bonfons.

When he went in Grandet found breakfast ready. Madame Grandet was already sitting in her raised chair, busy knitting sleeves for herself, for the winter. Eugénie ran to her mother and threw her arms round her neck with the sudden outburst of affection which is often the expression of a hidden trouble.

'You can have your breakfast,' said Nanon, coming bustling downstairs in a hurry. 'The lad's sleeping like a cherub. He looks a lamb with his eyes shut! I went in and called him, but I needn't have troubled, there wasn't a sound out of him.'

'Let him sleep,' said Grandet. 'He will waken soon enough today to hear bad news.'

'Why, what's the matter?' asked Eugénie, dropping two tiny lumps of sugar into her coffee. Goodness knows how many grains these lumps of sugar weighed: the worthy miser amused himself by cutting them up, as a spare-time relaxation.

Madame Grandet, who had not dared to ask this question herself, looked at her husband.

'His father has blown his brains out.'

'My uncle? ...' said Eugénie.

'Oh, that poor young man!' exclaimed Madame Grandet.

'Poor indeed!' retorted Grandet. 'He hasn't a penny.'

'Oh well, he's sleeping as though he was king of the earth,' said Nanon, pityingly.

Eugénie could eat no more. Her heart ached, as a woman's heart does ache when, for the first time in her life, her whole being is filled with compassion for the sorrow of someone she loves. She burst into tears.

'You didn't know your uncle, so what are you crying for?' inquired her father, giving her a look like the stare of a hungry lion, a stare he no doubt usually reserved for eyeing his heaps of gold.

'But who wouldn't feel sorry for the poor young man, sir?' said the servant. 'There he is sleeping like a top and knowing nothing about what's happened to him.'

'I wasn't speaking to you, Nanon! Hold your tongue.'

In that moment Eugénie learned that a woman in love must always hide her feelings. She made no answer.

'Till I come back you will say nothing about this to him, I hope, Madame Grandet,' the old cooper went on. 'I have to go and see after the ditch they are marking out in my meadows by the road. I'll be back for lunch at noon, and I'll talk to my nephew about his affairs then. ... As for you, Mademoiselle Eugénie, if it's that dressed up young puppy you're crying over, that's enough of that, child. He'll be off post-haste to the East Indies. You'll never set eyes on him again ...'

Her father took up his gloves from the brim of his hat, and put them on with his accustomed calm deliberation, pushing the fingers of each hand in turn well into place, dovetail fashion, with the fingers of the other hand, and then went out.

'Oh, mamma, I can't breathe!' cried Eugénie, when she was alone with her mother. 'I have never felt such pain before.'

Madame Grandet, seeing how white her daughter's face was, opened the window and let in some fresh air.

'That's better,' said Eugénie after a moment.

Madame Grandet was startled by this nervous agitation in a person usually so calm and self-possessed. She looked at her daughter in the intuitive sympathy mothers possess with those they love, and guessed everything. Indeed, the lives of the famous Hungarian sisters, attached to one another by one of nature's errors, could scarcely have been more closely joined in sympathetic feeling than those of Eugénie and her mother, living as they did always together in this recess by the window, together in church, breathing the same air even while they slept.

'My poor little girl!' said Madame Grandet, drawing Eugénie's head down to her breast.

At these words the girl raised her face with a questioning glance to her mother's, scrutinizing her inmost thoughts.

'Why should he be sent to the Indies?' she said. 'If he is in trouble should he not stay here? Is he not our closest relative?'

'Yes, my dear, it would be very natural for him to stay; but your father has his reasons, we must respect them.'

The mother and daughter sat in silence, the one on her raised chair, the other in her own little armchair, and together they resumed their work. Then suddenly, with a heart overflowing with gratitude for the loving understanding her mother had shown her, Eugénie took her mother's hand and kissed it, saying, 'How kind you are, dearest mamma!'

Her mother's tired face, worn with long suffering patiently endured, lit up when she heard these words.

'Do you like him?' asked Eugénie.

Madame Grandet answered her only with a smile. Then after a moment's silence, she said in a low voice, 'Surely you cannot be so fond of him already? That would be a pity.'

'A pity?' Eugénie repeated. 'Why? You like him, Nanon likes him, and why shouldn't I like him too? Come, mamma, let's go and lay the table for his breakfast.'

She threw down her work and her mother followed suit, saying as she did so, 'You're a mad girl!' In spite of her words she was happy to approve her daughter's giddiness, and even share it as she helped her.

Eugénie called Nanon.

'What are you wanting now, Mam'selle?'

'Nanon, you'll have cream by twelve o'clock, won't you?'

'Oh, by twelve o'clock, yes!' the old servant answered.

'Well, make his coffee very strong. I have heard Monsieur des Grassins say that they drink their coffee very strong in Paris. Put plenty in.'

'And where do you think I'll get it from?'

'Buy some.'

'And suppose the master meets me?'

'He is down in his meadows.'

'I'll just run over to the shop then. But when I went for the wax candle Monsieur Fessard asked me if the Three Holy

106

Kings were staying in our house. The whole town will be hearing about our goings-on.'

'If your father suspects anything,' said Madame Grandet, 'he will be ready to beat us.'

'Well, if he beats us, he can only beat us; we'll go down on our knees and take our beating.'

Madame Grandet could do nothing but raise her eyes to heaven in answer to this. Nanon took her cap and went out. Eugénie unfolded a clean white tablecloth and went to fetch some of the grapes which she had amused herself by hanging in clusters from strings in the loft. She walked along the corridor lightly, so as not to waken her cousin, and could not resist the temptation to stop outside his door to listen to his even breathing.

'Trouble is awake and watching while he sleeps,' she said to herself.

She took the greenest vineleaves that were left hanging on the vine, arranged her grapes as temptingly as any old professional hand, and bore the dish in triumph to the table. She laid predatory hands on the pears that her father had counted out in the kitchen, and piled them up in a pyramid with leaves among them. She came and went, ran in and out from one room to another, danced here and there. She would gladly have ransacked her father's house from top to bottom, but everything was locked up, and her father had the keys. Nanon came back with two new-laid eggs. When she saw them Eugénie could have flung her arms round the old servant's neck.

'The farmer from La Lande had eggs in his basket, and when I asked him for some he gave me these, the nice man, just to keep in with me.'

After two hours of busy occupation, in the course of which Eugénie left her work twenty times at least to go and watch the coffee boiling, or listen for sounds from her cousin's room announcing that he was getting up, she had succeeded in preparing a very simple, very inexpensive lunch, but one which was a terrible infringement of the immemorial customs and practice of the household. Midday lunch was a meal that no one thought of sitting down to table for. It consisted only of a little bread, some fruit or butter, and a glass of wine. Now as she looked at the table placed beside the fire, with one of the arm-chairs set before the place laid for her cousin, at the two plates of fruit, the egg-cups, the bottle of white wine, the bread, the sugar heaped up in a saucer, Eugénie trembled in every limb even to think of the stare her father would give her if he happened to come in at that moment. And so she kept looking at the clock to estimate if her cousin had time to finish lunch before the master of the house returned.

'Never mind, Eugénie. If your father comes in, I shall take the responsibility of doing all this on myself,' said Madame Grandet.

Eugénie could not keep back her tears. 'Oh! my darling mother,' she exclaimed, 'I have never loved you half enough!'

Charles, after strolling interminably about his room, humming and singing snatches of song to himself, came downstairs at last. Happily, it was still only eleven o'clock. True Parisian that he was, Charles had taken as much pains with his appearance as if he had been staying in the château of the noble lady who was travelling in Scotland. He came in with that affable laughing air that sits so well on a young man, and that made Eugénie rejoice and feel sorry for him in the same instant. He had taken the catastrophic collapse of his castles in Anjou as a joke, and greeted his aunt very gaily.

'Did you sleep well, my dear aunt? And you, too, cousin?'

'Yes, thank you. How did you sleep?' said Madame Grandet.

'Oh, I slept soundly.'

'You must be hungry, cousin,' said Eugénie. 'Sit down and have something to eat.'

'Oh, I never take breakfast before twelve o'clock, just after I get up. Still, I fared so badly on the way here that I'll place myself in your hands. Besides ...' He drew out the most charming little flat watch that Bréguet ever made. 'Why, it's only eleven o'clock. I was up early this morning.'

'Up early? ...' said Madame Grandet.

'Yes, but I wanted to put my things in order. Well, I am quite ready for something, anything will do, a bird, a partridge ...'

'Holy Virgin!' cried Nanon, as she heard this.

'A partridge,' said Eugénie to herself, wishing she could lay out all she had to buy a partridge.

The dandy sank gracefully into the armchair, like a pretty woman reclining on a divan. Eugénie and her mother drew their chairs forward and sat near him, by the fire.

'Do you always live here?' Charles inquired, finding the room even more hideous by daylight than it had seemed by candlelight the evening before.

'Always,' Eugénie answered, with her eyes on him, 'except during the vintage. We go to help Nanon then, and we all stay at the Abbey at Noyers.'

'You never take a walk?'

'Sometimes on Sunday after vespers, when it is fine, we walk as far as the bridge,' said Madame Grandet; 'or in the hay-making season we go to watch the hay being cut.'

'Have you a theatre here?'

'Go to the play!' exclaimed Madame Grandet. 'Go to see play-actors! But do you not know that that's a mortal sin?'

'Here, sir,' said Nanon, bringing in the eggs, 'we are giving you chickens in the shell.'

'Oh, new-laid eggs!' said Charles, who, after the manner of people who take luxury for granted, had not given another thought to his partridge. 'How delicious! Now, what about a little butter, eh, my good girl?'

'Butter now? That means no cake later on!' said the servant.

'But of course bring some butter, Nanon!' cried Eugénie.

The girl watched her cousin cutting his bread and butter into strips to dip into his egg, and was as happy in the sight as the most romantic shop-girl in Paris watching the triumph of innocence in a melodrama. It is true that Charles, who had been brought up by a gracious, charming mother, and polished by an accomplished woman of the world, was as dainty, elegant, neat in his ways as any little milliner. The compassion and tenderness of a young girl have a truly magnetic force, and Charles, seeing himself thus waited upon by his cousin and aunt, could not help yielding without a struggle to the influence of the overwhelming current of feeling, that was, as it were, brought to bear upon him. He cast a glance at Eugénie of radiant good humour, a caressing glance that held a smile. As he looked at her he noticed the exquisite harmony of line of the features in her pure face, her innocent attitude of attention to him, the magical clearness of her eyes, alight with young dreams of love but with no heaviness of passion.

'Upon my word, my dear cousin, if you were in a box at the Opéra, and dressed in full fig, my aunt would be quite right to think of deadly sin, for all the men would be envious and all the women jealous.'

This compliment made Eugénie's heart stop beating, and then beat fast with delight, although it did not convey much meaning to her mind.

'Oh, you're making fun of your little country cousin!' she said.

'If you knew me better, cousin, you would know that I detest mockery: it hardens the heart, deadens all the feelings ...' And he swallowed a strip of bread and butter with a very pleasant satisfaction.

'No, I never make fun of other people,' he went on, 'very probably because I haven't a keen enough wit, and I find this failing is a great disadvantage to me. In Paris they have a way of wiping a man out by saying, "He's so good-natured!" By which they mean, "The poor youth hasn't a spark -- he's as dense as a rhinoceros." But as I am well off and known to bring down my bird first shot at thirty paces, with any kind of pistol, anywhere, they don't poke fun at me.'

'What you say, nephew, shows that you have a kind heart.'

'You have a very pretty ring on your finger,' said Eugénie. 'Is it rude to ask if I may look at it?'

Charles held out his hand, pulling off his ring as he did so, and Eugénie blushed as the tips of her fingers touched her cousin's pink finger-nails.

'Look, mother, what fine workmanship!'

'There's a big lot of gold in that,' said Nanon, bringing in the coffee.

'What's that?' asked Charles, laughing. And he pointed to an oval pot of glazed brown earthenware, decorated outside with a border of cinders, in which the coffee grounds rose to the surface and fell again in the boiling liquid.

'It's piping hot coffee,' said Nanon.

'Oh, my dear aunt! I'll leave at least some useful remembrance of my stay here. You are very much behind the times! I will teach you how to make good coffee in a Chaptal coffee-pot.' And he endeavoured to explain the principle on which the Chaptal coffee-pot works.

'Well, bless me, if there's all that fuss about it you would have to spend all your time at it,' said Nanon. 'I'll never make coffee that way. No, indeed. And who would get grass for our cow while I was making the coffee?'

'I'll make it,' said Eugénie.

'My dear child!' said Madame Grandet, looking at her daughter.

At this, as they recalled the blow about to fall to overwhelm this unfortunate young man in misery, the three women fell silent and looked at him with an air of commiseration which caught his attention.

'What's the matter, cousin?' he asked.

'Hush!' said Madame Grandet, as Eugénie was going to answer. 'You know that your father means to speak to Monsieur —'

'Say "Charles",' said the young man.

'Oh, is your name Charles? What a nice name!' exclaimed Eugénie.

Dreaded misfortunes are nearly always sure to happen. Just at that moment Nanon, Madame Grandet, and Eugénie, who could not think of the old cooper's return without a shudder, heard a well-known knock echo through the house.

'That's Papa!' said Eugénie.

She swept away the saucer with the sugar, leaving a few lumps on the tablecloth. Nanon carried off the plate with the eggshells. Madame Grandet started up like a frightened deer. It was a scene of utter panic, to Charles's bewilderment and wonder.

'Why, what's the matter?' he asked.

'My father's here,' said Eugénie.

'But what of it? ...'

Monsieur Grandet came into the room, cast one piercing glance at the table, at Charles, saw everything.

'Aha! You've been treating your nephew to a banquet, I see. That's good, very good, excellent indeed!' he said, without any hesitation in his speech. 'When the cat is away, the mice may play.'

'A banquet? ...' Charles repeated to himself, quite unable to form any idea of the normal diet and customs of this household.

'Bring me my glass, Nanon,' said the winegrower.

Eugénie brought the glass. Grandet drew a large horn-handled clasp-knife from his pocket, cut a slice of bread, took a little butter and spread it carefully, and began to eat without sitting down. Charles was putting sugar into his coffee. Grandet noticed the lumps of sugar on the table-cloth; he looked narrowly at his wife, who turned pale and started backwards. He bent over to whisper in the poor old woman's ear:

'Where did you get all that sugar from?'

'Nanon went to Fessard's for some: we had none in the house.'

No one can imagine the painful interest that this tableau held for the three women. Nanon had left her kitchen and stood looking into the room to see how things were going there. Meanwhile Charles had tasted his coffee, and finding it rather strong was looking round the table for the sugar, which Grandet had already put away.

'What do you want, nephew?' the old man inquired.

'The sugar.'

'Put some more milk in,' said the master of the house, 'and your coffee will taste sweeter.'

Eugénie took up the saucer full of sugar, which Grandet had previously taken possession of, and replaced it on the table, looking her father calmly in the face as she did so. Certainly no Parisian lady, helping her lover to escape by holding the weight of his silk rope ladder with her weak arms, shows greater courage than Eugénie showed then, in putting the sugar back on the table. The Parisian will have her reward when she proudly displays to her lover a beautiful arm covered with bruises; each bruise will be kissed and bathed in tears, and pain forgotten in pleasure: while Charles would never have the remotest conception of the deadly terror that shook his cousin's heart, while she stood there stricken by the lightning of the old cooper's look.

'You are not eating anything, wife?'

The poor helot went to the table, miserably cut a piece of bread and took a pear. Eugénie recklessly offered her father grapes, saying as she held out the plate,

'Do taste some of my fruit, Papa! – cousin, you will have some, won't you? I went to fetch these fine clusters specially for you.'

'Oh! if they aren't stopped they will loot the whole town of Saumur for you, nephew. When you have finished we will take a turn in the garden together. I have things to tell you which sugar won't make any sweeter.'

Eugénie and her mother looked at Charles with an expression of concern on their faces that the young man could not mistake.

'What do you mean by that, uncle? Since my mother died' – his voice softened as he said this – 'nothing worse can happen to me ...'

'Who can know with what afflictions God may seek to try us, nephew?' said his aunt.

'Ta, ta, ta, ta!' said Grandet. 'Here's the usual rigmarole beginning. Nephew, I'm sorry to see that you have such nice white hands.' And he showed him the fists like shoulders of mutton that nature had furnished the ends of his own arms with.

'Those are hands fit for raking in the crowns! You have been brought up to wear on your feet the fine leather that we use for note-cases to keep our bills in. That's bad, bad!'

'What do you mean, uncle? I'm hanged if I understand a word you're saying.'

'Come along,' said Grandet.

The miser snapped his knife shut, swallowed what was left of his white wine and opened the door.

'Oh, take courage, cousin!'

Something in the girl's voice sent a chill through Charles, and he followed his terrible relative with deadly misgivings. Eugénie, her mother, and Nanon went into the kitchen, moved by an uncontrollable anxiety, to watch the two actors in the scene which was about to take place in the damp little garden, where the uncle walked, at first in silence, with his nephew.

It did not embarrass Grandet to tell Charles of his father's death, but he felt a kind of pity for him because he was left without a penny, and he was seeking for some form of words that might ease the breaking of the cruel news. 'You have lost your father!' It was nothing to tell him that. Fathers usually die before their children. But: 'You have no money at all!' All the woes in the world were summed up in those words. And so the worthy man was forced to walk the whole length of the middle path in the garden for the third time, in silence, with the gravel crunching under his feet.

In the crises of life, when we are overwhelmed by joy or sorrow, we see our surroundings with sharpened senses, and they remain for ever afterwards indelibly part of our experience. Charles scrutinized with strained intentness the box borders of the little garden, the faded autumn leaves floating to the ground, the crumbling walls, the grotesquely twisted branches of the apple trees, picturesque details which were to remain in his memory for ever, eternally bound up with the memory of that supreme hour of early sorrow, by a trick of memory peculiar to deep feeling.

'It's very warm, very fine,' said Grandet, taking a deep breath.

'Yes, uncle ... But why? ...'

'Well, my boy,' his uncle began again, 'I have some bad news to give you. Your father is very ill ...'

'What am I doing here?' exclaimed Charles. 'Nanon!' he shouted, 'order post horses directly! I can find a carriage of some sort about here, I suppose,' he added, turning to his uncle, who stood there without moving.

'Horses and carriage are of no use,' replied Grandet with his eyes fixed on Charles, who stared speechlessly back at him. 'Yes, my poor boy, you have guessed what I have to say. He is dead. But that's nothing; there is something worse. He shot himself through the head. ...'

'My father?'

'Yes. But that's nothing. The newspapers are commenting on that, as if it were any business of theirs! Here, read this.'

Grandet, who had borrowed Cruchot's newspaper, showed

Charles the fatal paragraph; and the poor young fellow, who was still just a boy, still at the age when feelings express themselves spontaneously, burst into tears.

'That's better,' said Grandet to himself. 'His eyes made me feel frightened. He will be all right now that he has begun to cry. – That's not all yet, my poor nephew,' Grandet went on aloud, not knowing whether Charles was listening to him or not. 'That's nothing, you will get over it in time; but ...'

'Never! never! My father! my father!'

'He has ruined you. You have no money whatever.'

'What does that matter? Oh, where is my father? ... oh, my father!'

The sound of his sobbing filled that narrow space enclosed by walls, and awoke ghastly echoes from the ramparts. The three women, full of pity, wept too; for tears are as infectious as laughter can ever be. Without waiting to hear more from his uncle, Charles dashed into the courtyard, found the staircase, ran upstairs to his room and threw himself across his bed to weep undisturbed, his head buried in the bedclothes, as far as possible from his relations.

'We must let the first shower pass,' said Grandet, returning to the parlour, where Eugénie and her mother had hastily resumed their places and, having dried their eyes, were working with trembling fingers. 'But that young man is good for nothing; his mind runs more on dead folk than it does on the money.'

Eugénie shuddered to hear her father speak in this fashion about the most sacred of all sorrows. From that moment she began to criticize her father in her mind. Charles's sobs, although they were stifled, echoed in that echoing house, a low-pitched groaning that seemed to rise from the very ground, and ceased only towards night-fall, after growing gradually fainter.

'Poor young man!' said Madame Grandet.

It was a fatal exclamation! The worthy Grandet looked

from his wife to Eugénie, and from Eugénie to the sugar bowl; he bethought himself of the extraordinary meal prepared for their unhappy relative, and stopped short in the middle of the room.

'Oh, by the way,' he said with his accustomed calm deliberation, 'I hope that you do not intend to continue your reckless squandering of my substance, Madame Grandet. I do not give you *MY* money in order to stuff that young scamp with sugar!'

'Mother had nothing to do with it,' said Eugénie. 'It was I who ...'

'Do you think because you have just come of age,' Grandet interrupted her, 'that you are free to set yourself against me? Think what you're about, Eugénie.'

'Father, in your house your own brother's son should not have to do without. ...'

'Ta, ta, ta, ta!' said the cooper, his voice rising a semitone with each 'ta', ' "My brother's son" here, "my nephew" there! Charles is nothing to us; he hasn't a penny to bless himself with. His father is a bankrupt. And when the fine gentleman has cried his fill he will clear out of this. I have no desire to see my house turned upside-down for him.'

'What is a bankrupt, father?' Eugénie asked.

'A bankrupt,' answered her father, 'has committed the most dishonourable deed that a man can dishonour his name by being guilty of.'

'It must be a very great sin,' said Madame Grandet, 'and our brother's soul may perhaps be eternally lost.'

'More of your church rigmaroles!' retorted her husband, shrugging his shoulders. – 'A bankrupt,' he went on, 'is a thief that the law unfortunately takes under its protection. People trusted Guillaume Grandet with their goods because of his reputation for honesty and fair dealing, and he has taken all they had and left them only their eyes to cry with. It's better to have an encounter with a highwayman than with a bankrupt; against a highwayman you can defend yourself, and he is risking his life in attacking you; but as for the other – in short, Charles is disgraced.'

These words fell heavily upon the poor girl's heart, in all their crushing weight. She was upright, as a flower growing in the depths of the forest is delicate, and knew nothing of the world's worldly-wise maxims, its specious arguments, its sophisms: and so she accepted at its face value her father's atrocious definition of bankruptcy, and he intentionally made no distinction between a failure from unavoidable causes and fraudulent bankruptcy.

'But, father, could you not have done something to prevent this dreadful thing happening?'

'My brother did not consult me. Besides, his debts amount to four millions.'

'How much is a million, father?' she asked, with the simplicity of a child who thinks it is a simple matter to supply what it wants at once.

'A million?' repeated Grandet. 'Why, it's a million francs worth twenty sous each. It takes five francs of twenty sous to make a five-franc piece, and there are two hundred thousand five-franc pieces in a million.'

'Good heavens!' cried Eugénie, 'how could my uncle have had four millions of his own? Can there be anyone else in France with as many millions as that?'

Grandet stroked his chin and smiled, and his wen seemed to expand.

'But what's going to become of Cousin Charles?'

'He will set out for the East Indies, and try to make his fortune there. That was his father's wish.'

'But has he enough money to take him there?'

'I will pay his passage ... as far as ... yes, as far as Nantes.'

Eugénie jumped up and threw her arms round her father's neck.

'Oh, father! How good you are!' she said. Her warm embrace made Grandet feel almost embarrassed. His conscience was pricking him a little.

'Does it take long to make a million?' she asked him.

'Bless me,' said the cooper. 'You know what a napoleon is, don't you? Well, it takes fifty thousand of them to make a million.'

'Mamma, we will have novenas said for him.'

'That is just what I was thinking,' replied her mother.

'That's right! Think of ways of spending money, as usual!' cried Grandet. 'Do you think we're made of money here?'

Just then a hollow groan, more desolate than all that had preceded it, came from the attics and made Eugénie and her mother shudder.

'Nanon, go up and see that he isn't killing himself,' Grandet called to the servant, and then turning to his wife and daughter, whose faces had grown pale as he spoke, 'Now, then, you two!' he went on. 'No nonsense, do you hear? I'll leave you now. I'm going to take a stroll round to see those Dutch fellows, who are going away today. Then I shall visit Cruchot and talk all this over with him.'

He went out. When Grandet had shut the door behind him Eugénie and her mother breathed more freely. The girl had never before that morning felt constraint in her father's presence; but in the last few hours her feelings and her ideas had been rapidly changing.

'Mamma, how many louis does a cask of wine fetch?'

'Your father sells his for between a hundred and a hundred and fifty francs, or sometimes for two hundred; so I have heard him say.'

'And if he has fourteen hundred casks at the vintage? . . .'

'Bless me, child, I don't know what it comes to. Your father never talks about his business affairs to me.'

'But, in that case, papa must be rich.'

'Maybe. But Monsieur Cruchot told me that your father bought Froidfond two years ago. That will probably have left him short of money.'

Eugénie, more in the dark than ever about her father's wealth, went no further with her calculations.

'He didn't even so much as see me, poor lamb!' said Nanon, returning from her mission. 'There he is lying like a calf on his bed, crying like a Magdalen, that you never heard the like of it! What's the matter with the poor young chap?'

'Come, mamma, let's go up and comfort him at once. If we hear a knock we can come down again.'

Madame Grandet could not oppose her daughter when she spoke in such a tone. Eugénie was no longer a mere girl, she had become a woman, and she was sublime. They went together, their hearts beating fast, to Charles's room. The door was open. The young man had neither eyes nor ears for anything outside himself. He was absorbed in his grief, and uttering an inarticulate lament.

'How he loves his father!' said Eugénie in a low voice, and the words came unmistakably from a heart full of unconscious passion, and held hopes she was unaware of. Madame Grandet at once looked at her daughter with a mother's immediate anxiety, and spoke in a low voice in her ear.

'Take care, you may fall in love with him,' she said.

'Fall in love with him!' repeated Eugénie. 'Ah! if you only knew what father said!'

Charles moved, turned his head, and caught sight of his aunt and cousin.

'I have lost my father,' he said. 'My poor father! If only he had not kept his losses secret, if he had only told me about them, we might have worked together to make them good. Oh, God! My father was so kind. And I was so sure of seeing him again that I think I must have said good-bye carelessly and indifferently, not knowing ...' He began to sob again, and could say no more.

'We will pray for him with all our hearts,' said Madame Grandet. 'Submit yourself to the will of God.'

'Be brave, cousin,' said Eugénie. 'Your father has gone and you have lost him for ever: now you must think of how to save your honour ...'

With that instinctive tact that never quite deserts a woman, who has all her wits about her in all she does, even when she is engaged in comforting the broken-hearted, Eugénie was trying to divert her cousin's thoughts from his sorrow and make him think of himself.

'My honour? ...' cried the young man, abruptly pushing his hair away from his face. And he sat upright on the bed and folded his arms. 'Ah, that's true. My uncle said that my father was a bankrupt.' He uttered a heart-rending cry and hid his face in his hands. 'Leave me to myself, Cousin Eugénie,' he begged her. 'Please leave me. Oh, God! God! forgive my father; he must have been so terribly unhappy.'

There was something desperately harrowing yet endearing in the sight of this youthful grief, so sincere, unaffected, and unreserved. It was a grief that shrank from observation, and the imploring gesture with which Charles begged to be left alone was understood by Eugénie and her mother, and moved their simple and sympathetic hearts. They went downstairs, took their seats near the window again in silence and worked for nearly an hour without exchanging a word.

Eugénie had cast a stolen glance at her cousin's personal belongings, and a girl's glance takes in everything in the twinkling of an eye. She had noticed the pretty odds and ends of his toilet fittings, his scissors and razors inlaid with gold. This glimpse of splendid luxury in a setting of misery had made Charles still more interesting in her eyes, by force of contrast perhaps. In lives passed in unbroken calm and seclusion Eugénie and her mother had never before been caught up in an event of such serious moment. Never before had their imaginations been stirred by a drama so tragical.

'Mamma,' said Eugénie, 'shall we wear mourning for my uncle?'

'Your father will decide that,' replied Madame Grandet. And they relapsed into silence again.

Eugénie plied her needle with a mechanical regularity which would have betrayed to any observer how far away and how busy her thoughts were. This adorable girl's first wish was to share her cousin's mourning. About four o'clock a sudden sharp knock made Madame Grandet start in terror.

'What can have brought your father back?' she said.

The winegrower came in, in the best of spirits. When he had taken off his gloves he rubbed his hands together briskly enough to have rubbed the skin off, if his epidermis had not resembled Russia leather in everything but its scent of larch bark and incense. He walked up and down for a time, and looked out at the weather. At last he could keep his secret no longer.

'Wife, I've got the better of them all,' he said, without stammering. 'Our wine is sold! The Dutchmen and Belgians were leaving this morning, so I just took a stroll round the market-place in front of their inn, looking as simple as I could. What's-his-name – you know the man I mean – came up to me. The best growers are hanging back and holding their wine: they want to wait, and I didn't stand in their way, they can wait if they like. Our Belgian was ready to give up. I saw that. Well, the business is settled; he takes all our vintage at two hundred francs per cask, half of it cash down. I have been paid in gold for half, and promissory notes have been made out for the rest. There are six louis for you. In three months' time the price of wine will fall.'

These last words were uttered quietly, but in a tone so sardonic that the people of Saumur, gathered at that moment in the market-place, discussing in dismay the news of Grandet's sale, would have shuddered if they had heard them, and a panic would have made wines fall by fifty per cent.

'You have a thousand casks this year, father, haven't you?' asked Eugénie.

'Yes, my girlie.'

This endearment indicated the highest degree of delight in the old cooper.

'That makes two hundred thousand francs?'

'Yes, Mademoiselle Grandet.'

'Well, then, father, you can easily help Charles.'

The astonishment, the wrath, the stupefaction of Belshazzar when he saw the writing *Mene Mene Tekel Upharsin* on the wall were nothing compared with Grandet's cold fury when he found the nephew he had forgotten all about occupying a place in the inmost thoughts and calculations of his daughter.

'Ah, is that so indeed? Ever since that puppy set foot in *my* house everything has been turned upside-down. You carry on as if there was a christening or a wedding in the house and all sorts of high jinks, and I will not have it. At my age I should know well enough how to manage my own affairs, I should think! At any rate I am not taking lessons from my daughter nor from anyone else. I shall do for my nephew whatever is right and proper for me to do, and you don't need to go poking your nose into the business. And as for you, Eugénie,' he added, turning towards her, 'don't say another word to me about him or I'll send you off to the Abbey at Noyers with Nanon, see if I don't; and not later than tomorrow if you forget what I say. Where is that boy? Has he come downstairs yet?'

'No, dear,' answered Madame Grandet.

'Well, what's he doing?'

'He is weeping for his father,' Eugénie said.

Grandet looked at his daughter, and could not find a word to say. He was, after all, a father too, in his own fashion. He took a turn or two up and down the room, and then went straight upstairs to his strongroom to consider whether he should make an investment in government stock. The timber felled in his two thousand acres of woodland had brought him in six thousand francs. Then there was the money from the sale of poplars, and money saved from his income of the year before and the current year. So that, leaving aside the two hundred thousand francs from the bargain just concluded, he had a lump sum of nine hundred thousand francs to dispose of. The twenty per cent to be made on his outlay in such a short time was very tempting. The stock stood at seventy francs. He jotted down his calculations on the newspaper in which his brother's death was announced, hearing as he did so, but not heeding, his nephew's lament. Presently Nanon thumped on the wall to summon her master downstairs, for dinner was on the table. On the last step of the staircase and as he passed under the archway Grandet was saying to himself; 'Since there is eight per cent interest as well, I'll do it. In two years I shall have fifteen hundred thousand francs from Paris in solid gold ... Well, where's that nephew of mine got to?'

'He says he doesn't want anything to eat,' replied Nanon. 'It isn't wholesome.'

'That's so much saved then,' remarked her master.

'Holy Mother, yes,' said she.

'Bah! he won't cry for ever. Hunger brings the wolf from the wood.'

It was a strangely silent meal that followed. When it was over and the tablecloth had been removed; 'We ought to go into mourning, dear,' said Madame Grandet.

'Really, Madame Grandet, you don't know what way of throwing money away to think of next. People mourn in their hearts and not in the clothes they wear.'

'But mourning for a brother is absolutely obligatory, and the Church lays it upon us to ...'

'Buy your mourning out of your six louis then. You can get me a crêpe band; that's enough for me.'

Eugénie raised her eyes to heaven but said nothing. For the first time in her life, she found her generous instincts, which had lain dormant and repressed and then been suddenly awakened, constantly and harshly thwarted. This evening to all appearances was exactly like a thousand others of their monotonous existence, but it was certainly the most unpleasant that Eugénie had ever spent. She sewed without raising her head, and made no use of the workbox which Charles had glanced at so disdainfully the evening before. Madame Grandet knitted her sleeves. Grandet sat twiddling his thumbs, lost in calculations the results of which were to astonish Saumur one day. Four hours went by. No one came to call on the family this evening. As they sat there the whole town was ringing with the news of Grandet's sharp practice, his brother's failure, and the arrival of his nephew. All the winegrowers, large and small, who formed the upper and middle classes of society in Saumur, were gathered under Monsieur des Grassins' roof to satisfy their common need of speaking their minds and exchanging views upon these matters of concern to all, and terrible were the curses being called down upon the head of their former mayor.

Nanon was spinning busily, and the whir of her wheel was the only sound that broke the silence that reigned beneath the dull grey rafters in the dismal sitting-room.

'We're not wasting words,' she said, showing strong white teeth like blanched almonds.

'Mustn't waste anything,' answered Grandet, rousing himself from his meditations.

He had been dreaming of an ocean of eight millions in three years, and mentally launching his ships on this long sheet of gold.

'Let's go to bed. I will go and say goodnight to my nephew for everybody, and see if he wants anything.'

Madame Grandet waited on the first-floor landing to hear what her worthy husband might have to say to Charles. Eugénie, bolder than her mother, went up two steps.

'Well, nephew, you're in great trouble, of course. Yes, it's natural enough to take on. A father is a father. Still, we must bear our misfortunes patiently. I've been thinking for you while you've been crying. I'm not a bad sort of relation, after all. Come, pluck up your courage. Will you drink a glass of wine? Wine costs nothing in Saumur. It's offered here as cups of tea might be in the Indies. – But you are all in the dark,' Grandet went on. 'That's bad! That's bad! we must see what we're doing.'

Grandet walked over to the chimneypiece.

'Bless my soul!' he exclaimed, 'a wax candle! Where the devil did they get hold of a wax candle? Those moonstruck women would tear up the very floor of my house to boil eggs for this boy!'

When they heard this, mother and daughter fled to their rooms and took refuge in their beds, with the celerity of frightened mice scurrying to their holes.

'So you've a secret store of money hidden somewhere, have you, Madame Grandet?' said the winegrower, walking into his wife's room.

'My dear, I'm saying my prayers. Wait a moment,' the poor woman replied, in a voice that shook.

'The devil take your prayers!' growled Grandet.

Misers hold no belief in a life beyond the grave, the present is all in all to them. This thought throws a pitilessly clear light upon the irreligious times in which we live, for today more than in any previous era money is the force behind the law, politically and socially. Books and institutions, the actions of men and their doctrines, all combine to undermine the belief in a future life upon which the fabric of society has been built for eighteen hundred years. The grave holds few terrors for us now, is little feared as a transition stage upon man's journey. That future which once awaited us beyond the *Requiem* has been transported into the present. To reach *per fas et nefas* an earthly paradise of luxury and vanity and pleasure, to turn one's heart to stone and mortify the flesh for the sake of fleeting enjoyment of earthly treasure, as saints once suffered martyr-

dom in the hope of eternal bliss, is now the popular ambition!
It is an ambition stamped on our age and seen in everything,
even the very laws whose enaction requires the legislator to
exercise not his critical faculty, but his power of producing
money. Not 'What do you think?' but 'What can you pay?'
is the question he is asked now. When this doctrine has been
handed down from the *bourgeoisie* to the people, what will
become of our country?

'Madame Grandet, have you finished?' asked the cooper.

'My dear, I am praying for you.'

'Very well! Good night. I shall have something to say to
you tomorrow morning.'

The poor woman prepared herself for sleep as uneasily as a
schoolboy who has not learnt his lessons and is terrified at the
thought of his master's angry face when he wakes. As she
muffled herself in the blankets to avoid hearing anything
further, Eugénie crept to her side, in her nightdress and bare-
foot, and kissed her mother's forehead.

'Oh, mother,' she said, 'dearest mother, tomorrow I will tell
him it was me.'

'No; he will send you to Noyers if you do. Leave it to me,
he can't eat me.'

'Do you hear, mamma?'

'What?'

'*He* is crying still.'

'Go to bed, child. You will catch cold, barefoot like that.
The floor is damp.'

Thus ended the solemn day which had brought a lifelong
burden to the poor rich heiress, whose sleep would never
again be so deep and so untroubled as it had been before that
day. Quite often the things that human beings do appear
literally incredible although in fact they have done them. We
might be less incredulous, perhaps, if we did not nearly always omit to throw a sort of psychological light on impulsive
decisions, by examining the mysterious birth of the reasons

that made them inevitable. Perhaps Eugénie's passion should be traced to the source from which its most delicate fibres sprang, its roots in the depths of her nature, and analysed there, for it became, as would be sneeringly said in the future, a disease, and influenced her whole existence. Plenty of people would rather declare an event incredible than follow the sequence of cause and effect, measure the strength of links in a chain, each arising from the one before it and inseverably joined with it, secretly, in the mind. In this case, to observers of human nature, Eugénie's past life shows sufficient cause for her unreflecting naïveté and the impulsiveness with which she gave expression to her feelings. The very fact that her life had been so untroubled made feminine pity, that most insidious emotion, take possession of her heart more overwhelmingly.

And so, disturbed and excited by the day's events, Eugénie slept lightly. She woke several times to listen to her cousin, thinking she heard the sighs which all day long had found an echo in her own heart. Sometimes she pictured him dying of grief; sometimes she dreamed that he was dying of starvation. Towards morning she did indeed, she was sure, hear a terrible cry. She dressed at once, and noiselessly in the dawn light ran to her cousin's room, whose door stood open. The candle had burned down to the socket of the candlestick. Charles, overcome with exhaustion, slept in his clothes, sitting in an armchair with his head fallen forward on the bed. He was dreaming as people dream who go to bed supperless. Eugénie could watch him undisturbed, and weep, could admire his handsome young face and sorrowfully note the traces left by grief, the closed eyes swollen with weeping, which even in sleep seemed to shed tears still. Charles became aware in his sleep of Eugénie's presence. He opened his eyes, and saw her watching him pityingly.

'I beg your pardon, cousin,' he said drowsily, obviously lost to all sense of time or place.

'There are hearts that sympathize with you here, Cousin

Charles, and *we* thought that you might be in need of something. You ought to go to bed. You will tire yourself out sitting up like that.'

'Yes. That's true.'

'Well, good-bye,' she said, and fled, feeling ashamed and yet at the same time glad that she had come. Only innocence dares to be so bold. Both vice and virtue (when it has acquired some knowledge) weigh their actions carefully.

Eugénie, who had not trembled in her cousin's room, could scarcely stand when she reached her own. The unreflecting freedom of her existence had suddenly come to an end. She blamed herself bitterly and reproached herself again and again. 'What will he think of me? He will believe that I love him.' And yet in her heart this was exactly what she most wished him to believe. A guileless passion has its own intuition, and knows by instinct that love kindles love. What an event it was in the girl's lonely life to have gone in secret to a young man's room! For certain souls do not some thoughts and actions, prompted by love, amount to solemn betrothal?

An hour later she went to her mother's room, and helped her to dress as usual. Then the two women went downstairs to their seats by the window, and waited apprehensively for Grandet, with the kind of fever or cold sweat, lump in the throat or constricted chest, that afflicts people expecting some scene or act of punishment – an emotion so common to flesh and blood that even domestic animals experience it, uttering cries when their master beats them, however slight the physical pain they suffer may be, although they make no sound when they hurt themselves badly by accident.

The cooper came downstairs, but he spoke to his wife absent-mindedly, kissed Eugénie, and sat down to table without apparently thinking of his threats of the evening before.

'What's happened to my nephew? The boy certainly doesn't get in our way.'

129

'He's asleep, sir,' replied Nanon.

'So much the better, he won't need a wax candle,' said Grandet in a bantering way.

His extraordinary forbearance and sour gaiety astonished Madame Grandet, and she scrutinized her husband closely. The worthy fellow (here perhaps it should be pointed out that in Touraine, Anjou, Poitou, and Brittany the designation *bonhomme* – a good sort, worthy fellow, so often applied to Grandet, has no implication of neighbourly kindliness or worth, and is bestowed on the dourest men as well as on the most genial and kindly disposed, as soon as they reach a certain age) ... the worthy fellow, then, took his hat and gloves and said,

'I am going for a stroll in the market-square, to meet our Cruchot friends.'

'Eugénie, your father has something on his mind. There's no doubt about it.'

As a matter of fact, Grandet, who slept little, was in the habit of spending half the night considering and reflecting, working out the preliminary calculations which made his views, observations, and plans so astonishingly accurate and clear, and ensured the unfailing success which the inhabitants of Saumur watched with perennial wonder. All human power is achieved by a compound of patience and time. The people who accomplish most are the people who exert their will to watch and wait. A miser's life is a constant exercise of every human faculty in the service of his own personality. He considers only two feelings, vanity and self-interest: but as the achievement of his interest supplies to some extent a concrete and tangible tribute to his vanity, as it is a constant attestation of his real superiority, his vanity and the study of his advantage are two aspects of one passion – egotism. That is perhaps the reason for the amazing curiosity excited by misers skilfully presented upon the stage. Everyone has some link with these persons, who revolt all human feelings and yet epitomize them. Where is the man without ambition? And what ambition can be attained in our society without money?

Grandet had indeed something on his mind, as his wife put it. Like all misers he had a constant need to pit his wits against those of other men, to mulct them of their crowns by fair legal means. To get the better of others, was that not exercising power, giving oneself with each new victim the right to despise those weaklings of the earth who were unable to save themselves from being devoured? Oh! has anyone properly understood the meaning of the lamb lying peacefully at God's feet, that most touching symbol of all the victims of this world, and of their future, the symbol which is suffering and weakness glorified? The miser lets the lamb grow fat, then he pens, kills, cooks, eats, and despises it. Misers thrive on money and contempt.

During the night the old fellow's thoughts had taken a fresh direction: that was the cause of his unusual mildness. He had woven a web to entangle the businessmen in Paris, he would twist them round his fingers, knead and mould them like wax in his hands, make them come and go at his command, sweat and hope and fear and change colour, all for the entertainment of the man who had once been a cooper, lurking in his dingy grey room at the top of the worm-eaten staircase in his house in Saumur.

He had been thinking about his nephew. He wanted to save his dead brother's name from dishonour without obliging either his nephew or himself to part with a sou. His money was about to be invested for the next three years, he had nothing to occupy his mind now beyond the management of his estate; he needed a field for his malicious energy to work in, and he had found it in his brother's bankruptcy. Having nothing at the moment to crush between his paws he was ready to pulverize the Parisians for Charles's benefit and show himself to be an excellent brother, at little cost. Saving the honour of the family name counted for so little in his plan, that his good offices in the matter might be put down to something like the need gamblers feel to see a game played well, even when they have no stake in it. The Cruchots were necessary to his scheme, yet he did not wish to go openly in search of them; they should come to his house, and that very evening the comedy he had just plotted should begin, and tomorrow the whole town would be talking of him admiringly; and his generosity would not cost him a farthing.

In her father's absence Eugénie had felt the pleasure of being free to busy herself openly about her beloved cousin, to lavish upon him without fear the wealth of her pity. In devotion woman is sublimely superior to man. It is the only superiority she cares to have acknowledged, the only quality which she pardons man for letting her excel him in.

Three or four times Eugénie went to listen to her cousin's breathing, to find out if he was sleeping, or if he had wakened. Then when at last he got up she set herself to see to the cream, the coffee, eggs, fruit, plates, glass; everything that was needed for her cousin's breakfast was given her special care. She ran lightly up the rickety staircase to listen to Charles again. Was he dressing? Was he still weeping? She climbed the last few stairs and reached his door.

'Cousin!'

'Yes?'

'Will you have breakfast downstairs or in your room?'

'Wherever you please.'

'How do you feel?'

'My dear cousin, I'm ashamed to say I feel very hungry.'

This conversation through the closed door seemed to Eugénie like some episode in a romance.

'Very well then, we will bring your breakfast up to your room, so as to avoid vexing my father.'

She sped downstairs to the kitchen, as light as a bird.

'Nanon, do go and do his room.'

The familiar staircase which she had run up and down so

often, which echoed to the slightest sound, no longer looked old and decrepit to Eugénie's eyes. It shone with radiant light, it spoke to her like a friend, was young like her, young like her love to which it lent its services. Then her mother, her kind and indulgent mother, willingly lent herself to the plans love had filled her brain with, and when Charles's room was ready they went together to keep him company. Was it not their duty in Christian charity to try to console the mourner? They drew from religious teaching a number of little sophistries to justify themselves.

And so Charles Grandet found himself the object of the most loving and tender solicitude. His bruised heart keenly felt the comfort of the kindness, as delicate and grateful as the touch of velvet, the sensitive sympathy that these two souls living under constant repression could feel and convey, when for once they found themselves free in their natural sphere, the realm of suffering. Using a relative's privilege Eugénie began to tidy her cousin's linen and arrange the articles on his dressing-table. She could admire the costly trifles he had brought with him, at leisure, and hold each finely made gold or silver knick-knack long in her hand under the pretext of examining its decoration.

Charles was deeply touched by the generous interest his aunt and cousin took in him. He was well enough acquainted with Parisian society to know that in his present circumstances he would have met with only coldness or indifference there. He noticed how radiantly good-looking Eugénie was in her own particular fashion. He began to admire the simplicity of manner he had laughed at the day before. And so when Eugénie took the earthenware bowl full of coffee and cream from Nanon's hands, with a frank eagerness to wait on her cousin herself, casting a look full of kindness at him as she did so, the Parisian's eyes were suddenly filled with tears. He took her hand in his and kissed it.

'Why, what's the matter?' she asked.

'They are tears of gratitude,' he answered.

Eugénie turned hastily to the chimney piece, took up the candles and held them out to Nanon.

'Here, Nanon, take these away,' she said.

When she looked at her cousin again her cheeks were still very red, but at least her eyes did not betray her; she was able to dissemble the overwhelming joy that filled her heart. But her cousin's eyes and hers expressed the same feeling, their souls were rapt by the same thought: the future was theirs. This thrill of happiness was all the sweeter to Charles in the midst of his deep sorrow because it was so unexpected.

A knock at the front door made the two women hurry to their places by the parlour window. It was lucky that they managed to get downstairs fast enough to be found at their work when Grandet came in, for if he had met them under the archway his suspicions would have been aroused at once. After lunch, which Grandet took standing, the keeper, who had not yet received the promised reward for his services, arrived from Froidfond, bringing a hare and partridges shot in the park, as well as some eels, and a couple of pike which the millers had sent.

'Aha! here comes old Cornoiller like fish in Lent, at just the right moment. Are those ready for eating?'

'Yes, sir. I thought you would be grateful for the obligement. They were killed the day before yesterday.'

'Come on, Nanon, look lively!' said the worthy cooper. 'Take them from him. They'll do for dinner. I have invited two Cruchots.'

Nanon opened her eyes wide in amazement, and looked from one face to another.

'Oh, indeed!' she said. 'And where will I get bacon and spice for seasoning from?'

'Give Nanon six francs, wife,' said Grandet, 'and remind me to go to the cellar to fetch up a bottle of good wine.'

'Well, now, Monsieur Grandet,' the keeper began, for he

wanted to get the question of his wages settled and had prepared a speech in advance, 'Monsieur Grandet ...'

'Ta, ta, ta, ta!' said Grandet. 'I know what you're going to say: you are a good fellow, we'll see about that tomorrow, I'm too busy today. Wife,' he added to Madame Grandet, 'give him five francs.' And with that he hastily departed.

The poor woman was only too happy to buy peace at the cost of eleven francs. She knew from experience that Grandet usually lay low for a couple of weeks after forcing her to pay out, coin by coin, the money he had given her.

'Here, Cornoiller,' she said, slipping ten francs into his hand. 'We shall not forget to repay you for your services one of these days.'

Cornoiller had nothing to say to this. He went off.

'I only need three francs, Madame,' said Nanon, who had put on her black bonnet and taken up her basket. 'Keep the rest. That will do very well.'

'Make it a good dinner, Nanon. My cousin will be coming downstairs,' said Eugénie.

'There's something out of the ordinary going on, I'm certain,' said Madame Grandet. 'This is only the third time since we were married that your father has invited people to dinner.'

About four o'clock, when Eugénie and her mother had just finished laying the table for six persons, and the master of the house had brought up several bottles of the exquisite wines which are jealously hoarded in their cellars by people who live in the winegrowing districts, Charles came into the room. The young man looked pale. His gestures, his face, his looks, the tone of his voice, expressed a sadness which was very touching. His grief was unaffected, sincere, and deeply felt, and the tense, drawn look of suffering gave him the pathetic charm women find so attractive. Eugénie found it so, and was more in love than ever. Perhaps, too, his misfortunes had brought him closer to her. Charles was not now the wealthy and handsome young man living in a sphere out of her reach that he had been when she first saw him; he was a relative in deep and terrible distress, and grief levels all distinctions. A woman has this in common with the angels, that all suffering human beings are her peculiar charge. Charles and Eugénie understood one another without a word being spoken. The fatherless boy, the poor dandy so fallen from his high estate, sat silent in a corner of the room, withdrawn in proud composure from the company; but from time to time his cousin's soft affectionate glance sought him out across the room, forcing him to leave his sad brooding and follow the flight of her thoughts to new realms of hope, and a future in which she loved to think that she might share.

The news of the dinner to which Grandet had invited the Cruchots was making a greater stir in Saumur at that moment than had the sale of his wine the day before, although that constituted a crime, an act of high treason against the wine-growing community. If the scheming old winegrower had given his dinner-party with the idea in his mind that once cost Alcibiades' dog his tail, he would perhaps have been a great man, but he felt himself too superior to the citizens of a town which he constantly exploited, to set any value on the opinion held of him in Saumur.

The des Grassins soon heard of the violent death and probable bankruptcy of Charles's father. They decided to visit their client that evening, to condole with him in his affliction and show their friendly interest, and at the same time find out what conceivable motives could have led him, in such circumstances, to invite the Cruchots to dinner.

At five o'clock precisely, President C. de Bonfons and his uncle the notary arrived, dressed up to the nines in their Sunday best. The guests took their seats at the table and began by making an uncommonly good meal. Grandet was solemn, Charles silent, Eugénie dumb, and Madame Grandet said no more than usual, so that the dinner was about as lively as a funeral repast. When they rose from the table Charles said to his aunt and uncle:

'With your permission, I will leave you now. I have a number of long and difficult letters that I must attend to.'

'By all means, nephew.'

When Charles had left the room, and it was safe to assume that he was out of earshot and must by that time be immersed in his correspondence, Grandet looked slyly at his wife.

'Madame Grandet, what we are going to talk about would be Greek to you. It is half-past seven, and the best thing you could do is go off to bed. – Good night, Eugénie.'

He kissed his daughter, and the two women left the room.

Then the play began, and Grandet, more cunningly than he had ever done before, made use of the skill he had acquired in his dealings with men, which had often earned him the nickname 'old wolf' from those who had suffered from his teeth at rather too close quarters. If the Mayor of Saumur's ambitions had been aimed higher, if by good fortune he had risen to a higher social sphere, where he might have become a delegate to the congresses that decide international affairs, and he had there used the genius developed in him by his striving to achieve his own narrow ends, there is little doubt that he would gloriously have served the interests of France. Yet, after all, it is equally possible that away from Saumur the worthy cooper would have cut but a poor figure. It may be true that minds, like certain animals, lose their fertility when taken from their native clime.

'Y-y-you were s-s-saying, M-M-Monsieur le P-P-Président, that b-b-b-bankr-r-r-ruptcy ...'

Here the stammer which had been assumed at will by the winegrower for so many years that it was accepted as due to natural causes, like the deafness which he complained of when the weather was wet, became so wearisome to the two Cruchots that as they listened they unconsciously grimaced, their features working painfully as if in an effort to get out the words which he was purposely floundering through.

This is perhaps the proper place to relate the history of Grandet's stammer and deafness. No one in Anjou had better hearing or could speak Angevin French more clearly than the wily winegrower. On one occasion, long ago, he had been outwitted in spite of all his shrewdness by a Jew, who in the course of their discussion cupped his hand behind his ear as an ear trumpet, the better to catch what was said, and talked such gibberish in his effort to find the right words that Grandet, a victim of his own humanity, felt himself obliged to suggest to the crafty Jew the words and ideas the Jew appeared to be groping after, to complete the Jew's arguments himself, to say for the Jew what that accursed fellow ought to be saying on his own behalf, until in the end he had fairly changed places with the Jew. The cooper emerged from this odd contest with the only bargain of his business life that he ever had reason to regret. But if he lost by it financially speaking, he gained morally, was taught a practical lesson and later reaped the fruits of it. And so he ended by blessing the Jew who had taught him the art of wearing out the patience of his business adversary, of keeping him so busy expressing Grandet's ideas that he entirely lost sight of his own. Now, never had the use of deafness, stammering, and the labyrinthine circumlocutions in which Grandet was accustomed to cloak his thoughts been more necessary than they were in the matter under consideration. For one thing, he wanted someone else to take the responsibility for his ideas; and then when his own ideas were proposed to him he did not wish to express either agreement or disagreement, but to say so little as to leave his true intentions in doubt.

'M-M-Monsieur de B-B-Bonf-f-f-fons ...'

This was the second time in three years that Grandet had called the younger Cruchot 'Monsieur de Bonfons'! The president might well believe himself to be the crafty cooper's son-in-law elect.

'Y-y-you were s-s-s-saying that b-b-b-b-bankr-r-ruptcies may in c-c-c-certain cases b-b-b-b-b-e p-p-p-prevented b-b-b-b-by ...'

'By the commercial tribunals themselves. That happens every day,' said Monsieur C. de Bonfons, grasping old Grandet's idea or thinking he guessed it, and amiably anxious to explain it to him. 'Listen!'

'I'm l-l-listening,' replied the worthy cooper humbly, his face expressing the malicious enjoyment of a small boy who is laughing up his sleeve at his teacher while ostentatiously giving him his most earnest attention.

'When a man in a large way of business who is greatly respected, like, for instance, your late brother in Paris ...'

'My b-b-b-brother, yes.'

'... Is likely to become insolvent ...'

'Ins-s-s-s-solvent? Is-s-s that what you c-c-c-call it?'

'Yes. If his failure is imminent, the commercial tribunal to whose jurisdiction he is subject (do you follow this?) has the power by a judicial decision to name liquidators to wind up his business. Liquidation is not the same thing as bankruptcy, you understand? A bankrupt has disgraced his name; but winding up his business does no harm to a man's reputation.'

'It's quite a d-d-d-d-different th-th-thing; if-f-f only it d-d-d-d-doesn't c-c-cost any m-m-more,' said Grandet.

'But a liquidation may be arranged even without having recourse to the Tribunal of Commerce. For,' said the president, taking a pinch of snuff, 'how is a man declared bankrupt?

'Indeed, yes. I've n-n-never thought ab-b-bout that,' replied Grandet.

'In the first place,' the magistrate went on, 'by the filing of a petition by the merchant himself, or his agent holding power of attorney, with the clerk of the court, and its registration in due course; or, in the second place, at the request of the creditors. Now if the merchant does not file a petition, and if no creditor makes application to the court for a declaration of his bankruptcy, what happens then?'

'Yes, let's s-s-s-see what h-h-happens.'

'Then the family of the deceased, or his representatives, or his residuary legatee, or the man himself if he is not dead, or his friends if he has absconded, wind up the business. Perhaps you may intend to liquidate the debts in your brother's case?' inquired the president.

'Ah, Grandet!' exclaimed the notary, 'that would be a fine thing to do. We have our own idea of honour in the provinces. If you saved your name from dishonour, for it is your name, you would be ...'

'Sublime!' cried the president, interrupting his uncle.

'Of c-c-course my b-b-brother's name was G-g-grandet just like m-m-mine, that's s-s-s-s-sure and c-c-c-c-c-certain, I d-d-don't s-s-say it wasn't. And anyhow a l-l-l-l-l-liquid-d-d-dation like that would b-b-b-b-be a very g-g-g-g-good thing f-f-for my n-n-nephew in every w-w-w-way, and I am f-f-f-fond of him. B-b-b-b-but I m-must s-s-s-s-see. I d-don't know those s-s-s-s-smart f-f-f-fellows in P-p-paris. And then you s-s-s-s-see I live h-h-h-here in S-s-saumur! M-m-m-m-my v-v-v-vine c-c-cuttings, my d-d-d-drainage w-w-w-work, all the other things h-h-h-have t-t-t-to b-b-b-b-b-be att-t-t-tended to. I have n-n-n-never d-d-d-d-d-drawn a b-b-b-bill. What is a b-b-b-bill? I have t-t-t-taken p-p-p-plenty b-b-but I have n-n-n-never p-p-p-put my n-n-n-n-name on any b-b-b-bit of p-p-p-p-aper. You t-t-t-t-take them, and you d-d-d-discount them, that's all I know about them. I h-h-h-have heard t-t-t-t-tell that you can b-b-b-b-b-buy b-b-back b-b-b-b-b-bills ...'

'Yes,' said the president. 'You can buy bills on the market, less so much per cent. Do you understand?'

Grandet cupped his hand behind his ear, and the president repeated his remark.

'B-b-b-but h-h-h-how can a m-m-m-m-man earn an honest l-l-living with all that?' replied the winegrower. 'I d-d-d-don't know anything about that s-s-s-s-sort of thing, at m-m-m-m-m-my age. I m-m-m-must s-s-s-s-stay h-h-here and l-l-l-look after the g-g-grapes. The w-w-w-work on the g-g-g-g-g-grapes p-p-p-p-p-piles up, and it's the g-g-g-g-g-g-g-g-grapes that have to p-p-p-p-p-pay for everything. L-l-l-l-looking after the v-v-v-v-vintage has to come f-f-f-f-first. I have a g-g-g-great d-d-d-deal to do at Froidfond, and things that can't b-b-b-be d-d-d-d-d-done by anyone else either. I can't l-leave h-h-h-home to s-s-s-s-see after t-t-t-t-t-tangled affairs and all k-k-k-k-k-k-kinds of *em-em-embrrrououillllamini gentes*, God bless my soul, and all s-s-s-s-s-s-sorts of d-d-d-d-d-d-d-devilry that I don't unders-s-s-s-stand a w-w-w-w-word of. You s-s-s-say that I ought t-t-to b-b-b-be in P-p-p-paris to l-l-l-l-l-l-liquidate the b-b-business, to s-s-s-s-s-stop the d-d-d-d-d-declaration of b-b-b-bankruptcy, b-b-b-but h-h-h-how c-c-c-can I be in t-t-t-two p-p-p-places at once? I'm n-n-not a little b-b-b-b-bird and ...'

'And I understand your position,' cried the notary. 'Well, old friend, you have friends, and friends of long standing too, ready to devote themselves to your interests.'

'Come, now!' said the winegrower to himself. 'Make up your minds! Take the plunge!'

'Suppose someone were to go off to Paris, find your brother Guillaume's largest creditor, and say to him ...'

'Here, h-h-hold on a minute,' interrupted the cooper. 'Say to him ... what? S-s-s-something like this: "Monsieur G-g-grandet of S-s-saumur is this, Monsieur G-g-grandet of S-s-saumur is that. He is f-f-f-fond of his b-b-b-b-brother, he is f-fond of his n-n-nephew. He thinks a l-l-lot of his r-r-r-relations, and means to d-d-d-do his b-b-best by them. He has made a good p-p-p-p-profit from his v-v-vintage. D-d-don't p-p-push the business into b-b-bankruptcy, c-c-call a meeting of c-c-c-creditors, app-p-p-point liquidators. Then G-g-grandet will s-s-s-s-s-s-see what he c-c-can d-d-do. You will come off much b-b-better by winding up the b-b-business yours-s-selves than you would if you l-l-let l-lawyers poke their n-noses into it ..." Eh? Isn't that true?'

'Quite so!' said the president.

'Because, you s-s-see, Monsieur de B-b-bonfons, a p-p-p-person must see what he's d-d-doing before he makes up his mind. You can't d-do more than you c-c-can. In a b-b-big b-b-business like this you have to know what's there in your h-hand and what you have to p-pay or you m-m-might ruin yourself. Isn't that s-s-so?'

'Certainly,' said the president. 'It's my opinion that in a few months' time you could buy up the debts for an agreed sum of money, and pay it all by instalments. Aha! you can lead dogs a long way with a piece of bacon in front of their noses. When there has been no actual declaration of bankruptcy and you hold the bills in your hands you're as white as snow.'

'As s-s-snow?' Grandet repeated, putting his hand to his ear again. 'I don't unders-s-stand what s-s-snow has to do with it.'

'Well,' cried the president, 'just listen to me, will you?'

'I'm l-l-listening.'

'A bill of exchange is a commodity that is subject to rises and falls in value. That's a deduction from Jeremy Bentham's theory of interest. He was a publicist who proved that people were very silly and stupid to disapprove of moneylenders.'

'Bless my soul!' said the worthy cooper.

'Seeing that, in principle, money is a commodity, according to Bentham, and whatever represents money becomes a commodity too; and as it is plain that following the ordinary fluctuations that all articles of commerce are subject to, the commodity known as a bill of exchange, bearing such and such a signature, may like such and such an article of commerce, be plentiful or scarce in the market, may command a high price or be worth nothing at all, this court decides that ...

Well, now, how stupid of me! I beg your pardon ... I mean, I am of the opinion that you will be able to redeem your brother's debts for twenty-five per cent of their value.'

'Je-je-jeremy Ben ... ben ... you called him?'

'Bentham, an Englishman.'

'That's a Jeremiah that will save us lots of lamentations in business,' said the notary, laughing.

'The English s-sometimes have very s-sensible notions,' said Grandet. 'Then, acc-c-cording to B-Bentham, how if my b-brother's b-b-bills are w-w-w-worth ... are n-n-not worth anything! If I'm r-r-r-right ... it s-s-s-s-seems clear, d-d-d-doesn't it? The creditors would ... no, w-w-w-would n-n-not ... I unders-s-s-stand.'

'Let me explain all this to you,' said the president. 'In law, if you hold all the outstanding bills of the firm of Grandet your brother and his heirs owe nothing to anyone. Well and good.'

'Well and good,' repeated Grandet.

'In all fairness, if your brother's bills are negotiated on the market (do you understand what "negotiated" means?) at a loss of so much per cent; if one of your friends chances to be there and buys up the bills, the creditors not being constrained by any violent means to give them up; then the estate of the late Grandet of Paris becomes honourably cleared of its debts.'

'That's t-t-true, b-b-b-business is b-b-b-b-business,' said the cooper. 'That's g-g-g-granted. But all the s-s-s-s-same you unders-s-s-stand it's d-d-d-difficult. I have n-n-no m-m-m-m-money, nor the t-t-t-time, n-n-nor the t-t-time, n-n-n-nor ...'

'Yes, yes, you can't trouble about it. Well, if you like I'll go to Paris for you. (You will pay my expenses – that's a mere trifle.) In Paris I can see the creditors and discuss the matter with them and talk them over, and everything can be arranged if you add something to the amount realized by the liquidation, in order to get the bills into your hands.'

'Well, we shall s-s-s-s-see ab-b-bout that. I c-c-c-can't, I w-w-w-w-w-w-w-won't undert-t-t-take ... If you c-c-can't, you c-c-can't. You unders-s-stand how it is?'

'Quite so.'

'My head is b-b-b-buzzing with all these n-n-notions you've s-s-s-s-sprung upon me. It's the f-f-first t-t-time in my l-l-life that I've h-h-had to th-th-think about s-s-s-s-such ...'

'Yes, you are not a legal expert.'

'I'm a p-p-poor w-w-wine g-g-grower, and I d-d-don't know anything about wh-wh-what you have just been s-s-s-saying. I m-m-must th-th-think it over and w-w-work it out.'

'Well ...,' began the president, settling himself as if he were about to begin the discussion all over again.

'Nephew! ...' interrupted the notary reproachfully.

'Yes, uncle?' answered the president.

'Let Monsieur Grandet explain what he means to do. It's a question, now, of your being empowered to act for him, and it's a serious business. Our dear friend should tell us definitely ...'

A knock at the door announcing the arrival of the des Grassins family, their appearance and the greetings that followed, prevented Cruchot from finishing his sentence. The notary was not sorry to be interrupted: already Grandet was looking askance at him, and his wen showed like a storm-signal of trouble brewing within. At the same time, the cautious notary was inclined to think it unbecoming that the president of a court of first instance should go to Paris to treat with creditors, and lend his services in a rather dubious business, hardly in accordance with the laws of strict honesty. Besides he had not heard Grandet express the slightest inclination to pay out anything whatsoever, and he trembled instinctively to see his nephew becoming involved in such an affair. He took advantage of the stir created by the entrance of the des Grassins, therefore, to take the president by the arm and draw him into the window recess.

'You have shown quite as much zeal as there is any need for, nephew,' he said. 'That's enough enthusiasm. Your anxiety to marry the girl is making you lose your judgement. What, the devil! there's no need to dash at it like a crow knocking down walnuts! Let me steer the ship now and you trim your sails to the wind. Is it a suitable part for you to play, compromising your dignity as a magistrate in such a ...?'

He stopped short. He heard Monsieur des Grassins saying to the old cooper as he held out his hand:

'Grandet, we have heard of the terrible misfortunes which have befallen your family, the failure of Guillaume Grandet's business and your brother's death, and we have come to express all our sympathy with you in these sad events.'

'There is only one sad event,' interrupted the notary, 'the death of the younger Monsieur Grandet. And he would not have killed himself if it had occurred to him to call on his brother for help. Our old friend here, who is a man of honour to his finger-tips, intends to meet the debts of the firm of Grandet in Paris, and my nephew, the president, in order to spare him all the worry of a purely legal matter, has offered to set off at once for Paris in order to settle with the creditors and meet their claims.'

The three des Grassins were completely taken aback by these words, which the attitude of the winegrower seemed to confirm as he stood there stroking his chin. On their way to the house they had been commenting freely and severely on Grandet's close-fistedness, almost going so far as to accuse him of fratricide.

'Ah! I was sure of it!' exclaimed the banker, looking at his wife. 'What was I saying on the way here, Madame des Grassins? Grandet is a man of honour, every inch of him, and will not endure the slightest shadow resting on his name! Money without honour is an affliction. Oh, we know what honour is, in the provinces! This is handsome of you, Grandet, very handsome indeed! I am an old soldier; I can't hide what I think; I must just say it straight out. This is, by Jove it is, sublime!'

'Then the s-s-s-sublime costs a l-l-lot of money,' the cooper replied, while the banker shook his hand enthusiastically.

'But this, my good Grandet, with all respect to Monsieur le Président,' des Grassins went on, 'is simply a business matter and needs an experienced businessman to look after it. The man who does the job should know how to deal with such matters as the expenses of protested and renewed bills, and know his way about tables of interest, shouldn't he? I have business of my own to see to in Paris, and I could take on ...'

'We m-m-must s-s-s-see then h-h-how we can arrange t-t-t-to s-s-s-settle th-th-things together f-f-for the best whatever m-m-may t-turn up, without t-t-t-tying m-me d-down t-t-t-to d-d-do s-something I w-w-w-w-w-wouldn't w-w-w-w-want to do,' stammered Grandet; 'because, you see, Monsieur le Président naturally wanted me to pay his travelling expenses.' These last words were said without a trace of hesitation.

'Oh, but it's a pleasure to stay in Paris!' said Madame des Grassins. 'For my part I would gladly pay my travelling expenses to go there.' And she made a sign to her husband, as if urging him on to cut their adversaries out of this commission, cost what it might; then she looked down her nose at the two Cruchots who, for their part, looked pitifully crestfallen. Grandet seized the banker by a coat-button and drew him into a corner.

'I should have much more confidence in you than in the president,' he said to him. 'Besides there's other fish to fry,' he added, his wen twitching a little. 'I have some thousands of francs to invest in the funds, and I don't want to pay more than eighty francs for them. That clockwork runs down at the end of every month, so they say. You know all about that, I suppose?'

'To be sure I do! Well, so I shall have a few thousand livres to invest in the funds for you?'

'Not a great deal to begin with. But mum's the word! I want to play this game without anyone knowing about it. You will put through the business for me at the end of the month, but say nothing to the Cruchots: it would only vex them. And since you are going to Paris we can see at the same time, for my poor nephew's sake, what cards are trumps.'

'Agreed! I shall travel post tomorrow,' des Grassins said aloud, 'and I will come round to take your final instructions at ... at what time?'

'Five o'clock, before dinner,' said the winegrower, rubbing his hands together.

The two rival parties remained facing each other for a few moments longer. After a pause des Grassins said, tapping Grandet's shoulder,

'It's a fine thing to have kind relatives like ...'

'Yes, yes, without m-making any f-fuss about it,' Grandet replied, 'I d-d-do what I can for the f-f-family. I was f-f-fond of my b-b-brother, and I w-will p-p-prove it if it does ... doesn't c-c-c-c-cost ...'

'We will leave you now, Grandet,' said the banker, fortunately interrupting him before he could finish his sentence. 'If I go off to Paris earlier than I meant to, I shall have a number of things to see after before I go.'

'Yes, very well. I h-h-have to go t-t-too, in connexion with y-y-y-you know what, to d-d-d-d-deliberations in p-p-private s-s-s-s-session, as P-p-president Cruchot would s-s-s-say.'

'Plague take it! I'm not Monsieur de Bonfons any more,' thought the magistrate, and his face took on the expression of a judge who is bored by Counsel's speech.

The heads of the two rival families went out together. On neither side was another thought given to the treason Grandet had committed that morning against the winegrowers of the region; and they all sounded each other, though without result, to find out what was thought about Grandet's real intentions in this new affair.

'Are you coming to Madame Dorsonval's with us?' des Grassins asked the notary.

'We are going there later,' the president replied. 'I promised Mademoiselle de Gribeaucourt just to call and say good-evening to her, and, with my uncle's permission, we will call with her first.'

'We shall see you again later on then,' said Madame des Grassins affably.

But when the Cruchots had moved on and were a few paces away Adolphe said to his father:

'They're in a nice stew, eh?'

'Hush!' said his mother. 'They are very likely still within hearing, and, besides, that remark is not in very good taste: it sounds like something picked up at the law school.'

'Well, uncle!' cried the magistrate, when he saw that the des Grassins were too far away to hear him, 'I began by being President de Bonfons and ended as plain Cruchot!'

'I saw very well that you were vexed about it, but the des Grassins took the wind out of our sails. How silly you are, for all your cleverness! ... let them launch out on the strength of old Grandet's "We shall see"; and don't you worry, my boy, Eugénie shall marry you for all that.'

In a few minutes the news of Grandet's magnanimous decision was circulating in three houses at once, and soon the only subject of conversation in the town was this act of brotherly devotion. Grandet was forgiven for selling his vintage in complete contempt of the agreement made by all the vine-growers, and everyone admired his sense of honour and praised a generosity they had not thought him capable of. It is in the French character to take fire, fly into a passion, in anger or delight, at the appearance of the meteor of the moment, for the sake of some distant floating stick which looks portentous. Have nations and men in the mass no memory?

As soon as Grandet had closed his front door on his departing guests he called Nanon:

'Don't let the dog loose, and don't go to bed: we have work to do. Cornoiller is to be at the door with the carriage from Froidfond at eleven. Watch for him and let him in so that he doesn't need to knock at the door, and tell him to come in quietly. The police don't like it if you create a disturbance at night. Besides there's no need to let the whole neighbourhood know that I'm going out.'

Having thus spoken his mind, Grandet went upstairs to his laboratory, where Nanon heard him moving about, rummaging among the furniture, going and coming, stealthily and cautiously. He was evidently anxious not to waken his wife or daughter, and especially not to excite the notice of his nephew, whom, to begin with, he had sworn at when he saw that there was a light in his room.

In the middle of the night Eugénie, whose thoughts were all for her cousin, thought she heard the groan of a dying man: and for her the dying man was Charles. When she had said good-night to him he had been so pale, in such despair! Perhaps he had killed himself! She hastily wrapped herself in a capuchin, a long cloak with a hood, and went to her door. A bright light streaming through the chinks in the boards made her afraid at first that the house was on fire, but she was quickly reassured when she heard Nanon's heavy footsteps and the sound of her voice mingled with the neighing of several horses.

'Can my father be taking Charles away?' she said to herself, opening her door cautiously, for fear it might creak, but widely enough to let her see what was going on in the passage.

Suddenly her eyes met her father's, which froze her in terror, absent and unfocused though their gaze was. The cooper and Nanon were yoked together by a stout wooden stick which they were carrying on their right shoulders. The stick supported the weight of a little barrel tied to it with a rope: it looked like one of the barrels that Grandet amused himself by making in the bakehouse when he had nothing better to do.

'Holy Mother! sir, isn't it heavy!' said Nanon in a whisper.

'What a pity that it's only full of pence!' replied the cooper. 'Take care not to knock against the candlestick.'

This scene was lighted by a single candle, set between two banisters on the staircase.

'Cornoiller,' said Grandet to his gamekeeper *in partibus*, 'have you got your pistols with you?'

'No, sir. Lord love you! Is there anything for a barrel of coppers to be afraid of?'

'Oh, nothing at all,' said the cooper.

'Besides we won't be long on the way,' the keeper went on. 'Your tenants have picked out their best horses for you.'

'Good. Good. You didn't tell them where I was going?'

'I didn't know myself.'

'Right. Is the carriage strongly made?'

'The carriage, mister? That's all right. It would take three thousand barrels the like of that. What does that rubbishy barrel weigh anyway?'

'I'll tell you,' said Nanon. 'I know what it weighs all right! There's nearly eighteen hundredweight in there.'

'Hold your tongue, Nanon! You can tell my wife I have gone into the country. I'll be back for dinner. Drive fast, Cornoiller: we must be in Angers before nine o'clock.'

The carriage went off. Nanon bolted the great door, unchained the dog, went to bed with a bruised shoulder, and no one in the district suspected either that Grandet had gone or the object of his journey. The worthy cooper's discretion was absolute. Nobody in that house full of gold ever saw a sou lying about. In the course of that morning he had learned from gossip on the quays that a number of ships were being fitted out at Nantes, and that as a result, because of its scarcity, gold was worth double its value there, and speculators had come to Angers to buy it; and simply by borrowing his tenants' horses he had put himself in a position to go to Angers, sell his gold and bring back in return an order upon the Treasury from the Receiver-General for the sum he needed for his purchase of funds together with his profit on the sale of his gold.

'My father is going away,' said Eugénie, who had heard everything that had passed from the top of the staircase.

Silence had fallen again on the house, and the distant rumbling of the carriage wheels, dying away by degrees, was soon no longer audible in sleeping Saumur. As she stood there Eugénie felt in her heart, even before it rang in her ears, the sound of a cry, which echoed through the walls above her and came from her cousin's room. A thin line of light, like the edge of a sabre, shone from underneath the door and cut a bright band along the banisters of the old staircase.

'He is in pain,' she said, and she went up a few steps further.

A second groan brought her up to the landing above. The door was ajar; she pushed it open. Charles was sleeping, his head leaning over one arm of the old arm-chair. His hand hung down, nearly touching the pen that had fallen from his fingers to the floor. His quick jerky breathing, which was due to his uncomfortable position, suddenly alarmed Eugénie, and she hastily entered the room.

'He must be very tired,' she said to herself, looking at a dozen sealed letters on the table. She read the addresses: 'MM. Farry and Co., coach builders; M. Buisson tailor,' and so on.

'I suppose he has been settling all his affairs so as to be able to leave France soon,' she thought.

Her eyes fell on two open letters, and on the words with which one of them began: 'My dear Annette ...' She felt giddy and the room swam round her. Her heart beat loudly and her feet seemed rooted to the ground.

'His dear Annette! He is in love, someone loves him! Then there is no more hope. ... What does he say to her?'

These thoughts flashed through her mind and heart. She

read the words written everywhere, on the very floor, in letters of fire.

'Must I give him up already? No, I will not read the letter. I must go away ... Yet, what if I read it?'

She looked at Charles, gently took his head in her hands and laid it against the back of the chair, and he yielded himself to her like a child who, even while he is asleep, recognizes his mother and without waking accepts her care and kisses. Like a mother, Eugénie raised the hanging hand, and like a mother gently kissed his hair. 'Dear Annette!' A demon cried the words in her ears.

'I know that I am perhaps doing wrong, but I will read the letter,' she said.

Eugénie turned her head aside, for her high sense of honour reproached her. For the first time in her life good and evil confronted each other in her heart. Until that moment she had never had reason to blush for any action she had done. Passion and curiosity won the day. As she read her heart beat more heavily with every phrase, and the painfully quickened sense of life that filled her drew her still more irresistibly along the path of first love's keen emotions.

My dear Annette,

Only one thing in the world could have separated us, and that is the overwhelming misfortune which has befallen me, and which no human care could have foreseen. My father has killed himself; his fortune and mine are completely lost. I am an orphan at an age when, with the kind of education I have received, I can pass for a child, but it will take a man to climb from the dark pit into which I have fallen. I have been spending part of my time tonight in reckoning how I stand. If I am to leave France as an honest man, as naturally I mean to do, I have not a hundred francs of my own to try my luck with in the Indies or America. Yes, my poor Anna, I shall seek my fortune in the deadliest climates. They say that under tropical skies fortune is easily and swiftly found. As for staying on in Paris, I could not do it. I haven't got the right kind of mind, I am not brazen-faced enough, to stand up to the insults, the coldness, the contempt that are bound to come the way of a ruined man, a bankrupt's son! Good God! to owe two millions! ... I should die in a duel within a week. So I shall not go back to Paris. Your love, the tenderest and most devoted that ever ennobled a man's heart, would not seek to draw me back there. Alas! my darling, I haven't enough money to take me to you, to give you and take from you a farewell kiss, a kiss in which I should find the strength I need for the task that lies before me ...

'Poor Charles, it is a good thing I read this! I have money, and I will give it to him,' said Eugénie. She wiped her eyes, and read on.

I haven't even begun to think yet of the worries poverty brings. Supposing I have the hundred louis needed to pay for my passage out, I shall not have a penny over to provide for a trading venture. But, indeed, I am not likely to have a hundred louis, or a single louis. I don't know what money will be left when my debts in Paris are paid. If there is nothing, I shall simply go to Nantes and work my passage out as an ordinary seaman. I shall begin like plenty of energetic men who have gone to the Indies young, without a penny, and have come back rich.

Ever since this morning I have been coolly looking my future in the face. It is much harder for me than it would be for anyone else, spoiled as I have been by a mother who adored me, indulged by the best of fathers, and loved at my first entrance into the world by a woman like Anna! I have only known the roses of life, and such good fortune could not last. Still, I have more courage now than a carefree young man can be expected to have, especially a young man accustomed to be flattered and spoilt by the most charming woman in Paris, enjoying from the cradle a happy family life, on whom everyone near him turned a smiling face, whose wishes were law to a father ... Oh! my father, Annette! He is dead ... Well, I have thought over my position, and yours too. I have grown a lot older in the last twenty-four hours. Dear Anna, if you were to sacrifice all the pleasures of the luxury you enjoy, your pretty clothes, your box at the Opéra, to keep me near you in Paris, we should still not have enough money for the extravagant life I am accustomed to. Besides I could not accept such a sacrifice. And so today we say good-bye for ever.

'He is leaving her! Oh, what happiness!'

Eugénie leapt for joy. Charles stirred, and her blood ran cold in terror. Happily, however, he did not waken. She read on:

When shall I come back? I do not know. The climate of the Indies ages a European very quickly, especially if he works hard. Suppose it to be ten years from now. Your daughter will be eighteen years old, your constant companion and a pair of watchful eyes on all you do. The world will judge you very harshly, your daughter perhaps more harshly still. There are plenty of examples of ingratitude on the part of a young girl, and we have seen the kind of judgement the social world passes on such things, so we should profit by what our experience has taught us. Only keep in your heart, as I shall keep in mine, the memory of these four years of happiness, and be faithful if you can to your poor lover. I shall not be in a position, however, to insist on it, because you understand, dear Annette, that I must adapt myself to my situation, see life through bourgeois spectacles, and make my calculations with the most prosaic realism. So I must consider marriage as a necessary step in my new existence; and I will confess that here in my uncle's house in Saumur I have found a cousin whose manners, appearance, mind, and heart you would approve, and who, moreover, seems to me to have . . .

'He must have been very tired to stop like that in the middle of a letter to her,' Eugénie said to herself, as she saw that the letter broke off there and the sentence was left unfinished. She was ready to find excuses for him.

How should this innocent girl see the coldness and calculation of the letter? Young girls brought up in the ways of religion are ignorant of the world and unsuspecting. They see love in all around them from the moment they set foot in love's enchanted kingdom. They walk surrounded by the light from heaven that their own soul reflects, which sheds its rays upon their lover: they see him clad in dazzling colour by the fire of their own feeling, and lend him their generous thoughts. A woman's blunders spring nearly always from her belief in goodness, her confidence in sincerity. The words 'My dear Annette – my darling' echoed in her heart like the most charming language of love: they stirred her soul like organ music, fell as gently and sweetly on her ear as the divine notes of the *Venite adoremus* had fallen in her childhood.

The tears, too, which had left visible traces round Charles's eyes, were surely evidence that he possessed all the sensibility and warmth of heart that are so attractive to girls. How could she know that if Charles loved his father so much and mourned him so sincerely, this tenderness was due less to the goodness of Charles's heart than to his father's goodness to him?

Monsieur and Madame Guillaume Grandet had always indulged their son's every whim, had let him enjoy all the pleasures that their wealth gave them access to, and so he had never had any reason to make the hideous calculations of which the younger members of most families in Paris are more or less guilty. With the delights of Paris all round them they wish for things that are beyond their present reach, and make plans which they are disgusted to see constantly held up, and they reflect that they will never be able to do as they wish so long as their parents are alive.

His father's generosity to him had created a strong and sincere affection for him in Charles's heart, an affection without any reservations. But Charles was a true child of Paris, with the Parisian's way of thinking; trained by Annette herself to study the consequences of every step before he took it, he was not a young man in mind though he wore the mask of youth. He had received the detestable education of a world in which in the course of a single evening more crimes are committed, in thought and word at least, than a court of justice has to consider in an entire session; in which the finest ideas are destroyed by an epigram, and a man is considered strong only if he sees things as they are. To see things as they are, there, means to believe in nothing: in no affection, in no man, not even in events – for events can be falsified or manufactured. To see things as they are you must weigh your friend's purse every morning, know the proper moment to intervene to twist whatever may turn up to your profit, suspend your judgement and be in no hurry to admire either a work of art or a fine achievement, in every action look for the motive of self-interest.

After many follies, the great lady, the beautiful Annette, had compelled Charles to think seriously. She spoke to him of his future position as she passed a scented hand through his hair, and, twisting a curl round her fingers, inculcated ideas about ways of getting on in the world. She made him both soft and materialistic, a twofold demoralization, but one wholly in accordance with the standard of good society, good manners, and good taste.

'You are very foolish, Charles,' she would say to him. 'I can see it will not be an easy task to teach you the ways of the world. You were very unkind to Monsieur des Lupeaulx. Oh! I know he's not a man one can have much respect for, but wait until he falls from power and then you can despise him as much as you like. Do you know what Madame Campan used to say to us? "My children, so long as a man is in office, adore him; if he falls, help to drag him to the refuse dump. When he has power he is a minor god, but when he has lost it and is ruined he is viler than Marat, for he is living, and Marat dead and put away. Life is a series of combinations, and you must study the various groups in society and follow their changing affiliations, if you are to succeed in maintaining a good position." '

Charles was too much a man about town, he had been too consistently spoiled by his parents, too much flattered by society, to have any lofty ideals. There had been a grain of gold in his heart, set there by his mother, but Parisian society had drawn it out to wire and beaten it to gilding, placed all on the surface where it must soon rub off. But Charles was only twenty-one. At that age it seems as if a freshness of heart must go hand in hand with the freshness of youth: it seems impossible that the young mind should not match the young face, the youthful voice, the frank look. Even the harshest judge, the most sceptical lawyer, the most hard-headed money-lender, will hesitate to believe that a wizened heart, a corrupt and cold-blooded nature, can dwell beneath a smooth forehead and eyes that still fill readily with tears.

Charles had never yet had occasion to put the maxims of Parisian morality into practice: he was virtuous because he was untried. But, unconsciously, he had imbibed all the principles of egoism. The seeds of this destructive political economy, as the Parisians know it, lay dormant in his heart, and could not fail to germinate as soon as he ceased to be an idle spectator and became an actor in the drama of real life.

Nearly all girls are ready to believe unquestioningly the fair promise of a pleasant outward appearance; but even if Eugénie had been as watchfully observant and cautious as country girls sometimes are, how could she have brought herself to mistrust her cousin when everything about him, everything he said and did, seemed the spontaneous expression of a noble nature? All her sympathies had been roused by a chance, fatal for her, which had let her witness the last outburst of real feeling in this young heart, and hear, as it were, the dying sighs of conscience.

So Eugénie laid down the letter, which seemed so full of love to her, and began to contemplate her sleeping cousin with the warmest kindness. The bright dreams and visions of youth found their mirror in his face: there and then she vowed to herself that she would love him always. Then she glanced over the other letter, without feeling herself at all indiscreet: if she read it, after all it was only to look for fresh proof of the fine qualities with which, woman-like, she endowed the man of her choice.

MY DEAR ALPHONSE,

By the time you read this letter all my friends will have left me; but I may tell you that though I have few hopes of my fashionable acquaintances, who so generously and easily call one their friend, I have never doubted your friendship. So I give you the task of settling my affairs, and count on you to turn all I possess to the best account.

You must by this time know my situation. I have nothing left at all, and mean to set out for the Indies. I have just written to everyone I can think of, to whom I owe money, and you will find the list enclosed: it is as exact as I can make it from memory. My library, furniture, carriages, horses, etc. should fetch enough, I believe, to pay my debts. I want to keep only the knick-knacks of no great value, which might serve as a beginning in gathering together a parcel of goods to trade with out there. I shall send you from here, my dear Alphonse, a proper power of attorney for the sale of my effects, in case there is any question about the matter. Please send me all my arms. And you must keep Briton yourself. Nobody will want to give the price this fine animal is worth, and I would rather offer it to you, as a substitute for the ring a dying man usually bequeaths to his executor.

Farry, Breilman and Co. built me a very comfortable travelling carriage, but they haven't delivered it yet: get them to keep it in settlement of my account with them, but if they refuse this don't do anything, in my present circumstances, that might cast a stain on my reputation.

I owe six louis to that fellow from the British Isles, which I lost to him at cards: don't forget to give him ...

'Dear Cousin Charles,' said Eugénie, laying down the letter and running off to her own room, but on tip-toe to make no noise, bearing one of the lighted candles with her.

Once there, it was not without a keen feeling of pleasure that she opened one of the drawers in an old oak chest, a beautiful piece of furniture, one of the finest examples of the craftsmanship of the Renaissance: the famous royal salamander could still be made out, half-effaced, on it. She took from it a large red velvet purse with gold tassels and a fringe of worn gold braid that had once belonged to her grandmother. For a moment she weighed her wealth very proudly in her hand, then joyously set to work to reckon up the total value, which she had forgotten, of her little store. She first sorted out twenty Portuguese moidores, as new-looking and bright as when they were struck in 1725, in the reign of John V: each was nominally worth five lisbonines, or a hundred and sixty-eight francs, sixty-four centimes on the exchange, so her father had told her, but actually they were worth a hundred and eighty francs because of the rarity and beauty of the coins, which shone like lesser suns. *Item*, five genovines, Genoese coins of a hundred livres each, also rare, worth eighty-nine francs in current value, but a hundred francs to collectors. These had come to her from old Monsieur de la Bertellière. *Item*, four Spanish gold quadruples, of the time of Philip V, bearing the date 1729, the gift of Madame Gentillet, who, as she gave them one by one, always used to say, 'This little canary-bird, this nice little yellowboy is worth ninety-eight livres! Take great care of it, my dear; it will be the flower of your flock.' *Item*, and these were the coins her father thought most of, for the gold was a fraction over the twenty-three carats, a hundred Dutch ducats, minted in 1756, and each worth about thirteen francs. *Item*, a great curiosity these! ... coins of a kind dear to a miser's heart, three rupees stamped with the Zodiacal sign of Libra, and five with the sign of Virgo, all pure gold of twenty-four carats, the magnificent coins of the Great Mogul. The weight of gold in them alone was worth thirty-seven francs forty centimes, but connoisseurs who love to handle gold would pay at least fifty francs for each of them. *Item*, the double napoleon which she had been given two days before, and which she had carelessly thrust into the red purse.

She had coins in mint condition among her treasures, minia-ture works of art, which Grandet often inquired about and asked to see, so that he could point out their intrinsic value to his daughter, and show her the beauty of the milling, the flawless bright condition of the background, the sharp-edged unworn relief of the ornate lettering. But she had not a thought to spare for their rarity and beauty. It did not occur to her either to reflect on her father's mania, and the risks she ran in parting with treasure so dear to his heart. No, she was thinking only of her cousin, and she managed at last, after making a few mistakes, to calculate that she was the possessor of gold worth about five thousand eight hundred francs at its face value, which could be sold to collectors for nearly two thousand crowns. She clapped her hands in delight at such riches, like a child who cannot help dancing about the room, working off his overflow of wild spirits by physical move-ment. So both father and daughter had counted their wealth that night; he, for the purpose of selling his gold; Eugénie, to cast it abroad upon an ocean of affection. She put the coins back in the old purse, took it up and went upstairs without hesitating for a moment. Her cousin's need made her forget the social conventions, the fact that it was night: she was strong, too, in the clearness of her conscience, in her devotion and in her happiness.

As she stood upon the threshold, the candle in one hand, her purse in the other, Charles woke, saw his cousin and stared in open-mouthed surprise. Eugénie came forward, set the light down on the table, and said in a shaking voice, 'Cousin Charles, I have to ask your forgiveness for a serious wrong I have done you; but I know that God will forgive me, if you are willing to overlook it.'

'What is it?' said Charles, rubbing his eyes.

'I have read those two letters.'

The colour rose in Charles's face.

'Are you wondering how I could do it?' she went on; 'why I came to your room? Indeed, now I don't know how or why, and I am almost tempted not to feel too sorry I read the letters, because they have shown me your heart, your soul, and ...'

'And what?' asked Charles.

'And your plans, how badly you need some money ...'

'My dear Eugénie ...'

'Hush! cousin, not so loud! We must not wake anyone. Here are my savings,' she went on, opening her purse, 'the savings of a poor girl who has no need of them. Do take them, Charles. This morning I simply did not know what money was: you have taught me; it is just a means of attaining one's ends, that's all. A cousin is practically the same thing as a brother, and surely you can borrow your sister's purse.'

Eugénie, in this a woman rather than a girl, had not foreseen a refusal, yet her cousin did not answer.

'What! are you going to refuse me?' she asked, hearing only the beating of her heart in the profound silence of the night. She found her cousin's hesitation wounding to her pride; but then the thought of his dire need returned with renewed force to her mind, and she fell on her knees.

'I will not rise until you have taken this money!' she said. 'Oh, cousin, for pity's sake, answer me! ... let me know if you respect me, if you are generous, if ...'

When he heard this cry, wrung from her by a noble despair, Charles shed tears: and when she felt these hot tears fall on the hands that he had seized to raise her to her feet, Eugénie grasped her purse and emptied it on to the table.

'Well, the answer is *yes*, isn't it?' she said, weeping with joy. 'Don't hesitate to take it, cousin; you will grow rich, never fear. This gold will bring you luck; some day you will give it back to me. Or we will form a partnership. I will agree to any conditions you may impose. But you ought not to make so much of this gift.'

Charles found words at last to express his feelings.

'Yes, Eugénie, I should have a petty spirit indeed if I did not accept it. But, nothing for nothing, trust for trust.'

'What do you mean?' she asked, startled.

'Listen, my dear cousin, I have here ...'

He interrupted himself, and pointed to the chest of drawers, on which stood a square box in a leather case.

'I have something here which is as dear as life itself to me. That box was a present from my mother. Ever since this morning I have been thinking that if she could rise from the grave she herself would sell the gold that in her tenderness she lavished on this dressing-case: but if I did it, I think it would be sacrilege.'

Eugénie clasped her cousin's hand tightly in hers when she heard these last words.

'No,' he went on, after a slight pause and an exchange of glances in which there was a hint of tears, 'no, I do not want to spoil it, or to risk taking it with me on my journey. Dear Eugénie, I will leave it in your keeping. Never did one friend confide anything more sacred to another. Judge for yourself.'

He took up the box, drew it from its leather cover, opened it and sadly showed his wondering cousin a dressing-case shining with gold, in which the fine workmanship of the fittings greatly enhanced the value of the precious metal.

'What you are admiring is nothing,' he said, pressing a spring which revealed a secret drawer. 'Here is what is worth more than the whole world to me.'

He drew out two portraits, two of Madame de Mirbel's masterpieces, richly set in pearls.

'Oh! how lovely she is! Is this the lady you were writing...?'

'No,' he said with a smile. 'That is my mother, and here is my father; your aunt and uncle. Eugénie, I ought to beg you on my knees to keep this treasure for me. If I should die and your little fortune be lost, the gold would compensate you; and you are the only person I can leave the two portraits with, you are the only person worthy to take charge of them, but destroy them rather than let them pass into other hands ...'

Eugénie was silent.

'Well, the answer is *yes*, isn't it?' he added charmingly.

When she heard him say this Eugénie looked at her cousin openly for the first time with the eyes of a woman in love, with a bright gaze that revealed the depth of her feeling. He took her hand and kissed it.

'You are an angel, robed in white! What can a question of money ever be between us two? But the feeling, which gives it its only value, will be everything for us.'

'You are like your mother. Was her voice as soft as yours?'

'Oh, much softer, and sweeter ...'

'Yes, to you,' she said, lowering her eyelids. 'Come, Charles, you must go to bed. I wish it. You are tired. Good-bye till tomorrow.'

She gently disengaged her hand from her cousin's, and he took the candle and lighted her to her door. When they had reached the threshold of her room he paused, and said,

'Ah! why am I a ruined man?'

'Oh, my father is rich, I believe,' she replied.

'Poor child,' said Charles, taking one step into the room and leaning against the wall; 'he would not have let my father die, he would not leave you in this poverty-stricken place, he would live in quite a different fashion, if he were rich.'

'But he has Froidfond.'

'And what is Froidfond worth?'

'I don't know; but there is Noyers too.'

'Some wretched farm-house!'

'He has vineyards and meadows ...'

'Not worth talking about,' said Charles scornfully. 'If your father had even twenty-four thousand livres a year would you be sleeping in this cold bare room?' he added, moving his other foot across the threshold. 'So that is where my treasures will stay,' he went on, looking at the old chest, trying to conceal what he was thinking.

'Go and sleep,' she said, anxious that he should not enter an untidy room. Charles drew back, and they said good night with a smile.

They fell asleep, to dream the same dream; and from that night Charles realized that there were still roses to be gathered in the world, and began to wear his mourning more lightly.

Next morning Madame Grandet found her daughter walking with Charles before breakfast. The young man was still depressed, as indeed any poor wretch must be whose fortunes appear to have reached their nadir. As Charles considered his troubles and measured the depth of the abyss he had fallen into, he felt the difficulty of the climb that lay before him weigh heavily upon his mind.

'Father will not be back before dinner,' said Eugénie, in answer to the disquiet expressed in her mother's face.

It was easy to see in Eugénie's manner, in the brightness of her face and the singular sweetness that her voice took on, the sympathy that lay between the cousins. Their hearts were ardently united, perhaps even before they had realized the force of the feeling that brought them together.

Charles stayed in the living-room, and his need for seclusion was respected. The three women had plenty to occupy them. Grandet had forgotten to make arrangements before he left, and a great many work-people came on various business, the slater, the plumber, the bricklayer, labourers, vine workers, tenants; some to settle bargains regarding repairs that were being done, others to pay rents or be paid wages: so Madame Grandet and Eugénie were obliged to bustle about, and reply to the interminable talk of the workmen and country folk. Nanon stowed away everything that was brought in, in her kitchen. She always waited for her master's orders about what produce was to be kept for use in the house and what was to be sent to market. Like a great many small country squires the worthy cooper was in the habit of drinking his poorer wines and eating his spoiled fruit himself.

About five o'clock in the evening Grandet returned from Angers, having made fourteen thousand francs on his gold, and with a government certificate in his note-case which would bear interest until the day when the money was transferred into the funds. He had left Cornoiller at Angers to attend to the half-foundered horses, and bring them back at a leisurely pace after they had had a good rest.

'I've been to Angers, wife,' he said. 'I'm hungry.'

Nanon called to him from her kitchen, 'Have you had nothing to eat since yesterday?'

'Nothing at all,' answered the cooper.

Nanon brought in the soup. Des Grassins came to take his client's instructions just as the family were sitting down to the meal. Old Grandet had not even seen that his nephew was there.

'Go on with your dinner, Grandet,' said the banker. 'We can have a little chat. Do you know what gold is fetching at Angers, and that they have been sending from Nantes to buy it there? I am going to send some over.'

'Don't send it,' replied the old fellow. 'They have plenty of gold there now. I can't let a good friend like you waste your time.'

'But they are selling gold there at thirteen francs fifty centimes.'

'You mean they *were* selling it.'

'Where the devil can they have got the gold they wanted?'

'I was in Angers myself last night,' Grandet told him in a low voice.

The banker gave a start of surprise. Then a whispered conversation took place between them, in the course of which des Grassins and Grandet several times looked at Charles. At one point, probably when the former cooper told the banker to invest sufficient money in the funds to bring him in one hundred thousand livres, a gesture of astonishment again escaped des Grassins.

'Monsieur Grandet,' he said, addressing Charles, 'I am going to Paris; and, if there is anything I can do for you there....'

'There is nothing, thank you, sir,' Charles replied.

'You must thank him more warmly than that, nephew. This gentleman is going to wind up the business of Guillaume Grandet, and settle with the creditors.'

'Can there be any hope of doing that?' asked Charles.

'But are you not my nephew?' cried the cooper, with a fine assumption of pride. 'Your honour is our own. Is your name not Grandet?'

Charles rose to his feet, flung his arms round Grandet and embraced him, turned pale and left the room. Eugénie looked at her father admiringly.

'Well, good-bye, des Grassins, my good friend,' said Grandet. 'I am very much obliged to you. See that you wheedle those folk in Paris properly!'

The two diplomatists shook hands, and then the cooper showed the banker the door. When it had shut behind him he came back into the room, flung himself into his chair, and said to Nanon, 'Bring me some blackcurrant cordial.'

But he was too much excited to stay still in his chair. He got up, looked at Monsieur de la Bertellière's portrait, and began to 'dance a jig' as Nanon called it, singing,

> 'In the *Gardes françaises*
> I had a grandpapa ...'

Nanon, Madame Grandet, and Eugénie exchanged glances, but said nothing. The vinegrower's ecstasies of delight always filled them with dismay.

The evening soon came to an end. Old Grandet felt inclined go off to bed early, and when he went to bed, everyone in the house was obliged to go to bed too; just as in Poland in the days of Augustus, when the king drank the whole of Poland got drunk. In any case, Nanon, Charles, and Eugénie were just as tired as the master of the house. As for Madame Grandet, she was accustomed to sleep or wake, eat or drink, according to her husband's pleasure. During the couple of hours after dinner which he devoted to digestion, however, Grandet was more genial than he had ever been before, and he delivered himself of a number of his favourite apophthegms. One example will be enough to give the measure of his wit. When he had finished his cordial, he looked thoughtfully at the glass.

'You have no sooner put your lips to a glass than it is empty!' he said. 'Such is life. You cannot eat your cake and have it too. You can't use your money and keep it in your purse. Life would be too good if you could.'

He was not only convivial but kindly as well. When Nanon came in with her spinning-wheel, he said to her, 'You must be tired. Let your hemp alone.'

'Oh, well,' the servant answered, 'if I did, *quien!* I should only be sitting there like a lady with nothing to do.'

'Poor Nanon! Would you like some cordial?'

'Oh, if you ask me to have cordial I won't say no. Madame makes it much better than the apothecaries. What they sell is just like physic.'

'They put too much sugar in it, and spoil the flavour,' said the cooper.

The party gathered in the living-room for breakfast at eight o'clock next morning, for the first time looked like a really intimate family group. These troubles had quickly drawn Madame Grandet, Eugénie, and Charles together, and Nanon herself sympathized with them, without being consciously aware of the fact: the four of them were beginning to be almost like one family. As for the old winegrower, his greed for gold had been satisfied and he had the assurance that 'that young puppy' would soon be off, and that he would have nothing to pay but travelling expenses as far as Nantes, so that he hardly knew or cared that Charles was in the house. The two children, as he called Charles and Eugénie, were free to do as they liked. They were under Madame Grandet's eye, and he had complete confidence in her in all matters of conduct and religion. Besides, there were other matters to engage his entire attention: the ditches draining his meadows were to be laid out along the roads, there were rows of poplars to be planted along the Loire, and he had all the ordinary winter work at Froidfond and in the vineyard on his hands.

That time was the springtime of love for Eugénie. Since that scene by night when she had given her gold to her cousin, her heart had followed the gift. When they looked at one another their glances, speaking of the secret they shared, drew them together, deepened their feeling for each other and made it less ordinary, more intimate, as their secret set them apart, as it were, from everyday life. And did not the relationship justify a certain gentleness in the voice and tenderness in the eyes? Eugénie was delighted to make her cousin forget his grief in the childish joys of a dawning love-affair.

The beginning of love and the beginning of life have a pleasing likeness to one another. Is it not everyone's concern to lull a child with soothing songs and kind looks, to tell him stories of wonders that paint the future with gold for him? Are not hope's dazzling wings always spread for his delight? Does he not shed tears of joy as well as grief, and grow impatient about nothing, about the stones with which he tries to build an unsteady palace, about the flowers forgotten as soon as picked? Is he not eager to grasp time and put it behind him, to get on with his business of life? Love is the soul's second metamorphosis.

Childhood and love were the same thing for Eugénie and Charles: theirs was a first passion with all its childish ways, all the more tender and dear to their hearts because their hearts were surrounded by shadows. The mourning crêpe in which their love had been wrapped at its birth only brought it into closer harmony with their surroundings in the tumbledown old country house. As he exchanged a few words with his cousin in that silent courtyard, or sat with her on a moss-grown bench in the little garden until the sun had set, absorbed in saying and hearing the sweet nothings that lovers think so important, or content to sit wrapped in the stillness that brooded over that space between ramparts and house, as a person lingers meditatively in church cloisters, Charles learned to think of love as something sacred. His great lady, his dear Annette, had acquainted him only with love's tempests and storms; but now he had done with passion as they know it in Paris, flirtatious, vain, and dazzlingly empty: he had found love in purity and truth.

He grew fond of the old house, and the household ways no longer seemed absurd to him. He took to coming downstairs early in the morning to have the chance of talking with Eugénie for a few moments before her father came to dole out the provisions for the day; and when Grandet's heavy footstep echoed on the stairs, he escaped into the garden. The slightly criminal nature of this secret meeting, kept secret even from Eugénie's mother, and apparently unnoticed by Nanon who made as though she did not see it, lent to the most innocent love-affair in the world the excitement of forbidden pleasures. Then, after breakfast, when old Grandet had gone to inspect his lands and the work being done on them, Charles stayed in the parlour with the mother and daughter, and experienced a pleasure he had never known before in holding skeins of thread for them to wind, in watching them sew and listening to their talk. He found something that appealed to him strongly in the simplicity of the almost cloistral life they led, in which he had discovered the beauty of the nature of these two women who had never known the world. He had believed such lives as these to be impossible in France, outside legend and Auguste Lafontaine's novels, and only admitted that they might exist in Germany. Soon in his eyes Eugénie was the ideal he had found in Goethe's Marguerite, Marguerite without Marguerite's sin.

And so day after day his looks, his words, enchanted the poor girl, and she let herself drift deliciously with the tide of love. She snatched her happiness like a swimmer seizing a willow branch overhanging the river to draw himself to land and rest for a while. Did not the grief of parting already cast its shadow on the happiest hours of those fleeting days? Every day something occurred to remind them of the approaching separation.

For instance, three days after des Grassins had left for Paris Grandet had taken Charles before a magistrate, with all the solemnity provincial people think due to such an act, and he had signed a deed renouncing any claim to his father's property. A terrible repudiation! An unfilial deed amounting to apostasy! Charles went to Maître Cruchot to obtain two powers of attorney, one for des Grassins, and the other for the friend who had been commissioned to sell his personal effects. Then he had formalities to comply with before he could obtain his passport. And, finally, when the simple mourning which Charles had ordered from Paris arrived, he sent for a tailor in Saumur and sold him his now useless wardrobe. This act was peculiarly pleasing to old Grandet.

'Ah! now you look like a man setting out, and ready to make his way in the world,' he said, when he saw Charles wearing a plain black overcoat of coarse material. 'Good! Very good!'

'I beg you to believe, sir,' Charles replied, 'that I know very well how to face my altered circumstances.'

'What's that?' said his worthy uncle, his eyes lighting up at the sight of a handful of gold that Charles held out to him.

'I have gathered together my studs and my rings and all the trifles I have that I haven't much use for now, which may have some value; but I know no one in Saumur, and this morning I thought I would ask you ...'

'To buy them from you?' Grandet interrupted.

'No, uncle, to tell me the name of an honest man who ...'

'Give them to me, nephew; I will go upstairs and value the gold and let you know to a centime what it's worth. Jeweller's gold,' he remarked, examining a long chain, 'jeweller's gold. Eighteen or nineteen carats, I should say.'

The worthy fellow held out his huge hand and went off with the pile of gold.

'Cousin Eugénie,' said Charles, 'allow me to offer you this pair of clasps, which you could use to fasten ribbons at your wrists. That kind of bracelet is very fashionable just now.'

'I have no hesitation in accepting, Cousin Charles,' she said, with a look of private understanding.

'And, aunt, this is my mother's thimble. I have treasured it in my dressing-case till now,' Charles went on, and he handed a pretty gold thimble to Madame Grandet, who had been longing for one for the last ten years.

'We can't possibly thank you in words, my dear boy,' said the old mother, her eyes filling with tears; 'but morning and evening when I say my prayers, when I repeat the prayer for travellers I will pray most fervently for you. If anything should happen to me, Eugénie will keep this jewel safe for you.'

'This is worth nine hundred and eighty-nine francs seventy-five centimes, nephew,' said Grandet, opening the door; 'but to save you the trouble of selling it, I will give you the money ... in livres.'

The expression 'in livres' means among inhabitants of the Loire valley that a crown of six livres is to be accepted as worth six francs, without deduction.

'I did not like to suggest that,' Charles replied; 'but I hated the thought of hawking my ornaments in the town you live in. Dirty linen should be washed in private, as Napoleon used to say. Thank you for your kindness in obliging me.'

Grandet scratched his ear, and there was a moment's silence.

'And, uncle,' Charles went on, looking at him rather nervously as if he was afraid of hurting his susceptibilities, 'my cousin and aunt have been good enough to accept a small remembrance from me; will you in your turn please accept these sleeve-links, which are useless to me now? They will remind you of a poor boy far away, who will certainly be thinking of those who are all that remain to him now of his family.'

'My boy, my boy, you must not strip yourself like that ...'

'What have you got, wife?' said Grandet, turning to her greedily. 'Ah! a gold thimble. And you, little girl? Well, now, diamond clasps! Well, I'll take your links, my boy,' he went on, grasping Charles's hands; 'but ... you will allow me to ... pay ... your, yes ... your passage to the Indies. Yes, I mean to pay for your passage. Besides, you see, my boy, when I was valuing your jewellery I only counted the value of the gold; it is perhaps worth a trifle more on account of the workmanship. Well, that's that. I will give you fifteen hundred francs ... in livres. Cruchot will lend it to me, for I haven't a brass farthing here; that is unless Perrotet pays me – he is in arrears with his rent. Well, well, I think I'll go and see him.' And he took up his hat, put on his gloves, and went there and then.

'So you are going away?' said Eugénie, with a look in which admiration was mingled with sadness.

'I can't help myself,' he answered, his eyes on the ground.

For some days past Charles had looked, spoken, and behaved like a man who, though in deep trouble and feeling that he bears the weight of heavy obligations, is able to draw fresh courage from his very need for it, and brace himself to meet his misfortunes. His self-pitying phase was over: he had become a man. Never had Eugénie been more sure of the nobility of her cousin's character than when she watched him coming downstairs in the plain black coat that set off his pale face with its sad expression so well. The two women had gone into mourning that day too, and they went with Charles to a Requiem mass celebrated in the parish church for the repose of the soul of the late Guillaume Grandet.

When they were at lunch Charles received letters from Paris, which he opened at once and read.

'Well, cousin, are you pleased with the way your affairs are going on?' said Eugénie in a low voice.

'Never ask questions of that kind, my girl,' observed Grandet. 'What, the devil! I don't tell you *my* business; why should you poke your nose into your cousin's? Leave the boy alone.'

'Oh! I have no secrets,' said Charles.

'Ta, ta, ta, ta! You will soon learn that businessmen have to bridle their tongues.'

When the two lovers were alone in the garden, Charles drew Eugénie to the old bench under the walnut tree, and said as they sat down, 'I felt sure I could trust Alphonse, and I was right. He has done wonderfully well, and carried through my business prudently and loyally. I owe nothing now in Paris; all my furniture has been sold and sold well, and he tells me that he has taken the advice of an old sea captain and used the surplus money, three thousand francs, to buy a quantity of knick-knacks and European odds and ends that will sell very well in the Indies. He has sent my packages to Nantes where there is a vessel loading for Java. In five days, Eugénie, we will have to say good-bye, perhaps for ever, but at any rate for a very long time. My trading goods and ten thousand francs which two of my friends have sent me make a very small start. I cannot hope to return for many years. My dear cousin, do not let us consider ourselves bound to each other in any way: I might die, you are very likely to have an opportunity of settling yourself comfortably ...'

'You love me? ...' she said.

'Oh! indeed I do,' he replied with a warmth and sincerity which showed the warmth and sincerity of his feeling.

'Then I will wait for you, Charles. Good heavens! my father is looking out of his window,' she exclaimed, warding off her cousin who was about to put his arms round her.

She fled to the archway, and when Charles followed her there, ran to the foot of the staircase and flung open the folding door; then, without knowing very clearly where she was making for, Eugénie found herself near Nanon's sleeping closet, in the darkest part of the passage. There Charles, who was close behind her, took her hand and laid it on his heart, put his arm round her waist and drew her gently to him. Eugénie made no further resistance; she received and gave the purest, sweetest, but most whole-hearted of kisses.

'Dear Eugénie, a cousin is better than a brother, he can marry you,' said Charles.

'Amen, so be it!' cried Nanon, opening her door behind them.

The two lovers fled in fright to the living-room, where Eugénie took up her sewing and Charles seized Madame Grandet's prayer-book and began to read the litanies of the Virgin.

'Bless us!' said Nanon, 'we're all at our prayers.'

As soon as Charles had fixed the date of his departure, Grandet exerted himself to make it appear that he was much concerned about him. He was liberal with everything that cost nothing, made it his business to find a packer for Charles's goods, and then declaring that this man wanted too much for his cases, overruled all objections and set about making cases himself from some old planks. He was up early every morning, planing, fitting, smoothing, nailing his boards together, and made some very good cases and packed all Charles's property in them. He undertook to send them down the Loire by steamer to Nantes in good time to go by the merchant ship, and to insure them for the voyage.

Since that kiss in the passage, the hours had slipped away for Eugénie with terrifying swiftness. Sometimes she thought she must follow her cousin. Anyone who has known the binding force of a passion soon to be cut short, and watched the span of a love-affair shortened day by day by passing time, by age or mortal sickness, by any one of the number of fatalities that human flesh is heir to, will understand the agony that Eugénie endured. She often wept as she walked in the garden, which had grown too narrow for her; the courtyard, the house, the town were all too narrow; her thoughts ranged already over the vast stretches of the sea.

At last the eve of the day of departure arrived. In the morning, when Grandet and Nanon were out of the house, the precious casket that held the two portraits was solemnly placed in the only drawer of Eugénie's chest that could be locked, beside the now empty purse. The safe bestowal of this treasure was not effected without many tears and kisses. When Eugénie put the key in her bosom she had not the strength of will to prevent Charles from kissing its hiding-place.

'The key shall always stay there, dearest.'

'Well, my heart will always be there too.'

'Oh, Charles, that isn't right,' she said, rather reproachfully.

'Are we not married?' he replied; 'I have your promise. Take mine.'

'I am yours for ever!' they said together, and repeated again. No more sacred promise was ever made on earth: Eugénie's transparent sincerity had momentarily sanctified Charles's love.

Breakfast next morning was a sad occasion. Nanon herself, in spite of the golden gown and a gilt cross that Charles had given her, had tears in her eyes. She alone was free to express what she felt.

'That poor dear delicate young man going off across the sea ... May God look after him!' she said.

At half past ten the whole family left the house to go with Charles to the diligence for Nantes. Nanon had let the dog loose and locked the door, and she meant to carry Charles's bag with his night things. All the shopkeepers in the ancient street were at their doors to see the little procession pass, and Maître Cruchot joined them in the market-place.

'You mustn't cry, Eugénie,' said her mother.

'Well, nephew,' said Grandet at the inn door, kissing Charles on both cheeks; 'you go poor, return rich; you will find your father's honour in safe keeping. I, Grandet, will answer for that; it will only depend on you ...'

'Oh! Uncle, you make parting less bitter for me. Is that not the finest gift you could make me?'

Not properly understanding the old cooper's remarks, which he had interrupted, Charles dropped tears of gratitude on his uncle's leathery cheeks, while Eugénie took her cousin's hand in one of hers and her father's in the other, and gripped them tightly. Only the notary smiled to himself in admiration of Grandet's artfulness, for he alone had entirely understood him. The four Saumurois with a group of other onlookers stayed by the diligence until it left; then it disappeared across the bridge, and the sound of its wheels could be heard only faintly in the distance.

'Good luck to your travels, and good riddance!' said the cooper.

Luckily, only Maître Cruchot heard this exclamation. Eugénie and her mother had walked along the quay to a point from which they could still see the coach, and stood there waving their handkerchiefs and watching Charles's waved in reply until he was gone from their view.

'Oh, mother, if only I could have God's power for one moment!' said Eugénie, when he was out of sight.

To save interrupting the story of events in the Grandet family circle, we must cast a glance into the future at the worthy cooper's operations in Paris through the agency of des Grassins. A month after the banker had gone Grandet was in possession of a certificate for Government stock worth a hundred thousand livres per annum, bought at eighty francs. No information was ever forthcoming on the means the close-mouthed and suspicious miser employed to change his gold for stock: even the inventory and statement of his affairs left by Grandet at his death shed no light on the matter. Maître Cruchot imagined that Nanon in some way or other, and ignorant of exactly what she was doing, must have been Grandet's faithful instrument in the transfer; for about that time the servant was away from home for four or five days, on the pretext of setting things in order at Froidfond. As if its worthy owner was likely to leave any ends loose there! As for the affairs of the firm of Guillaume Grandet, everything happened just as the cooper had foreseen and planned that it should.

As everyone knows, the most exact and detailed information about large fortunes in Paris and the provinces is held by the Bank of France. The names of des Grassins and Félix Grandet of Saumur were known there, and accorded the respect due to wealthy men whose wealth is based on great estates unencumbered by mortgages. The arrival of the Saumur banker with instructions, so it was said, to make the firm of Grandet of Paris solvent, as a matter of family honour, was sufficient to spare the dead wine-merchant's shade the disgrace of protested bills. The seals were broken in the presence of the creditors, and the family notary proceeded in due order to the inventory of the estate.

Presently des Grassins called a meeting of creditors, who unanimously appointed the Saumur banker and François Keller, the head of a large business firm and one of the principal creditors, as joint trustees; and empowered them to do anything they thought necessary to prevent any doubt being cast on the good name of the family, or the bills. The credit Grandet of Saumur enjoyed, the hopes des Grassins roused in the hearts of the creditors as his agent, made things go smoothly. There was not a single dissentient voice among the creditors. Nobody dreamed of passing his bill to his profit and loss account, and each man said to himself, 'Grandet of Saumur will pay!'

Six months went by. The Parisians had withdrawn the bills from circulation, and had put them away underneath all their other business papers. This was the first result the cooper was looking for. Nine months after the first meeting the two trustees distributed forty-seven per cent of the amount owing to each creditor. This sum had been raised by the sale of valuables, property, goods and chattels belonging to the late Guillaume Grandet, a sale made with most scrupulous honesty. The delighted creditors acknowledged the undeniable and admirable integrity of the Grandet brothers. Having praised them and circulated their praises for a suitably decorous length of time, the creditors began to ask when the remainder of their money would be forthcoming. It became necessary to write a collective letter to Grandet.

'Now we're getting somewhere,' said the old cooper, throwing the letter in the fire. 'Have patience, my little friends.'

In reply to the propositions put forward in the letter, Grandet of Saumur asked that all the documents involving claims against his late brother's estate should be deposited with a notary, together with receipts for payments already made, in order, so he said, that the accounts might be audited, and to establish correctly just how much money was owed by the estate.

This matter of depositing the documents raised innumerable difficulties. Generally speaking, a creditor is a sort of maniac: no one can tell what he will do. If he is ready to compound a matter today, he is breathing fire and vengeance tomorrow; a few days later and he is all sweet reasonableness. Very likely, his wife is in a good temper today, his youngest born has finished cutting his teeth, everything is going well at home, he is in no mind to give up a penny of his claims. But when to-morrow comes it is raining and he cannot go out, he is in bad form, he says yes to any proposal that will settle a matter. The day after he has to have guarantees. By the end of the month he has a good mind to demand an execution, he would send you to the scaffold if he could! The creditor is like the sparrow on whose tail small children are encouraged to try to sprinkle salt, but he turns the simile against his debtors, for he can lay his hands on nothing when he tries to pin them down. Grandet had observed this barometric variation of creditors, and his brother's creditors acted exactly as he had expected. Some flew into a rage, and refused point-blank to deposit their bills.

'Good! that's going nicely,' said Grandet, rubbing his hands as he read the letters which des Grassins wrote to him about the business.

Others consented to the depositing of their documents only on condition that their position was clearly defined, and that it was noted that they renounced none of their rights, and reserved even the right to declare the estate bankrupt. More letters passed, and in the end, after further delay, Grandet agreed to all the conditions. Armed with this concession the creditors who were ready to yield made the more recalcitrant creditors see reason, and the deposit was made, not without some grumbling.

That fellow,' they said to des Grassins, 'is laughing at you, and at us too.'

Twenty-three months after Guillaume Grandet's death, many of the merchants, in the rush of business life in Paris, had forgotten their claims against his estate, or thought of them only to say,

'I'm beginning to think that the forty-seven per cent is all I'll see of that debt.'

The cooper had counted on the power of Father Time, who, so he used to say, is a good fellow, to help him. At the end of the third year des Grassins wrote to tell Grandet that in consideration of ten per cent of the sum of two million four hundred thousand francs still owed by the firm of Grandet, he had induced the creditors to give up their bills. Grandet replied that the notary and the stockbroker whose dreadful failures had been the death of his brother were still alive, it hadn't killed *them!* that they might well be solvent again by this time, and should be proceeded against, to get something out of them and reduce the figure of the deficit.

Towards the end of the fourth year the deficit was duly and finally fixed at twelve hundred thousand francs. Then six months were spent in correspondence between the trustees and the creditors and between Grandet and the trustees. To cut the matter short, strong pressure being brought to bear on Grandet of Saumur to make him pay up, he wrote to the two trustees, about the ninth month of the same year, that as his nephew, who had made a fortune in the East Indies, had signified his intention of paying his father's debts in full, he could not take it upon himself to defraud the creditors by winding up the business without consulting him: he awaited a reply.

The middle of the fifth year found the creditors still being held in check by the words 'in full', let fall from time to time by the sublime cooper, who was laughing up his sleeve at them, and who never spoke of 'those PARISIAN folk!' without a knowing smile and an oath. But a fate unheard of in the annals of commerce was reserved for the creditors. When next they appear in the course of this story they will be found still in exactly the same position that Grandet had left them in.

When his Government stock reached a hundred and fifteen Grandet sold out and received from Paris about two million four hundred francs in gold, which went into his wooden kegs to join the six hundred thousand francs of interest which his investment had brought in.

Des Grassins remained in Paris, for the following reasons. In the first place he was appointed a deputy. In the second, he fell in love, father of a family though he was, but bored with the boring dullness of existence in Saumur, with Florine, one of the prettiest actresses of the Théâtre de Madame. The quartermaster was resurgent in the banker. It serves no purpose to discuss his conduct; at Saumur it was judged to be profoundly immoral. It was very lucky for his wife that she had brains enough to carry on the business at Saumur in her own name, and could take her own fortune from her husband's hands, and do her best to repair the breaches made in it by his extravagance and folly. The Cruchot party did all they could to criticize the quasi-widow's false position, and succeeded so well in making matters worse for her that she married her daughter very badly, and had to give up all hope of the match with Eugénie Grandet for her son. Adolphe joined des Grassins in Paris, and there, so rumour said, went entirely to the bad. The triumph of the Cruchots was complete.

'Your husband has taken leave of his senses.' This was Grandet's comment, as he helped Madame des Grassins with a loan (on good security). 'I am very sorry for you; you are a good little woman.'

'Ah!' sighed the poor lady. 'Who could have believed, that day when he left your house to go to Paris, that he was rushing to his ruin?'

'Heaven is my witness, Madame, that to the very last

moment I did everything I could to prevent him from going. Monsieur le Président was dying to do the business in Paris, and if your husband was so set on going, we now know why.'

And so it was clear that Grandet owed no obligation to des Grassins.

In every situation women are bound to suffer more than men, and feel their troubles more acutely. Men have physical robustness, and exercise some control over their circumstances. They are active and busy, can think of other matters in the present, look forward to the future and find consolation in it. That was what Charles was doing. But women stay at home, alone with their grief, and there is nothing to distract them from it. They plumb the depths of the abyss of sorrow into which they have sunk, and fill it with the sound of their prayers and tears. And that was Eugénie's fate. She was taking the first steps along her destined path. In love and sorrow, feeling and self-sacrifice, will always lie the theme of women's lives, and Eugénie was to be in everything a woman, save in what should have been her consolation. Her moments of happiness, picked up haphazard as a wall acquires a scattered collection of nails, when collected together, to use Bossuet's graphic image, were not enough to fill the hollow of the hand. Troubles never keep us waiting for them, and for Eugénie they came at once.

The day after Charles had gone, the Grandet household took up its accustomed routine again, and looked the same as it had always done to everyone but Eugénie, who found it suddenly grown very empty. She wanted Charles's room to remain exactly as he had left it; but her father must not know. Madame Grandet and Nanon lent themselves to this whim of hers, and willingly helped her to maintain the *status quo*.

'Who knows? He may come back sooner than we think,' she said.

'Ah! I would like to see him back here again,' replied Nanon.

'I was getting nicely used to him! He was a lovely little gentleman, with his hair curling up over his ..ead just like a girl's.'

Eugénie gazed at Nanon.

'Holy Virgin, miss, you have eyes like a lost soul! Don't go looking at people that way.'

From that day Mademoiselle Grandet's beauty took on a new character. The solemn thoughts of love which slowly filled her soul, the dignity of a woman who is loved, gave to her face the sort of radiance which painters represent by the aureole. Before her cousin's coming Eugénie might have been compared with the Virgin before the Annunciation. When he had passed from her life she seemed like the Virgin Mother. She carried love like an unborn child. Spanish art has finely represented these two Marys, who in their difference from each other constitute one of the most glorious of the symbols in which the Christian religion abounds.

On her way back from mass on the day after Charles had gone, for she had resolved to go to mass every day, Eugénie bought a map of the world in the town's only bookshop. This she pinned beside her mirror, so that she could follow on it the course of her cousin's voyage to the Indies, so that night and morning she might go in her imagination aboard that distant vessel, and see her cousin, and ask him all the innumerable questions she longed to ask:

'Are you well? Are you not sad? Are you thinking of me as you watch that star, whose service to lovers you showed me and whose beauty you made me see?'

In the morning she used to sit lost in a dream under the walnut tree, on the worm-eaten bench patched with grey lichen where they had said so many pleasant and foolish things to each other, talking nonsense, building happy castles in Spain in which to live. She thought of the future as she watched the narrow span of sky that the walls enclosed, and as her eyes wandered to her favourite corner of the old buttressed wall, and to the roof, under which lay Charles's room. In short, her solitary, lonely, true, enduring love entered into every thought, and became the very substance, or as our forefathers would have said, the 'stuff' of her life.

When Grandet's friends, so-called, came to play cards in the evening, she was gay, she hid her feelings; but all morning she talked of Charles with her mother and Nanon. Nanon had come to see that she might feel for her young mistress in her troubles without falling short in her duty towards her old master, and she said to Eugénie,

'If I had had a man of my own, I would have ... I would have gone after him down to hell. I would have ... well, I would have wanted to lay down my life for him; but ... it's no use. I'll die without knowing what it's like to live. Believe it or not, Mam'selle, that old Cornoiller, and he's not a bad man all the same, is sniffing round my savings, just like those folk who come here courting you with an eye on the master's pile. I may be as big as a house, but I've still got eyes in my head; I can see what's there in front of my nose. And yet you know. Mam'selle, I can't help liking it, though you can't call it love.'

Two months went by in this dream-like fashion. The absorbing interest of their secret bound the three women together in a closer intimacy, and infused new life into their dull domestic existence, which had been so monotonous before Charles's coming. For them Charles still dwelt under the discoloured grey rafters of the parlour and came and went as before. Morning and evening Eugénie opened the dressing-case and gazed at her aunt's portrait. One Sunday morning she was surprised by her mother when she was engaged in trying to trace a likeness to Charles in the features of the portrait, and Madame Grandet then learned the terrible secret of how Eugénie had parted with her precious coins, and been given the dressing-case in exchange.

'You gave him everything!' said her mother, aghast. 'What

will you say to your father on New Year's Day when he asks to see your gold coins?'

Eugénie's eyes grew fixed and staring; and for half the morning the two women went about in a state of mortal terror. They were in such a state of agitation that they forgot the time and found themselves too late for high mass, and went later to the military mass. In three days the year 1819 would end. In three days a terrible drama would begin, a bourgeois tragedy undignified by poison, dagger, or bloodshed, but to the protagonists more cruel than any of the tragedies endured by the members of the noble house of Atreus.

'What's to become of us?' said Madame Grandet to her daughter, laying her knitting down on her knee.

There had been so much disturbance of the normal routine in the last two months that little knitting had been done, and the woollen sleeves the poor lady needed for winter wear were not finished yet; and this homely and apparently unimportant fact was to have sad consequences for her. For want of warm sleeves she caught a severe chill after a violent perspiration brought on by one of her husband's appalling outbursts of rage.

'I have been thinking, my poor child, that if you had only told me your secret we should have had time to write to Monsieur des Grassins in Paris. He might have been able to send us gold coins like yours, and though Grandet knows the look of them so well, perhaps ...'

'But where could we have got so much money?'

'I would have raised it on my own property. Besides, Monsieur des Grassins would certainly have ...'

'There's no time now,' Eugénie interrupted in a strained, half-stifled voice. 'We're bound to go to his room tomorrow morning to wish him a happy New Year, aren't we?'

'But, Eugénie, why shouldn't I go and see the Cruchots about it?'

'No, no, I should be in their hands then. It would mean putting ourselves in their power. Besides, I have made up my mind. I have acted quite rightly; I don't regret anything. God will protect me. May His holy will be done! Oh, if you had read that letter, mother, you wouldn't have thought of anything but him!'

The next morning, the first of January, 1820, the sheer terror which had taken possession of both mother and daughter, and which they could not hide, inspired them with the most natural of excuses for omitting their solemn visit to Grandet's room. The winter 1819–20 was one of the severest for years before and after, and snow lay deep on the roof-tops.

Madame Grandet called to her husband, as soon as she heard him stirring in his room,

'Grandet, do tell Nanon to light a little fire in my room. It's so cold that I'm freezing under the bedclothes. I've come to a time of life when I need taking care of. Besides,' she went on after a slight pause, 'Eugénie can come and dress here. The poor girl might easily catch a chill, dressing in her own room in such weather. Then we will go downstairs and wish you a happy New Year by the fire in the parlour.'

'Ta, ta, ta, ta, what a tongue! What a way to begin the year, Madame Grandet! I've never heard you say so much in your life. You haven't had a sop of bread in wine, I suppose?'

There was a moment's silence.

'Oh, well,' he went on, his wife's proposal no doubt suiting him well enough; 'I'll do what you wish, Madame Grandet. You are really a good sort of a woman, and I wouldn't like any harm to come to you in your old age, although, generally speaking, the La Bertellières are pretty tough – they're built to last. Hey, aren't they?' he cried, after a pause. 'Never mind; we've had their money in the end. I forgive them.' And he coughed.

'You're very gay this morning,' said the poor woman gravely.

'Who, me? I'm always gay ...

> Gay, gay, gay, your daily task,
> Cooper, gaily mend your cask!'

He had finished dressing and came into his wife's room. 'Yes, by all that's shiversome, it's a pretty hard frost, like it or not. We shall have a good breakfast, wife. Des Grassins has sent me some *pâté de foie gras* with truffles! I'm going to meet the diligence to fetch it. He has probably sent a double napoleon for Eugénie with it,' the cooper added, coming closer and speaking in a lower voice. 'I have no gold left, wife. I did have a few old coins, I can tell you that between ourselves, but I had to let them go in the way of business.' And by way of celebrating the first day of the year, he kissed his wife on the forehead.

'Eugénie,' cried her mother, 'I don't know what's come over your father, but he's in a good temper this morning.'

'Bah! we'll get on all right.'

'What's up with the master this morning?' cried Nanon, coming into her mistress's room to light the fire. 'First of all he says to me, "Good morning, a happy New Year to you, you great noodle! Go and light a fire in my wife's room; she's cold." And then you should have seen my mouth open when I saw him holding out his hand to give me a six-franc piece that's hardly clipped at all! Here, Madame, look at that. Oh, he's a fine man, never mind! There are some ones who, the older they get, the harder-hearted they get; but him, he gets sweeter like your black-currant cordial, and improves with keeping. He's a very good, very perfect man ...'

The secret source of Grandet's high spirits lay in the complete success of his speculation. Monsieur des Grassins, after deducting various amounts that the cooper owed him, for discounting Dutch bills amounting to a hundred and fifty thousand francs, and for sums of money advanced to enable the cooper to purchase a hundred thousand livres' worth of Government stock, was sending him by the diligence thirty thousand francs in crowns, the remainder of the half-yearly dividend from his investment, and he had informed Grandet that Government stocks were rising in value. They stood then at eighty-nine; and the best-known capitalists were buying them for the end of January at ninety-two. In two months Grandet had made twelve per cent on his capital, he had paid off his expenses, and from that moment would collect fifty thousand francs every six months, with no taxes to pay and no property concerned to keep in repair. In short, he began to understand the possibilities of Government stock, a kind of investment of which provincial people fight exceedingly shy, and looking ahead he foresaw that within five years he would be master of a capital of six millions, six millions that would go on growing without much trouble on his part, and that added to the value of his landed property would make a colossal fortune. The six francs given to Nanon were perhaps in settlement of an immense service the girl had unwittingly rendered her master.

'Oho! Where's old Grandet off to, dashing off at break of day as if he were running to a fire?' said the shopkeepers that morning, as they took down their shutters.

Then a little later, when they saw him coming back from the quay, followed by a porter from the coach-office wheeling bulging bags on a wheelbarrow,

'Ah!' one man said, 'water always makes for the river; the old boy was going to his crowns.'

'They roll in from Paris, and Froidfond, and Holland,' said another.

'He will buy Saumur before he has finished,' cried a third.

'He doesn't care how cold it is, he is always looking after his business,' said a woman to her husband.

'Hey! Monsieur Grandet, if those are a nuisance to you I can help you to get rid of them,' said his next-door neighbour, a cloth merchant.

'Oh, aye! they're only coppers,' said the winegrower.

'Silver ones,' said the porter under his breath.

'If you want anything from me, keep a still tongue in your head,' said the worthy winegrower, as he opened the door.

'Oh! the old fox! I thought he was deaf,' said the porter to himself. 'He can hear in cold weather, so it would seem.'

'Here, here's twenty sous for your New Year's present, and mum's the word! Off with you now! Nanon will take your wheelbarrow back. — Nanon, are the womenfolk gone to mass?'

'Yes, sir.'

'Come on, shake a leg, lend a hand here!' he cried, and loaded her with the bags. In another minute the crowns were safely stowed in his room, and he had locked himself in with them.

'When breakfast is ready, thump on the wall,' he said, before he shut the door; 'and take the wheelbarrow back to the coach office.'

It was ten o'clock before the family breakfasted.

'Your father won't ask to see your gold here,' said Madame Grandet, as she came back from mass with Eugénie. 'If he does, you can pretend to feel shivery and say it is too cold to go and fetch it. We will have time to make up the money before your birthday.'

As Grandet came downstairs he was planning the prompt translation of the crowns he had ust received from Paris into good and solid gold, and thinking with satisfaction of how well his speculation in the funds had turned out. He had decided that he would go on investing money in the funds until they rose to a hundred francs. Such plans as these boded ill for Eugénie.

As soon as he came in the two women wished him a happy

New Year, his daughter lovingly, with her arms round his neck, Madame Grandet with a grave dignity.

'Aha! child,' he said, kissing her on both cheeks, 'I am working for you, if you only knew! ... I want you to be happy, and you can't be happy if you have no money. Without money, it's no go! Look, here's a brand-new napoleon I sent for to Paris for you. By all that's holy, there's not a speck of gold in the house, except yours. You are the only one that owns gold. Show me your gold, little girl.'

'Bah! it's too cold; let's have our breakfast,' replied Eugénie.

'Well, we'll see it afterwards, eh? That will help our digestion. That great des Grassins sent us this, believe it or not,' he went on, 'so eat up, children, it costs us nothing. He's doing well, des Grassins. I'm pleased with him. He's managing the affairs of poor dear Grandet very cleverly. He's doing Charles a great service, and free at that. – Ououh! ououh!' he mumbled, with his mouth full, after a pause. 'This is good. Eat your fill, wife; there's enough here to do us for two days, at least.'

'I am not hungry. I am not in the best of health, as you know.'

'Oh! Ah! well, but you can afford to put plenty away without fear of splitting the cask. After all, you're a la Bertellière, a good solid woman. You may be a trifle on the sallow side, but I'm fond of yellow, myself.'

A condemned prisoner looking forward to a public and ignominious death probably feels less horror than Madame Grandet and Eugénie felt as they thought of what must follow this family meal. The more gaily and noisily the old winegrower talked and ate, the lower sank their hearts. Yet the girl had one support she could rest on at this crisis: she drew strength from her love.

'For his sake,' she said to herself; 'for his sake I would die a thousand deaths.'

And as she thought this she looked at her mother, her eyes ablaze with courage.

'Clear everything away,' Grandet told Nanon when the meal was finished, at about eleven o'clock; 'but leave us the table. We can lay out your little treasure more comfortably on it,' he said, looking at Eugénie. '*Little* treasure, did I say? Well, indeed, it's not that. Actually what you have is worth five thousand nine hundred and fifty-nine francs, and another forty this morning makes six thousand francs all but one. Well, I'll give you the franc you need to make up the sum myself, because, you see, little girl … – Why are you listening to us? Show me your heels, Nanon, and go and do your work!'

Nanon vanished.

'Listen, Eugénie, you will have to give me your gold. You won't refuse your dada, little girl, will you, eh?'

The two women said not a word.

'I haven't any gold now, myself. I had some, but it's all gone. I will give you six thousand francs in livres for it, and you shall invest it; I'll show you how. There's no need to worry about a *dozen*. When you are married, which will be before very long, I'll find a husband for you who can give you the finest *dozen* that has ever been heard of in these parts. Listen now, my dear. There's a wonderful opportunity at the moment: you can put six thousand francs in the Government, and every six months you will get about two hundred francs in interest, free of tax, free of expenses, come hail, frost, or flood, or any of the other things that eat into your profits if you invest your money in land. Perhaps you hate parting with your gold, eh, is that the trouble, little girl? Never mind, let me have it all the same. I will find some more gold coins for you, ducats from Holland, and Portuguese moidores, and genovines, and rupees, the Mogul's rupees; and with what I shall give you on your birthday and other holidays, within three years you will have half your jolly little hoard of gold back again. What do you say, little girl? Come, hold up your head, now. Run and fetch the jolly little yellowboys. I think I deserve a good kiss for telling you these secrets and mysteries of life and death for five-franc pieces. In sober truth crowns live and breed like men: they come and go and sweat and bring in wages.'

Eugénie rose and took a few steps towards the door, then turned abruptly, looked her father in the face, and said,

'*My* gold is gone.'

'What! your gold is gone?' cried Grandet, rearing like a horse when a cannon is fired ten paces off

'Yes, I haven't got it.'

'You're dreaming, Eugénie!'

'No.'

'By my father's pruning-hook!'

When the cooper thus swore, the rafters shook.

'Mercy upon us!' cried Nanon. 'Look how white the mistress is!'

'Grandet, your rages will be my death,' said the poor woman.

'Ta, ta, ta, ta! in your family you never die! – Eugénie, what have you done with your gold?' he burst out, turning on her.

The girl was on her knees beside Madame Grandet.

'My mother is ill,' she said, 'Look ... Don't kill her.'

Grandet was scared by the pallor of his wife's usually dark, sallow face.

'Help me to bed, Nanon,' she said in a feeble voice. 'This is killing me ...'

Nanon came at once to lend her arm to her mistress. Eugénie helped her on the other side, and they managed to get her upstairs to her room; not without the greatest difficulty, for she was half-fainting and needed their support at every step. Grandet was left alone. After a few minutes, however, he came halfway up the first flight of stairs and called,

'Eugénie! When your mother is in bed, come down.'

'Yes, father.'

She did not linger upstairs, once she had soothed her mother.

'Now, my girl, you are going to tell me where your money is,' said Grandet.

'If I am not free to do as I choose with the presents you give me, father, please take them back again,' Eugénie replied coldly, and she took the napoleon from the mantelpiece and held it out to him. Grandet pounced upon it and slipped it into his waistcoat pocket.

'I certainly won't ever give you anything again – not a farthing piece!' he said, biting his thumb at her. 'So you despise your father, do you? You have no confidence in him? You don't know the meaning of the word "father"? If your father isn't everything to you, he is nothing. Where is your money?'

'Father, I do love and respect you, in spite of your anger; but I would very humbly point out to you that I am twenty-two years old. You have told me often enough that I'm of age, for me to know it. I have done what I chose to do with my money, and you may be sure that it is in good hands ...'

'Whose?'

'That's an inviolable secret,' she said. 'Have you not secrets of your own?'

'Am I not the head of my family? Can I not have my business affairs?'

'This is my affair.'

'It must be a pretty poor investment you have made, if you can't tell your father about it, Mademoiselle Grandet!'

'It is an excellent investment, and I can't tell my father about it.'

'At least tell me, when did you part with your gold?'

Eugénie shook her head.

'You still had it on your birthday, eh?'

But if cupidity had made Grandet wily, love had taught his daughter to be wary; she shook her head again.

'Has anyone ever seen such obstinacy, or a robbery like

this?' said Grandet in a voice which went *crescendo* and began to ring through the house and make it echo. 'What! here in my own house, in my own home, someone has taken your gold! the only gold there was! and I am not to know who? Gold is a precious thing. The best of girls can make mistakes and throw themselves away, that happens among the great folk and even sometimes to decent people; but to throw gold away! For you did give it to somebody, didn't you?'

Eugénie made no sign.

'Was there ever a daughter like this before! Can you be a child of mine? If you have invested your money, you have a receipt ...'

'Was I free, yes or no, to do as I pleased with it? Was it mine?'

'But you are a child!'

'I'm of age.'

Dumbfounded by his daughter's daring to argue with him, and by the arguments she used, Grandet turned pale, stamped on the ground, swore; then finding words at last, he shouted,

'Accursed viper of a daughter! Ah! you wicked girl, you know I'm fond of you and you take advantage of it! She cuts her own father's throat! By heaven! you have thrown all we've got at the feet of that good-for-nothing beggar with the morocco boots. By my father's pruning-hook! I don't want to disinherit you, by all my casks! but I curse you, you and your cousin and your children! You will never see anything good come of this, do you hear? If it was Charles you ... But, no, it's not possible. What! that puppy rob me? ...'

He stared at his daughter, who stood cold and silent.

'She won't budge! She won't bat an eyelid. She's more of a Grandet than I am myself. You didn't give your gold away for nothing, at least. Go on, did you?'

Eugénie stared at her father, with a satirical look in her eye which he found shocking.

'Eugénie, you are in my house, under your father's roof. If

you want to stay there, you must do as he tells you. The priests command you to obey me.'

Eugénie bowed her head.

'You strike at me in the things that are dearest to me,' he went on. 'I don't want to set eyes on you until you are ready to obey me. Go to your room, and you can stay there until I give you leave to come out of it. Nanon will bring you bread and water. You hear what I say. Be off with you!'

Eugénie burst into tears, and rushed off to her mother. Grandet paced round and round his garden in the snow, without noticing how cold it was, and then suspecting that his daughter must be in his wife's room, and delighted to catch her disobeying his orders, he ran up the stairs with the agility of a cat and suddenly appeared at Madame Grandet's door. Eugénie lay with her head buried in her mother's breast. Madame Grandet was stroking her hair and saying,

'Never mind, my poor child, your father will calm down.'

'She hasn't got a father now!' said the cooper. 'Was it really you and I, Madame Grandet, who brought a daughter as disobedient as this one into the world? A pretty bringing-up she had, and religious too! Well, why aren't you in your room? Off to prison with you, to prison, miss!'

'Will you take my daughter from me, sir?' said Madame Grandet, raising a face flushed with fever.

'If you want to keep her, take her with you, and clear out the pair of you ... Thunder and lightning! where is the gold? What has become of the gold?'

Eugénie got to her feet, looked her father proudly in the face, and went into her room; and the worthy cooper turned the key in the lock.

'Nanon!' he called. 'Rake out the fire in the parlour.' Then he came back to his wife's room, and took an easy-chair by her fire, saying, 'I suppose there is no doubt she has given it to that miserable fascinator of a Charles, and all he wanted was our money.'

In the danger that threatened her daughter, Madame Grandet found strength in her love for her to remain to all appearance unresponsive, dumb and deaf to Grandet's meaning.

'I knew nothing about all this,' she replied, turning her face to the wall to escape her husband's smouldering glances. 'Your violence makes me feel so ill that if what I foresee comes true I shall leave this room only when they carry me out feet first. You might have spared me at such a time, sir. I have never given you any cause for annoyance, or at least so I believe. Your daughter loves you, and I am sure she is as innocent as a new-born babe, so don't wound her feelings, reconsider your decision about punishing her. This cold is very sharp, you could easily do her some harm – she might contract a serious illness.'

'I won't see her and I won't speak to her. She can stay in her room on bread and water until she has done what her father bids her. What the devil! the head of a family has a right to know where gold goes when it goes out of his house. She had perhaps the only rupees that there are in France, and genovines and Dutch ducats ...'

'Eugénie is our only child, and even if she had thrown them into the river ... '

'Into the river?' shouted the worthy cooper. 'What! into the river? You are off your head, Madame Grandet. When I say a thing, I say it once for all, you ought to know that. If you want to have peace in your home, make your daughter confess to you, worm her secrets out of her. Women are better at that sort of thing than we men are; they understand each other better. Whatever it is she has done, I shall not eat her. Is she scared of me? Even if she has covered her cousin with gold from head to foot, he's on the high seas, isn't he? Ha! we can't run after him ...'

'Well then, ...'

As she was in the act of replying Madame Grandet saw her

husband's wen twitch terribly. The overwrought state of her nerves and her daughter's unhappiness had sharpened Madame Grandet's perceptions, developed the protective element in her affection, and made her wary. She changed what she had been about to say, without changing her tone.

'Well, then, have I any more authority over her than you have? She has said nothing to me. She takes after you.'

'Bless me! your tongue is hung in the middle and wags at both ends this morning! Ta, ta, ta, ta! you defy me, eh? You and she have put your heads together, perhaps?'

He stared hard at his wife.

'Really, Monsieur Grandet, if you want to kill me you have only to go on like this. I tell you this, and even if it were to cost me my life I would say it again: you are too hard on your daughter, she has more common sense on her side than you have. This money was hers, she can only have made a good use of it, and God alone has a right to know what our good works are. Sir, I implore you, take Eugénie back into favour again! ... If you do, I shall suffer less from the effect of the shock of your anger, and perhaps my life may be spared. My daughter, sir, I beg you to give me back my daughter!'

'I'm clearing out,' he said. 'I can't bear to stay in this house any longer. Mother and daughter argue and talk as if ... – Brooouh! Pouah! A cruel New Year's present you've given me, Eugénie!' he shouted to her. 'Yes, yes, cry! You'll be sorry for what you have done, do you hear? What's the good of receiving the Sacrament half a dozen times a quarter if you give your father's gold away on the sly to an idle good-for-nothing fellow who will play ducks and drakes with your heart when you have only that left to lend him? You will see what your Charles is worth with his morocco leather boots and his innocent looks, as if butter wouldn't melt in his mouth. He can have no heart or conscience either, to dare carry off a poor girl's money without her parents' consent.'

When the street door had shut behind him, Eugénie left her room and came to her mother's bedside.

'You were very brave for your daughter's sake,' she said.

'You see where undutiful ways lead us, child ... You have made me tell a lie.'

'Oh, mother! I will pray to God to let all the punishment fall on me.'

'Is it true,' inquired Nanon, appearing in a state of bewilderment and dismay, 'that we have Mam'selle put on bread and water for the rest of her days?'

'What does it matter, Nanon?' Eugénie said tranquilly.

'Ah! you think I'll be ready to guzzle *frippe* and let the daughter of the house sup on dry bread! No, I know better.'

'There mustn't be a word about all this, Nanon,' said Eugénie.

'I'll keep my tongue between my teeth, but you shall see!'

Grandet dined alone for the first time in twenty-four years.

'So here you are a widower, sir,' Nanon said to him. 'It's a very disagreeable thing to be a widower, and two women in the house.'

'I wasn't speaking to you, was I? Put a bridle on your tongue or I'll turn you out. What have you got in that saucepan I can hear simmering on the stove?'

'It's some fat I'm melting down ...'

'There will be people in this evening; light the fire.'

The Cruchots, Madame des Grassins, and her son appeared at eight o'clock, and expressed some surprise when they saw neither Madame Grandet nor her daughter.

'My wife is not very well this evening; Eugénie is upstairs with her,' said the old winegrower, with a wooden face.

An hour was spent in trivial conversation, and then Madame des Grassins, who had gone upstairs to see Madame Grandet, came down to the parlour again, and everyone asked her, 'How is Madame Grandet?'

'She's not at all well, not well at all,' she replied. 'She seems to me to be in a really worrying state of health. At her age you need to take the greatest care of her, Papa Grandet.'

'We shall see,' answered the winegrower in an absent-minded way, and the whole party said good night to him and took their leave.

When they were in the street, Madame des Grassins turned to the Cruchots and said, 'Something fresh has happened at the Grandets'. The mother is very ill; she doesn't know herself how ill she is. And the girl's eyes are red as if she had been crying for some time. Could they be trying to marry her off against her will?'

That night when the winegrower had gone to bed, Nanon crept silently in her old worn-out shoes to Eugénie's room, and displayed a *pâté* baked in a casserole.

'Here, Mam'selle,' said the kind soul. 'Cornoiller gave me a hare. You eat so little that this *pâté* will surely last you for a week; and it's not likely to spoil in this frost. At least you won't be kept on dry bread. That's not wholesome at all.'

'Poor Nanon!' said Eugénie, and she pressed the maid's hand.

'I made it very nice and very dainty, and *he* never noticed nothing. I got the bacon and the bay-leaves and all out of my six francs. It's my own money and I've a right to do what I like with it.' And the old servant rushed away, thinking she heard Grandet moving.

Over a period of several months the same state of affairs continued. The winegrower came constantly to see his wife at various times in the day, without ever uttering his daughter's name, or seeing her, or making the slightest reference to her. Madame Grandet never left her room, and from day to day her health deteriorated. Nothing made the old cooper give way. He remained immovable, harsh and cold as a granite pile. He continued to come and go according to his usual habit; but he did not stammer now, talked less, and showed himself harder in business matters than he had ever been. Yet he often, at this time, made mistakes in his bookkeeping.

'Certainly something has happened in the Grandet family,' repeated the Cruchot adherents and the Grassinists alike; and 'What can be the matter at the Grandets'?' became a stock question which people asked each other at every social gathering in Saumur.

Eugénie continued to go to church, escorted by Nanon. If Madame des Grassins spoke to her on their way out, after the service was over, she answered evasively and gave her no information that could satisfy her curiosity. But it became impossible after two months of this to hide the fact of Eugénie's isolation from Madame des Grassins or the three Cruchots. A time came when no pretext would serve to explain why she was always absent. A little later the secret was a secret no longer, although no one knew who had given it away; but the whole town knew that ever since New Year's Day Mademoiselle Grandet had been, by her father's orders, living on bread and water, locked in her room, without a fire; and that Nanon cooked dainties for her and brought them to her during the night. It was even known that the girl could only see and care for her mother when her father was out of the house.

Grandet's conduct was commented on very unfavourably. The whole town, as it were, outlawed him. His double-dealing and his hard-heartedness were remembered against him, and he was shunned by everyone. When he went by people pointed at him and whispered, and when his daughter walked down the crooked street, escorted by Nanon, on her way to mass or vespers, they came to their windows in curiosity, to see how the rich heiress bore herself and stare at her face.

Eugénie's face expressed only sadness and a divine sweetness. For some time she, like her father, had no knowledge of the town gossip about them. Her isolation, her father's displeasure, were trifles easily borne, for had she not her map of the world? From her window could she not still see the little bench, the garden, the angle of the old wall? Did not her lips remember the sweetness of love's kisses? So sustained by love and her religion, her consciousness of her innocence in God's sight, she patiently bore her father's anger and ill-treatment. One deep sorrow, which made all others seem meaningless, she found hard to bear: her gentle, tender mother was gradually sinking; her soul shone through the flesh in beauty more clearly every day, as she drew near the tomb. Eugénie often bitterly blamed herself for being the innocent cause of her mother's illness, as she watched her cruel malady slowly consume her; and although her mother did all she could to comfort her, the remorse she felt bound her still more closely to the love she was to lose. Every morning, as soon as her father had gone out, she went to sit at her mother's bedside, and Nanon brought her breakfast to her there. But poor Eugénie, sad and suffering with her mother's pain, silently looked at her mother's face and then at Nanon, wept, and dared not even mention her cousin's name. It was always Madame Grandet who began to talk about him. 'Where is *he*?' she would say. 'Why does *he* not write?' Neither mother nor daughter had any idea of the distance that separated them.

'Let's think of him, and not talk about him, mother,' Eugénie would answer. 'You are ill; you come before everyone.' 'Everyone' to Eugénie meant '*him*'.

'I don't regret leaving life, children,' Madame Grandet would say. 'God in His goodness has made me look forward with joy to the end of my sorrows.'

Everything this woman said was inspired by Christian feeling. During the first months of the year, when her husband came to take his breakfast by her bedside, and walk restlessly up and down in her room, she always made him the same speech, which she repeated with angelic gentleness, but with the firmness of a woman given the courage she had lacked all her life by the knowledge of approaching death.

'Thank you for the interest you take in my health,' she would say when Grandet had made the most conventional of inquiries; 'but if you wish to sweeten the bitterness of my last moments and lighten my pain, forgive our daughter and act like a Christian, a husband and a father.'

When he heard this, Grandet always sat down beside the bed, resignedly, like a man seeing a shower about to fall and calmly taking shelter under an archway. He listened silently to his wife, and said nothing. When he had heard what she had to say, to the most pathetic, loving and fervent prayers he would reply, 'You're looking a bit palish today, my poor wife.'

To judge by his stony face and set mouth, a kinder thought of his daughter never crossed his mind: he seemed to have effaced her from his memory. Even the tears which his vague answers, hardly varying in their terms, drew from his wife, and her pallid face, did not move him.

'May God forgive you, sir,' she would say, 'as I forgive you. You will have need of mercy some day.'

Since his wife had fallen ill, Grandet had not ventured to make use of his terrible 'Ta, ta, ta, ta!' but his wife's divine gentleness had not disarmed him or induced him to abate his tyranny at all. Madame Grandet's plain face grew in beauty day by day, made lovely by the spiritual loveliness that shone in it. Her soul was shining through its earthly envelope, and seemed to purify and refine her homely face and make it radiant. This transfiguration of the faces of the saintly is a phenomenon we have all observed. The soul accustomed to dwell among noble and lofty thoughts sets its seal on the most rough-hewn features in the end.

The sight of the transformation brought about by suffering, which consumed the last shreds of earthly being in this woman, had its effect, however feeble, on that man of bronze, the old cooper. He dropped his old habit of speaking contemptuously and did not speak at all, preserving by imperturbable silence his dignity as head of the household.

As soon as the faithful Nanon showed her face in the market-place, jokes and disparaging remarks about her master were apt to whistle suddenly about her ears; but even though public opinion loudly condemned old Grandet, in her concern for the family honour the servant stoutly defended him.

'Well, now,' she would say to the worthy winegrower's detractors, 'don't we all get harder as we get older? Why can't you allow the man to have his crochets like everybody else? Quit telling lies now: Mam'selle lives like a queen. She stays all by herself. Well, that's what she likes doing. Besides my master and mistress have very good reasons for what they do.'

At last, one evening towards the end of spring, Madame Grandet, feeling that sorrow was having more effect in shortening her days than her malady, and having made no headway in spite of all her prayers in her attempts to reconcile Eugénie and her father, confided her troubles to the Cruchots.

'To put a girl of twenty-three on bread and water!...' exclaimed the Président de Bonfons. 'And without just and sufficient cause! But that constitutes actionable cruelty; she can proceed against him; *inasmuch as* ...'

'Come, nephew,' said the notary, 'that's enough of your legal jargon. Make your mind easy, Madame, I will get a stop put to this imprisonment tomorrow.'

Eugénie heard them talking about her, and came out of her room.

'Gentlemen,' she said, as she came forward with great dignity, 'I beg you not to do anything about this matter. My father is master in his own house, and so long as I live in his house I must obey him. What he does should not be subject to the approval or disapproval of other people; he is answerable only to God. If you have any friendly feeling for us, you will say nothing whatever about this: I beg you not to talk about it. To criticize my father is to belittle us all in the eyes of the world. I am very grateful for the interest you have taken in me, but you would oblige me much more if you would silence the offensive rumours that are going about the town: I heard of them only by accident.'

'She is right,' said Madame Grandet.

'Mademoiselle, the best means of preventing people from chattering is to have your liberty restored to you,' the old notary replied respectfully. He was struck by the beauty which solitude, sadness, and love had developed in Eugénie's face.

'Well, dear, leave the matter in Monsieur Cruchot's hands, since he answers for his success. He knows your father, and knows how to approach him. You and your father must be reconciled at all costs, if you want me to be happy in the short time that remains.'

Next day Grandet went to take a few turns round his little garden, as he had formed the habit of doing ever since Eugénie had been locked up. He chose for his walk a time when Eugénie was accustomed to brush her hair, by the window. When the cooper had walked to the big walnut tree and beyond it, he used to stand there hidden by its trunk for several minutes, watching his daughter brushing out her long chestnut locks, torn, no doubt, by conflicting emotions, between his obstinate will on the one side and his natural desire to put his arms round his child on the other.

He often sat for some time on the crumbling wooden seat where Charles and Eugénie had sworn that they would love each other for ever, while Eugénie in her turn stole stealthy glances at her father or watched him in her mirror. If he rose and resumed his pacing up and down the garden, she would sit contentedly at her window, contemplating the corner of the old wall where the prettiest flowers hung from the crevices: maidenhair fern, convolvulus, and a plant with thick leaves and yellow or white flowers, a stonecrop, very common in vine-yards at Saumur and Tours.

Monsieur Cruchot came early in the morning and found the

old winegrower sitting, in the sunshine of a fine June day, on the little bench with his back against the wall, absorbed in watching his daughter.

'What can I do for you, Maître Cruchot?' he said, when he caught sight of the notary.

'I've come to talk about a business matter.'

'Aha! have you brought me some gold coins to exchange for crowns?'

'No, no, it's not a money matter, it's about your daughter Eugénie. Everybody's talking about her, and about you.'

'What business is it of theirs? A man is master in his own house.'

'Agreed. A man is free to kill himself if he chooses, or what's worse, to throw his money out of the windows.'

'What do you mean?'

'Only that your wife is very ill, my friend. You ought to call in Monsieur Bergerin; her life is in danger. If she should die without having been properly looked after, you would not feel very comfortable, I imagine.'

'Ta, ta, ta, ta! You know what is wrong with my wife, and once these doctors set foot in your house they come five or six times a day.'

'Well, Grandet, you will do as you think best. We are old friends; there's not a man in all Saumur who has your interests more at heart than I have, and that's why I had to say this to you. Now, let happen what may, you are not a child, you know how to manage your own business, let it go. That's not the business that brought me here, anyway. It's something rather more serious for you, perhaps. After all, you are not anxious to kill your wife – she is too useful to you. But just think what your position would be, with regard to your daughter, if Madame Grandet should die. You would have to give an account to Eugénie of her mother's share in your joint property. She is her mother's heiress, and she and not you will inherit it. Your daughter could legally claim her mother's fortune – you would have to divide your property, sell Froidfond ...'

These words struck the worthy cooper like a bolt from the blue, for cunning as he might be in business he was not so strong in legal matters. It had never crossed his mind that the property of joint owners might be sold by a forced sale.

'So I strongly advise you to treat her kindly,' said the notary in conclusion.

'But do you know what she has done, Cruchot?'

'What has she done?' asked the notary, full of curiosity and surprise at the thought of receiving a confidence from Grandet, and anxious to learn the cause of the quarrel.

'She has given away her gold.'

'Oh! well, wasn't it hers?'

'That's what they all say to me!' said the cooper, letting his arms fall with a tragic gesture.

'And for the sake of a mere trifle are you going to put a stumbling-block in your path, when there are concessions you will have to ask her to make if her mother dies?'

'Ah! you call six thousand francs in gold a mere trifle?'

'Well, my friend, do you know what the valuation and division of your and your wife's property will cost, if Eugénie demands it?'

'Well?'

'Two or three, perhaps four, hundred thousand francs! Don't you see that to find out the real value it will have to be put up for public auction? Whereas if you came to an agreement ...'

'By my father's pruning-hook!' cried the vinegrower, turning pale and leaning back against the wall. 'We shall see about this, Cruchot.'

After a moment of silent agony the worthy cooper fixed his eyes on the notary and spoke again. 'Life is very hard,' he said. 'It is full of troubles. Cruchot,' he went on, very solemnly, 'you would not deceive me, would you? Swear to me on your honour that this story of yours is based on legal fact. Show me the Code: I want to see it in the Code!'

'My poor friend,' the notary answered him; 'don't I know my own profession?'

'It is really true? I shall be stripped, cheated, murdered, robbed by my daughter!'

'She's her mother's heiress.'

'Why do we have children? Ah! my wife, I love my wife. Luckily, she is tough: she's a la Bertellière.'

'She hasn't a month to live.'

The cooper struck his brow, paced up and down, returned to Cruchot, threw a terrible glance at him, and said, 'What's to be done?'

'Eugénie might quite simply give up her claim to her mother's property. You don't mean to disinherit her, do you? But if you want her to make you a concession of that kind, you shouldn't treat her harshly. I'm doing myself out of a job by telling you all this, old friend, for how do I make my living? – by winding up estates, making inventories, arranging sales, divisions of property …'

'We shall see, we shall see. Don't let's talk about it, Cruchot. It's more than flesh and blood can stand. Have you collected any gold for me?'

'No, but I have a few old louis, about nine or ten, which you can have. See here, my good friend, make your peace with Eugénie. You know, all Saumur is speaking ill of you.'

'The blackguards!'

'Come now, the funds have risen to ninety-nine; so be content for once in your life.'

'Ninety-nine, Cruchot?'

'Yes.'

'Eh! Eh! ninety-nine!' repeated the old man, as he went with the notary to the street door. Then, too much agitated by what he had just heard to sit down again or even to stay at home, he went to his wife's room. 'Well, mother,' he said to her, 'you may spend the day with your daughter. I'm going to Froidfond. Be good, the pair of you. This is our wedding anniversary, dear wife. Look, here's ten crowns for you, for the Corpus Christi altar. You have wanted one long enough. Well, give yourself a treat! Enjoy yourselves; keep your spirits up; get well! Hurra for a merry heart!'

He threw ten crowns of six francs each on his wife's bed, took her face in his hands, and planted a kiss on her forehead.

'Dear wife, you are feeling better, aren't you?'

'How can you think of receiving the God of forgiveness into your house, when you shut your daughter out of your heart?' she said, with deep feeling.

'Ta, ta, ta, ta!' said her husband soothingly. 'We shall see about that.'

'Thank God for His goodness! Eugénie!' cried her mother, her face flushing with joy. 'Come and give your father a kiss. He has forgiven you!'

But the worthy cooper had disappeared. He was off at full speed to his vineyards, trying as he went to set his shaken ideas in order after the earthquake that had upset his world.

Grandet had just entered upon his seventy-sixth year. During the last two years especially his avarice had gained a stronger hold upon him. All engrossing passions increase in strength with time: and all who devote their lives to one over-ruling idea, so observers note, whether they be misers or simply ambitious men, cling with the whole force of their imagination to one symbol of their passion. In Grandet's case, gold, the sight of gold, the possession of gold that he could touch and handle, had become a monomania. The tyrannical strain in his nature had grown with the growth of his love of money, and it seemed to him a thing *against nature* that he should be required to give up control of even the least part of his property on his wife's death. What! render an account of his fortune to his daughter! Make an inventory of all he possessed, both land and personal estate, and put it all up to auction? ... 'It would be just the same as cutting my throat,' he said aloud, as he stood in the middle of a vineyard, examining the young vines.

At last he came to a decision, and went back to Saumur at dinner-time with his mind made up. He would give way to Eugénie, coax and humour her, so that he might die royally at last, in control of his millions to his last gasp.

He chanced to have his pass-key with him, and he let himself in and crept stealthily upstairs to his wife's room. It happened that just at that very moment Eugénie had taken the handsome dressing-case from its hiding-place and laid it on her mother's bed. The two women, in Grandet's absence, were giving themselves the pleasure of tracing a likeness to Charles in his mother's portrait.

'It's just his forehead and his mouth!' Eugénie was saying, when the winegrower opened the door.

When she saw the look her husband cast at the gold Madame Grandet cried, 'God have pity on us!'

The winegrower pounced on the dressing-case, like a tiger pouncing upon a sleeping child.

'What have we here?' he said, carrying off the treasure to the window, and settling himself down with it there. 'Gold! Solid gold! and plenty of it too! There's a couple of pounds weight in this. – Aha! Charles gave you this in exchange for your beautiful coins, eh? But why didn't you tell me? That was a good stroke of business, little girl. You're your father's daughter, so I see.' Eugénie shook in every limb. 'That's so, isn't it – it belongs to Charles?' Grandet repeated.

'Yes, father. It is not mine. That case is a sacred trust.'

'Ta, ta, ta,.ta! he took your fortune; you must make good the loss of your little treasure hoard.'

'Father! ...'

The old man put his hand in his pocket for his knife, in order to split off a fragment of the gold, and was obliged, for a moment, to lay the case on a chair. Eugénie rushed forward to seize it; but the cooper, who had kept an eye on both his daughter and the dressing-case, stretched out an arm to prevent her, and pushed her back so violently that she staggered and fell across her mother's bed.

'Sir, sir!' shrieked Madame Grandet, starting up from her bed.

Grandet had drawn out his knife, and was about to prise off the gold.

'Father!' cried Eugénie, throwing herself on her knees, and dragging herself over to kneel at his feet and stretch out her hands imploringly towards him. 'Father, in the name of the Virgin and all the saints, for the sake of Christ who died on the cross, for the salvation of your own soul, father, and if you have any care for my life, do not touch it! That case is neither yours nor mine; it belongs to an unhappy relative of ours who entrusted me with it, and I must give it back to him intact.'

'Why were you looking at it if it was entrusted to you to keep? Examining it is worse than touching it.'

'Oh, father! don't damage it, or you will bring disgrace upon me! Father, do you hear?'

'For pity's sake, sir!' said her mother.

'Father!' cried Eugénie in a voice that rang through the house, and brought Nanon upstairs in a fright. She caught up a knife that lay within her reach and held it like a dagger.

'Well?' Grandet said calmly, with a cold smile.

'You are killing me!' said Madame Grandet.

'Father, if your knife so much as scratches off a particle of gold I will stab myself with this. It's your fault that my mother is dying, now my death will be laid at your door too. Go on, we'll strike blow for blow!'

Grandet held his knife over the case, looked at his daughter and hesitated.

'Would you really do that, Eugénie?' he asked.

'Yes!' said her mother.

'She would do what she says,' cried Nanon. 'Be sensible, sir, for once in your life.'

The cooper looked from the gold to his daughter and from his daughter to the gold, and wavered for a long moment. Madame Grandet fainted.

'There! Do you see, sir; the mistress is dying!'

'Here, child, don't let's fall out over a box. Take it then!' cried the cooper hastily, throwing the case on the bed. 'Nanon, you go and fetch M. Bergerin. Come now, mother,' and he kissed his wife's hand, 'there's nothing wrong; there, there: we have made it up, isn't that so, little girl? No more dry bread, you can eat whatever you like ... Ah! she's opening her eyes. Well, now, mother, good little mamma, dear little mamma, never mind! Look, do you see? I'm kissing Eugénie. She loves her cousin, well and good. She shall marry him if she likes. She shall keep his little box for him. But you must live for a long time yet, my poor wife. Come now, show us that you can move a little. Listen! you shall have the finest altar for Corpus Christi that has ever been seen in Saumur.'

'How can you treat your wife and child so?' said Madame Grandet feebly.

'I'll never do it again, never!' exclaimed the cooper. 'You shall see, my poor wife.'

He went to his strong-room and came back with a handful of louis, which he scattered on the bed.

'Here, Eugénie, here, wife, these are for you,' he said, fingering the coins. 'Come, cheer up, my dear! Take care of yourself and get well. You shan't lack for anything, nor Eugénie either. There are a hundred louis for her. You won't give those away, will you, hey?'

Madame Grandet and her daughter looked at each other in astonishment.

'Take them back, father; it's only your affection we need.'

'Oh, well, just as you please,' he said, pocketing the coins. 'Let's be good friends together. Let's all go down to the parlour and have dinner, and play lotto every evening, and stake our two sous, and be as jolly as sandboys, eh, wife?'

'Indeed, I wish I could, if that would please you,' said the dying woman; 'but I have not the strength to get up.'

'Poor mother,' said the cooper. 'You don't know how much I love you – and you too, child!'

He put his arms round his daughter, and kissed her fervently.

'Oh, how good it is to kiss your daughter after a squabble! My little girl! Look, you see, mamma, we are almost like one person now. Go and lock that away now,' he said to Eugénie, pointing to the dressing-case. 'Go on, don't be afraid. I will never say another word to you about it, never.'

Monsieur Bergerin, who was known as the best doctor in Saumur, soon arrived. When he had made his examination he told Grandet, without mincing matters, that his wife was very ill indeed, that all excitement must be avoided, but that with quiet, a light diet, and careful nursing her life might be prolonged until about the end of autumn.

'Will her illness cost much?' asked the worthy cooper. 'Will she need a lot of drugs?'

'Not many drugs, but a great deal of care,' replied the doctor, unable to restrain a smile.

'After all, Monsieur Bergerin,' Grandet went on, 'you are a man of honour, aren't you? I put myself in your hands. Come and see my wife as often and as many times as you think you should. Keep my good wife safe for me. I love her dearly, you see, though I may not show it, because I'm not one to wear my heart on my sleeve; but everything is shut inside and I feel things terribly. I have my own troubles too. It began with the death of my brother, and I'm spending money in Paris on account of him that amounts to ... oh! I'm paying the eyes out of my head for him; and there's no end to it! Good day, sir. If you can save my wife, save her, even if I have to spend a hundred francs, or even two.'

In spite of Grandet's fervent wishes for his wife's restoration to good health – his uncertainty about her fortune was like a foretaste of death to him – in spite of his readiness to indulge his wife and daughter, to their astonishment, in every possible way and grant their slightest wish; in spite of Eugénie's most tender and devoted care, Madame Grandet's life moved swiftly towards its close. Every day she grew feebler: like most women of her age she had no resistance to illness, and her strength ebbed rapidly. She had as frail a hold on life as the leaves now hanging in their fleeting autumn glory on the trees, and like the leaves when the sunlight strikes across and gilds them she shone with reflected light from heaven. Her death was worthy of her life. It was a death wholly Christian – is that not the same as saying it was sublime? Her virtues, her angelic patience, and her love for her daughter had never shone more brightly than they did in that October month in 1822 when she passed away. No complaint had ever passed her lips throughout her illness, and her spotless soul left earth for heaven with no regrets, except for her daughter, the sweet companion of her dreary life, for whom her dying eyes seemed to foresee untold ill-fortune. She trembled at the thought of leaving this ewe lamb, as innocent as she herself was, alone in a selfish world which sought to shear her fleece and take her treasure.

'My child,' she said before she died, 'there is happiness only in heaven. You will know that one day.'

When her mother was gone Eugénie found that she had new reason for clinging to the house where she had been born, where she had suffered so much, where her mother had just died. She could not look at the parlour window and her mother's raised chair without shedding tears. She believed she had misjudged her old father's nature when she found herself the object of his most tender care. He came to her room to take her down to breakfast on his arm. He watched her with an almost benevolent eye for hours at a time. In fact, he brooded over her as if she had been gold. The old cooper was so unlike himself, he was in such a state, almost of apprehension, before his daughter, that Nanon and the Cruchot party, noting these signs of weakness, put them down to his great age and thought that the old man's mind might be giving way. But on the day when the family first put on mourning, after dinner, to which Maître Cruchot, who alone was in his client's confidence, was invited, the old cooper's conduct was explained.

'My dear child,' he said to Eugénie, when the table had been cleared and the doors were carefully shut, 'now you are your mother's heiress, and we have some little business matters to arrange between us – eh, isn't that so, Cruchot?'

'Yes.'

'Is it really necessary to settle them today, father?'

'Yes, yes, little girl. I can't stay on pins and needles any longer. I don't believe you would want to make things harder for me.'

'Oh, father!'

'Well, we must decide everything this evening.'

'What do you want me to do?'

'Well, little girl, it's not for me to say. Tell her, Cruchot.'

'Mademoiselle, your father would rather not divide or sell his land, or pay a heavy succession duty on the ready money he may happen to have in hand. And so we would have to dispense with the making of an inventory of all the property which has not yet been divided between you and your father...'

'Cruchot, are you quite sure of what you are saying, to talk like this before a child?'

'Let me say what I have to say, Grandet.'

'Yes, yes, my friend. Neither you nor my daughter want to rob me. Do you want to rob me, little girl?'

'But, Monsieur Cruchot, what do you want me to do?' Eugénie asked, losing patience.

'Well,' said the notary, 'it would be necessary for you to

sign this deed, by which you renounce your claim to your mother's estate, and leave to your father the usufruct of all the property which remains undivided between you, and of which he guarantees you the reversionary interest ...'

'I don't understand what you are saying at all,' said Eugénie. 'Give me the deed, and show me where I am to sign it.'

Grandet looked from the deed to his daughter, and from his daughter to the deed, under such pressure of feeling that he wiped sweat from his forehead.

'Little girl,' he said, 'instead of signing that deed, which will cost a great deal to register, I would like it much better if you simply waived all claim to your poor dead mother's estate, and trusted to me for the future. I would give you a nice big allowance every month – say a hundred francs. You could pay for as many masses as you wanted out of that, you see, for anyone whom ... Eh? What do you say? A hundred francs a month in livres!'

'I will do whatever you please, father.'

'Mademoiselle,' said the notary, 'it is my duty to point out to you that you are reducing yourself to beggary ...'

'Oh!' she answered. 'What does that matter to me?'

'Be quiet, Cruchot. That's settled and done with!' exclaimed Grandet, taking his daughter's hand and clapping it with his own. 'You won't go back on your word, Eugénie, you are a good girl, eh?'

'Oh, father! ...'

He kissed her effusively, holding her so tightly that he nearly suffocated her.

'There, child, you have given new life to your father; but you are only giving back what he gave you, so we are quits. That is how business matters ought to be settled, and life itself is a matter of business. Bless you! You are a good girl, and really love your papa. Do as you like now. I'll meet you tomorrow, then, Cruchot,' he added looking at the horrified notary. 'You will see to the proper drawing up of the deed of renunciation for the clerk of the court.'

The next day, before noon, the declaration was signed, and Eugénie had stripped herself of her heritage with her own hand ... Yet in spite of all the cooper had said, a year went by without his daughter receiving a sou of the monthly allowance so solemnly promised her. When Eugénie spoke to him about it, half jokingly, he could not but blush. He went hastily to his strong-room, and when he came back he presented her with about a third of the jewellery which he had bought from his nephew.

'Here, child,' he said, with a sarcastic note in his voice; 'would you like to take these instead of your twelve hundred francs?'

'Oh, father! Will you really give them to me?'

'I shall give you as much again at the end of next year,' he said, throwing them into her lap; 'and so before long you will have all *his* trinkets,' he added, rubbing his hands together, in high good humour at being able to make a bargain thanks to his daughter's attachment to the jewellery.

Yet, although he was still robust and hale, the old man began to feel that he ought to initiate his daughter into the mysteries of his housekeeping and his other concerns. For two successive years he made her deal in his presence with the daily household expenses, and receive the part of the rents that were paid in kind. He patiently taught her the name and showed her the area covered by each vineyard and farm in turn. By the third year she had grown so accustomed to all his miserly ways, she had accepted them so unquestioningly and they had become so much a matter of habit with her, that he could give the keys of the larder into her keeping without misgivings, and he installed her as mistress of the house.

Five years went by in this way, and no event occurred to distinguish one day from another in the monotonous life that Eugénie and her father led. Every day in an unvarying succession they did the same thing at the same time with a chrono-metrical regularity like the movement of the works of the old clock. Everyone knew that there had been a deep sorrow in Mademoiselle Grandet's life, and everyone could guess at its cause; but nothing she ever said could be taken as justifying the suspicions of the different social circles in Saumur, as to the state of the rich heiress's heart.

She saw no one but the three Cruchots, and a few of their friends whom they brought one after another as visitors to the house. They taught her to play whist, and dropped in every evening to play a few rubbers.

In the year 1827, her father felt the infirmities of age weigh heavily upon him, and was obliged to take her more fully into his confidence, and tell her all the things he had always kept secret concerning his landed property. He told her to refer any difficulty she might find herself in to Cruchot, the notary, whose integrity he could vouch for. The worthy winegrower had now reached the age of eighty-two, and towards the end of that year he had a stroke, and his condition rapidly deteriorated. Monsieur Bergerin gave no hope of his recovery, and Eugénie, reflecting that she would shortly find herself alone in the world, was drawn closer to her father, felt more deeply the strength of this last link of affection that bound her to another human being. Love was the whole world for her, as it is for all women in love; and Charles was gone. She nursed her old father with the most devoted care. Though Grandet's understanding was impaired, his greed for gold remained un-diminished: it had become an instinct that survived the decline of his faculties.

Grandet died as he had lived. Every morning during these last few days he had himself wheeled to a place beside the fire near his strong-room door, behind which, no doubt, lay piles of gold. There he would sit, inert and passive, with no move-ment except of his eyes, which anxiously scanned the faces of the people who came to see him, and then looked uneasily at the iron-lined door beside him. Every sound he heard, however faint, had to be accounted for; and to the notary's amazement he could hear his dog yawning in the yard. He would rouse himself from his apparent stupor on the day and at the usual hour when rents were received, accounts settled with the vinedressers, and receipts given. Then he moved his chair round on its castors until he was facing the door of his strong-room, and watched while his daughter opened it, after taking precautions against being interrupted, and put away the little bags of money one on top of the other, with her own hand, and locked the door again. As soon as she had given him back the precious key, he would turn silently towards the fire again, putting the key in his waistcoat pocket, where he felt for and touched it from time to time.

His old friend the notary felt sure that the rich heiress was bound to marry his nephew the president, unless Charles Grandet came back, and redoubled his attentions to Grandet, and his exertions on his behalf. He came every day to take Grandet's instructions, went as he bade him to Froidfond, to farms, meadows, or vineyards, sold his crops, and changed all money received for gold and silver, which went secretly to join the bags piled up in the strong-room.

At last death drew near, and the cooper's strong frame wrestled with destruction. Even then he obstinately sat in his accustomed seat by the fire, in front of his strong-room door; and he would pull off all the blankets they tried to keep round him, and roll them up, saying to Nanon, 'Lock it up, lock that away, so that it won't be stolen.'

So long as he could open his eyes, which still looked wide awake and full of life, in contrast to his inert body, he would turn them at once to the door of his strong-room where all his treasure lay, and say to his daughter, 'Are they there? Are they there?' in a voice which betrayed a kind of panic fear.

'Yes, father.'

'Watch over the gold! ... Let me see some gold!'

Eugénie would spread some louis on a table for him, and he would sit for hours at a time with his eyes fixed on the coins, with the blank, fascinated gaze of a child who is just beginning to notice objects, and like a child he would painfully smile. 'That warms me!' he said from time to time, with an expression of perfect contentment on his face.

When the curé came to administer the last sacraments, his eyes, which for several hours had looked dull and lifeless, lit up at the sight of the crucifix, the candlesticks, and the silver holy-water vessel. He stared with concentration at the precious metal, and his wen twitched for the last time. When the priest held the gilt crucifix before his lips so that he might kiss the image of Christ, he made a frightful effort to clutch it, and this last effort cost him his life. He called to Eugénie, whom he could not see, although she was kneeling by his side, bathing his cold hand with her tears. 'Give me your blessing, father,' she begged him. 'Take good care of everything! You will have to give me an account of it all some day,' he said, his last words proving that Christianity is the religion for misers, after all.

And so Eugénie Grandet found herself alone in the world, alone and desolate in her house, having only Nanon to comfort her. At Nanon she might cast a glance with the certainty of finding understanding and response. Big Nanon was the only human being who loved her for herself, and to whom she could talk about her troubles: she was a providence for Eugénie, and no mere servant now, but a humble friend.

After her father's death, Maître Cruchot informed Eugénie that she had three thousand francs a year from property in and near Saumur, six millions invested in the three per cent fund, which had been bought at sixty francs and now stood at seventy-seven, plus two millions in gold and a hundred thousand francs in silver, not counting arrears which were still to come in. Her possessions amounted in all to about seventeen million francs.

'Where can my cousin be?' said Eugénie to herself.

On the day when Maître Cruchot had given his client this account of her possessions, and told her that the estate was now clear and free of all liabilities, Eugénie was sitting alone with Nanon, one on each side of the hearth in the parlour, which now seemed so empty, where everything was a reminder of the past, from the chair raised on blocks of wood where her mother used to sit, to the glass out of which her cousin had once drunk.

'Nanon, we're all alone now!' she said.

'Yes, Mam'selle; and if I only knew where he was, the darling young gentleman, I would go on my own two feet and fetch him.'

'There is the sea between us,' said Eugénie.

While the poor heiress sat mourning in her old servant's company in the cold dark house which was all the world she knew, there was no subject of conversation from Nantes to Orléans but Mademoiselle Grandet's seventeen millions. One of her first acts was to settle an annuity of twelve hundred francs on Nanon who, as she already had six hundred francs a year of her own, became a desirable match. In less than a month she had changed her state of life and condition from that of spinster to that of wife to Antoine Cornoiller, who was appointed head keeper and bailiff of Mademoiselle Grandet's lands and properties. Madame Cornoiller had an immense advantage over her contemporaries: although she was fifty-nine years old she did not look more than forty. Her large heavy features had stood up well to the assaults of time. Her almost monastic way of life had endowed her with a healthy colour and an iron constitution, and she set old age at defiance. Perhaps she had never looked so well in her life as she did on her wedding day. Her homeliness had its own attractiveness, and she cut a pleasant figure, with her sturdy, well-built, well-covered body, and an expression of happiness on her strong, indestructible face that made several people envy Cornoiller.

'Fast colour,' said the draper.

'She might have a family yet,' said the salter. 'She's as well-preserved as if she had been kept in brine, begging your pardon.'

'She has plenty of money, and that fellow Cornoiller is doing very well for himself,' said another neighbour.

Nanon was well liked by all her neighbours, and when she left the old house and walked down the winding street on her way to the church, she met with nothing but congratulations and good wishes. For a wedding present Eugénie gave her three dozen spoons and forks. Cornoiller was overcome by such munificence, and spoke of his mistress with tears in his eyes; he would have let himself be cut in pieces for her. In her new position as Eugénie's confidential housekeeper Madame Cornoiller found as much joy as she did in possessing a husband. She had at last a storeroom of her own to lock and unlock as she chose, and the right to give out provisions every morning, as her late master had done. Then she had two underlings to look after; a cook, and a housemaid who also did needlework, kept the household linen in repair, and made Mademoiselle Grandet's dresses. As for Cornoiller, he combined the duties of keeper and land steward. It goes without saying that the cook and housemaid chosen by Nanon were real *jewels*. And so Mademoiselle Grandet had four servants who were completely devoted to her. The tenant farmers scarcely noticed the change of administration: the worthy cooper had established with a firm hand the usages and customs that suited him long before he died, and they were conscientiously followed by M. and Madame Cornoiller.

At thirty years of age Eugénie knew nothing yet of the happiness of life. Her dull and cheerless childhood had been spent with her mother as her only companion, and Madame Grandet's sensitive and unappreciated nature had made her find life full of pain. As she joyfully said good-bye to life she pitied her daughter who had to go on living. When Eugénie thought of her, she had little to reproach herself with, but a great deal that she must for ever regret.

Eugénie's first and only love had been a fresh source of sadness. She had seen her lover for a few days, and given him her heart between two stolen kisses; then he had gone, and put the whole world between her and himself. Her father had cursed her for her love, and her mother had almost died because of it; and now she was left with nothing but grief and a few faint hopes. All her life she had been spending her strength in striving towards happiness, and nothing had come to sustain her and renew her strength.

The spirit, like the body, must breathe to live: it needs to take in love, from another soul, like oxygen, make it part of itself, and give it back, enriched. Without that wonderful process the heart dies: it suffers from lack of air and ceases to beat. Eugénie was beginning to suffer from her lack of love.

For her, her money was neither a source of power nor a consolation; her whole life lay in love, in her religion, in her faith in the future. Love was teaching her the meaning of eternity. Her heart and the Gospels revealed to her two worlds to look to. Night and day she lost herself in two dreams of infinity, eternal life, enduring love, which to her were perhaps one and the same. She withdrew into herself, loving and believing herself to be loved. For the last seven years her passion had completely absorbed her.

Her treasures were not her millions, with the income they brought in still piling up, but Charles's dressing-case, the two portraits hanging above her bed, the jewellery she had bought back from her father, now proudly displayed on a bed of cotton-wool in a drawer of the old chest, and her aunt's thimble, which her mother had used, and which she devotedly took up every day to work at a piece of embroidery, a Penelope's web, undertaken only for the sake of putting this gold thimble, so endeared to her by memory, on her finger.

It seemed hardly likely that Mademoiselle Grandet would

wish to marry while she still wore mourning. Her sincere piety was well known. And so the Cruchot family, its policy directed by the astute old abbé, confined its tactics to laying siege to the heiress, surrounding her with the most affectionate attentions. Her dining-room was filled every evening with an assemblage of the warmest and most devoted partisans of the Cruchots, who vied with each other in singing the praises of the mistress of the house in every key. She had her physician in ordinary, her grand almoner, her chamberlain, her mistress of the wardrobe, her prime minister, and above all her chancellor, a chancellor whose first desire it was to keep her informed of everything. If the heiress had wished for a train-bearer they would have found one for her. In fact, she was a queen, and never was queen more adroitly flattered.

The great never stoop to flattery : it is the resource of mean and petty natures, who diminish themselves still further in order to creep more easily into the heart of the person round whom they wish to revolve. Flattery implies a self-interested motive. So it was that the people who adorned Mademoiselle Grandet's sitting-room every evening (they called their hostess Mademoiselle de Froidfond) did their best, with results which were truly surprising, to heap praises upon her. This chorus of praise was something quite new to Eugénie, and embarrassed her at first, but little by little her ear attuned itself to hearing her beauty acclaimed, however gross the flattery might be, so that if some newcomer had considered her plain, the criticism would have touched her more nearly than it would have done eight years before. In the end she came to love this homage, which she secretly laid at her idol's feet. So, by degrees, she became accustomed to allowing herself to be treated as a queen, and to seeing her court full every evening.

M. le Président de Bonfons was the hero of the little circle, and his wit, his good looks, his learning, his amiability were incessantly cried up. One of the courtiers would draw attention to the fact that in the last seven years he had greatly improved his financial position, that Bonfons was worth at least ten thousand francs a year and lay, like all the Cruchot property, enclosed within the boundaries of the heiress's vast estates.

'Do you know, Mademoiselle,' another courtier would say, 'the Cruchots have forty thousand livres a year among them!'

'As well as what they have saved!' Mademoiselle de Gribeaucourt, a trusty old Cruchot follower, took up the story. 'A gentleman came from Paris lately to offer Monsieur Cruchot two hundred thousand francs for his office. He ought to sell it, if he could get an appointment as justice of the peace.'

'He means to succeed Monsieur de Bonfons, and is smoothing the way for himself,' remarked Madame d'Orsonval; 'for Monsieur le Président will be a councillor, and then president of the court of appeal. He is so gifted that he is bound to succeed.'

'Yes, he's a very remarkable man,' said another. 'Don't you think so, Mademoiselle?'

Monsieur le Président had tried to adapt himself to the part he wished to play. In spite of his forty years and his dark, forbidding face, which was wizened and dried up like the faces of most lawyers, he dressed like a young man, sported a Malacca cane, never took snuff in Mademoiselle de Froidfond's house, and always went there wearing a white cravat, and a shirt with an enormous frill which gave him a family resemblance to members of the turkey family. He talked to the lovely heiress in familiar terms as an intimate friend, and spoke of 'our dear Eugénie.'

In fact, but for the increase in the number of persons present, the substitution of whist for lotto, the absence of Monsieur and Madame Grandet, the scene of this new episode in the story was almost the same as it had been on that first evening long ago. The pack still pursued Eugénie and her millions; but it had grown in numbers, gave tongue in chorus, and hunted down the prey according to a plan. If Charles had arrived back from the distant Indies he would have found the same people, actuated by the same motives. Madame des Grassins, to whom Eugénie showed nothing but kindness and pity, still teased and vexed the Cruchots. Eugénie's face still shone in beauty against her dingy surroundings; and Charles, if he had joined the company, would have appeared a king, as he had done before.

Still, there had been some progress in the situation. The bouquet that the president had once presented to Eugénie on her birthday had become a daily offering. Every evening he brought the rich heiress a large and showy bunch of flowers, which Madame Cornoiller publicly placed in a vase, and privately flung into a corner of the yard as soon as the visitors had gone.

In the early spring Madame des Grassins made an attempt to disturb the Cruchot party's felicity by talking to Eugénie of the Marquis de Froidfond, whose noble name had fallen on evil days but might be re-established if the heiress wished to restore his estate to him by a marriage contract. She expatiated on the advantages of being a member of the peerage and possessing the title of marquise, and, taking Eugénie's quiet smile to mean approval, she went about saying that M. le Président Cruchot's marriage was not such a settled thing as some people seemed to think.

'Monsieur de Froidfond may be fifty years old,' she would say, 'but he doesn't look any older than Monsieur Cruchot. He's a widower, with children, it's true; but he's a marquis, he will be a peer of France some day, and nowadays matches of that kind aren't found under every bush. As a matter of fact, I know for certain that when old Grandet added his lands to the Froidfond estate, he had every intention of grafting his family tree on the Froidfonds'. He often told me so himself. Oh! Grandet knew what he was about.'

'How can it be, Nanon,' said Eugénie one evening, as she went to bed, 'that he hasn't written to me once in seven years?'

While these events were taking place in Saumur, Charles was making his fortune in the East Indies. His first trading venture, to begin with, had been very successful, and he had quickly realized a sum of six thousand dollars. Crossing the line cured him of many prejudices; he perceived that the best way to make money in the tropics, as in Europe, was to buy and sell men; so he made a descent upon the coast of Africa and bargained for Negroes and other merchandise which could be profitably disposed of at the various markets his interests led him to. He had no thought or time to spare for anything but business. His one idea was to return to Paris clothed in all the glamour of great wealth, and to achieve a position there even more splendid than the one from which he had fallen.

Knocking about and rubbing shoulders with different kinds of men in many different countries, he had observed how greatly customs and ideas vary, and he had grown sceptical; his own ideas had changed. When he saw what was held to be crime in one country regarded as admirable in another, his own moral judgements grew less rigid and he no longer held fixed views on what was right or wrong. Constantly associating with people who thought only of their own selfish interests, he too became selfish and distrustful: his heart grew cold, insensible, indifferent. Charles was a Grandet, and the fatal weaknesses of his Grandet blood did not fail to reveal themselves: he became hard, grasping, and greedy. He made money out of Chinese coolies, Negroes, swallows' nests, children, theatrical entertainers. He became a money-lender on a large scale. As he grew accustomed to disregarding a country's rights in the matter of customs duties he grew less and less scrupulous about respecting the rights of man; and he had no hesitation in going to St Thomas to buy stolen goods from the pirates for a fraction of their value, which he would then transport to the markets where they would fetch the highest price.

Eugénie's pure and noble face may have gone with him on

his first voyage, like the image of the Virgin that Spanish sailors place on the prow of their ships; he may have attributed his first successes to the almost magical power of the vows and prayers of a girl of such sweetness and gentleness of heart; but as time went on, Negresses, mulattoes, whites, dancing women of different lands, experiences of every kind and adventures in many countries completely effaced the memory of his cousin, of Saumur, the house, the bench, the kiss in the passage. He only remembered the little garden enclosed by the old walls because it was there that life had first become a hazardous business for him; but he repudiated all connexion with his family: his uncle was an old twister who had robbed him of his jewellery; Eugénie had no place either in his heart or in his thoughts. She had a place on his ledger as a creditor for six thousand francs. Such conduct and such ideas explain Charles Grandet's silence.

Everywhere he had gone, the East Indies, St Thomas, the coast of Africa, Lisbon, the United States, Charles Grandet, the adventurer, was known as Carl Sepherd, a pseudonym he had adopted in order not to compromise his real name. Carl Sepherd need wear no mask, could safely show himself everywhere, a daring, indefatigable, insatiable man, resolved to make his fortune *quibuscumque viis*, but in haste to wash his hands of villainy and be a respected and respectable man for the rest of his life.

With such methods his rise to prosperity was swift and dazzling, and in 1827 he was on his way back to Bordeaux aboard the *Marie-Caroline*, a fine brig belonging to a Royalist firm. He had with him nineteen hundred thousand francs in gold dust, packed in three casks strongly bound with iron, and he hoped to make a profit of seven or eight per cent by selling it to a mint in Paris. A fellow-passenger aboard the brig was Monsieur d'Aubrion, a gentleman in ordinary to His Majesty King Charles X, a worthy old man who had been foolish enough to marry a lady of fashion. Madame d'Aubrion's money was invested in land in the West Indies, and her extravagance was such that he had been obliged to go to the Indies to sell these estates.

Monsieur and Madame d'Aubrion were members of the family of d'Aubrion de Buch, whose last *captal* or chief had died just before 1789, and who were now in reduced circumstances: they had an income of barely twenty thousand francs and had a very plain daughter to get off their hands. Her mother hoped to find a husband for her who would not want a dowry, as they found that their money was hardly enough to live on, in Paris; but that was an enterprise whose success any man of the world would have considered problematical, in spite of the cleverness he usually credits a woman of fashion with. Even Madame d'Aubrion herself, when she looked at her daughter, almost despaired of passing her on to anyone, even to the most besotted worshipper of rank and blue blood.

Mademoiselle d'Aubrion was a damsel as long of body, as thin and slender, as the insect, her namesake. She had a disdainful mouth, over which hung a nose which was too long, thick at the tip, pasty in its normal state but blossoming out into a display of red immediately after meals, a kind of botanical phenomenon peculiarly disagreeable when appearing in the middle of a pale, bored face. She was all that a mother aged thirty-eight, who was still beautiful herself and felt she had still some claims to admiration, could wish, in fact. Yet the Marquise d'Aubrion had provided her with some compensations for all these disadvantages. She had inherited her mother's very distinguished bearing to begin with. Then she had undergone a regimen that kept her nose for the time being reasonably flesh-coloured, had learned how to dress, acquired charming manners and the pensive expression that catches a man's attention, and makes him think that he has at last met the angel he has sought so long in vain. She had been instructed in foot tactics – had learned how to make her foot peep out and let its smallness be admired if her nose had the impertinence to turn red. Indeed Madame d'Aubrion had made the very best of her daughter. By means of wide sleeves, deceptive bodices, full flowing dresses with trimming carefully applied, and a high-pressure corset, she had produced very curious results, a feminine figure that she should have displayed in a museum for the edification and instruction of mothers.

Charles became very intimate with Madame d'Aubrion, whose precise aim it was to become very intimate with him. People say that during the voyage the beautiful Madame d'Aubrion neglected no means of capturing a son-in-law so rich. At all events, when they landed at Bordeaux, in June 1827, Monsieur, Madame, and Mademoiselle d'Aubrion and Charles stayed in the same hotel, and travelled together to Paris. The Hôtel d'Aubrion was mortgaged to the hilt, and Charles was marked down to clear it. The mother had already said how happy she would be to give up the ground floor to her son-in-law and daughter. She did not share Monsieur d'Aubrion's prejudices in the matter of aristocratic descent, and had promised Charles Grandet to obtain from good King Charles X letters patent which should authorize him, Grandet, to take the name and bear the arms of the d'Aubrions, and to succeed, by buying the entail, to the property of Aubrion, worth thirty-six livres a year, with the titles of Captal de Buch and Marquis d'Aubrion. With their joint establishment they could be very useful to one another, and with a little mutual help and one or two sinecure posts about the court they might count on enjoying a net income of a hundred thousand francs and more, at the Hôtel d'Aubrion.

'And when a man has an income of a hundred thousand francs, a name, a family, a position at court (for I shall see that you are appointed a Gentleman of the Bedchamber), everything is open to him,' she told Charles. 'You could be Master of Requests in the Council of State, Prefect, Secretary to an Embassy, or even Ambassador, if you like. Charles X is very fond of d'Aubrion; they have known each other since child-hood.'

In confidential heart-to-heart talks during the voyage she fired and gave an aim to his ambitions, with a practised hand, and fairly turned his head. He never doubted but that his uncle had settled his father's debts; and he had a sudden vision of himself immediately and safely in harbour in the Faubourg Saint-Germain, at that time the cynosure and goal of high society, reappearing in the social world under the protective screen of Mademoiselle Mathilde's blue, blue-blooded nose as the Comte d'Aubrion, as the Dreux had reappeared one day transformed to Brézès. He was dazzled by the prosperity of the restored dynasty, which he had left apparently tottering, and the enticing dreams of aristocratic splendour which had been born during the voyage found nothing to dim their brilliance in Paris, where he finally made up his mind that he would stop at nothing to attain the giddy heights that his egotistical would-be mother-in-law had pointed out to him. In the panorama of his career, with this brilliant prospect before him, his cousin was nothing to him now but a distant speck. Yet he went to see Annette. As a woman of the world Annette strong-ly advised her old friend to make the match, and promised him her help in all his ambitious schemes. She was delighted to marry Charles off to such a plain and uninteresting girl. During his stay in the Indies he had grown much more attractive: his complexion had darkened, his manner had be-come self-possessed and decided, the manner of a man accustomed to settle matters for himself, to dominate other men, and to succeed. Charles breathed more freely in Paris when he saw that there was a part he could play there.

When des Grassins heard of his return, his approaching marriage, and the fortune he had made, he came to see him to talk about the three hundred thousand francs required to dis-charge his father's debts. He found Charles closeted with a goldsmith from whom he had ordered pieces of jewellery for his wedding present to Mademoiselle d'Aubrion, who was showing him the designs he had made for them. Charles had brought magnificent diamonds from the Indies, but, leaving them out of account, the cost of the settings, of massive silver plate and decorative pieces for the new establishment amounted to more than two hundred thousand francs. He did not recognize des Grassins, and received him with the arrogance of a young man of fashion who has killed four men in as many duels in the Indies. Monsieur des Grassins had already knocked at his door three times. This time, although he was admitted, Charles listened to him coldly and replied without paying any attention to what he had said.

'My father's debts are not mine,' he said. 'I am obliged to you, sir, for the trouble you have been good enough to take – to no purpose so far as I'm concerned. I have not scraped a couple of millions together by the sweat of my brow to chuck at the feet of my father's creditors.'

'Suppose your father were to be declared bankrupt within the next few days?'

'Within the next few days, sir, I shall be the Comte d'Aubrion; so yc 1 will understand that the matter leaves me cold. Besides, you know better than I do that when a man has a hundred thousand francs a year his father has never been bankrupt.' As he added these last words he politely edged Monsieur des Grassins towards the door.

One day early in the month of August of that same year, Eugénie was sitting on the little wooden bench where her cousin had sworn eternal love for her, in the garden where she often breakfasted when the weather was fine. It was a bright fresh morning, and the poor girl was pleasantly engaged in passing in review her memories of the great and small events of her love-affair and the catastrophes that had followed. The sun shone full on the picturesque old wall, revealing its cracked and almost ruinous condition: it had been her whim to leave it untouched, although Cornoiller kept prophesying to his wife that someone would be buried beneath it one fine day.

The postman knocked at the door and handed a letter to Madame Cornoiller, who hurried into the garden calling out, 'A letter, Mademoiselle! Is it the one you have been expecting?' she added, as she gave it to her mistress.

The words seemed to echo in Eugénie's heart as audibly as their real echo ringing from the garden wall and the ramparts.

'Paris! ... It is his writing! Then he must have come back!'

Eugénie turned pale, and held the letter unopened in her hand for several seconds: her heart was beating so fast that she could not break the seal and read it. Big Nanon stood there watching her, her hands on her hips, and joy seemed to emanate visibly like smoke from the wrinkles in her brown face.

'Do read it, Mam'selle! ...'

'Oh! Nanon! why does he come back by Paris, when he went away by Saumur?'

'Read it, and it will tell you.'

Eugénie opened the envelope with fingers that shook. Out of it there fell a draft on the firm of *Madame des Grassins et Corret* of Saumur. Nanon picked it up.

'MY DEAR COUSIN ...'

'I am not "Eugénie" now,' she thought; and her heart stood still.

'You ...'

'He never used to address me like this, like a stranger!' She folded her arms, dreading to read any further, and great tears rose to her eyes.

'Is he dead?' asked Nanon.

'He would not write, if he were!' said Eugénie, and she read the letter through. Here it is:

MY DEAR COUSIN,

You will learn with pleasure, I am sure, that my enterprise has succeeded. You brought me good luck, and I have come back a rich man, as my uncle advised me to. M. des Grassins has just told me of his death, and that of my aunt. The death of our parents is in the natural order of things, and we must follow them in our turn. I hope that you are consoled by this time. Time cures every pain, as I have found by experience. Yes, my dear cousin, I'm sorry to say boyhood's illusions are over for me. Well, well! it happens to everyone. Knocking about the world as I have done, I have had to think about life. I am a man now, where I was a child when I went away, and I have many things to consider which I did not even dream of then. You are free, cousin, and I am free still too. There is apparently nothing to prevent us from carrying out our youthful plans. But my nature is too honourable to allow me to hide my present position from you. I have not forgotten for a moment that I am bound to you. In all my wanderings I have always remembered the little wooden bench ...

Eugénie jumped up, as if she had sat down on blazing coals, and went to find a seat on one of the courtyard steps.

... the little wooden bench where we swore we would love each other always, the passage, the grey parlour, my attic bedroom, and the night when you in your thoughtful kindness made my future easier for me. Yes, indeed; those memories kept up my courage, and I told myself more than once that you were always thinking of me, as I often was of you, at the time we agreed upon. Did you look up into the darkness of the sky at nine o'clock? Yes, I am sure you did. Far be it from me to betray a friendship I hold so sacred. It would be wrong indeed of me to mislead you – not to be completely sincere with you.

A marriage has been proposed to me which is in accordance

with all the views I have come to hold about what is required of marriage. Love, in marriage, is just a wild dream. I know now – I have learned from experience – that it is advisable to obey all the social laws and conform with all the social conventions when one marries. There is some difference of age between us which would be likely to affect you in the future, my dear cousin, more than it would me. I say nothing about your tastes, your bringing up, the mode of life to which you are accustomed, which has few points of contact with life as it is lived in Paris, and would hardly fit in with the existence I am planning. I intend to maintain a household with a certain amount of state and entertain a great deal, and I seem to remember that you like quiet ways. No, I will be quite open with you, and will abide by your decision: you must know how I am situated since the verdict rests with you.

At present I have an income of eighty thousand livres. This fortune makes it possible for me to marry into the d'Aubrion family. In marrying their only daughter, a girl of nineteen, I should take their name, and would acquire a title, the post of Gentleman of the Bedchamber to His Majesty, and a most brilliant position in society. I will confess to you, my dear cousin, that I don't care in the least for Mademoiselle d'Aubrion; but in marrying her I secure a social position for my children of incalculable value in the future. Every day monarchical ideas seem more strongly established. A few years hence my son, the Marquis d'Aubrion, with an entailed estate and an income of forty thousand livres, will be able to choose his own position in the State. We owe it to our children to consider only them.

You see, cousin, how frankly I lay bare before you the state of my heart, my hopes, and my fortune. It is possible that after a separation of seven years you, for your part, have forgotten our childish fancies; but I have never forgotten either your kindness or the promise I made. I remember every word, even those spoken most lightly, which a young man less conscientious than I am, with a heart not so youthful and upright, would hardly feel bound by. When I say that my projected marriage is only a marriage of convenience, and that I still remember our childish love-affair, that shows you, doesn't it, that I am entirely at your disposal? It makes you mistress of my fate, and assures you that if I must renounce my social ambitions I will gladly content myself with the simple and pure happiness which the thought of you so touchingly recalls to my mind ...

'Tra la la! Tra la lee! Tro la la! Boom!' sang Charles Grandet to the air of *Non più andrai*, as he signed himself,

Your devoted cousin,

CHARLES.

'That's doing it handsomely, with a vengeance!' he said to himself. Then he had looked out the cheque, and added this postscript:

P.S. – I enclose a draft on the firm of des Grassins for eight thousand francs, payable in gold to your order, comprising interest and capital of the sum you were so kind as to lend to me. I am expecting a case from Bordeaux with a few things which you must allow me to offer you as a token of my eternal gratitude. You can send back my dressing-case by the diligence, to the Hôtel d'Aubrion, rue Hillerin-Bertin.

'By the diligence!' said Eugénie. 'A thing for which I would have given my life a thousand times!'

The shipwreck was complete and disastrous. The vessel foundered leaving not a rope nor a plank for hope to cling to in the vast ocean. Some women when they find themselves forsaken will tear their lover from a rival's arms and murder her, then fly to the ends of the earth, or seek oblivion on the scaffold or in the tomb. There is something one cannot but admire in that, no doubt. The motive for such a crime is a passion so exalted that human justice is silenced by it. Other women bow their heads and suffer in silence. They go on living, mortally wounded but resigned, weeping often but with no desire to strike back against the person who has injured them, praying for him and cherishing their memories until their last breath. That is love, true love, the love the angels know, the love sustained by pride that feeds on its own grief and dies of it at last. This was the emotion that Eugénie felt when she had read that horrible letter.

She raised her eyes towards heaven, remembering the last words of her mother, who had looked into the future with the clear far vision of the dying; then thinking of her mother's death and the life which had preceded it, which seemed to foretell what her own would be, she looked at her destiny face to face, and read it at a glance. There was nothing left for her to do but to develop her wings, aspire towards heaven, and live a life of prayer until the day of her deliverance.

'My mother was right,' she said weeping. 'One can only suffer and die.'

She went slowly from her garden to the parlour, avoiding her usual walk through the passage; but memories of her cousin lay in wait for her in the old grey room. There on the mantelpiece there always stood a certain saucer which she used at breakfast every morning with the old Sèvres sugar-bowl.

It was to be a memorable and eventful morning for Eugénie. Nanon announced the curé of the parish church. He was related to the Cruchots and so a supporter of the Président de Bonfons' interest, and for several days the old abbé had been urging him to speak to Mademoiselle Grandet of her duty, from a religious point of view, to marry.

When she saw her pastor Eugénie thought he had come for the thousand francs which she gave him for the poor of the parish every month, and she sent Nanon to fetch the money;

but the curé said with a smile, 'I have come this time, Mademoiselle, to talk about a poor girl in whom the whole town of Saumur takes an interest, who from a want of charity towards herself is not living as a Christian should.'

'Indeed, Monsieur le Curé, just now I can't possibly think of my neighbour, I can only think of myself. I am very miserable. My only refuge is in the Church. The Church has a heart large enough to hold all our sorrows, and from her inexhaustible well of love we may draw without fear.'

'Well, Mademoiselle, if we try to help that girl, we shall be helping you. Listen! If you wish to work out your salvation there are only two courses open to you to follow, either you must leave the world or you must live in it and obey its laws, you must follow either your earthly destiny or your heavenly vocation.'

'Ah! your voice speaks to me at a time when I looked for a voice. Yes, God has sent you here, Monsieur. I will bid farewell to the world and live for God alone in silence and seclusion.'

'But you must consider and reflect for a long time before you make such a drastic decision, my daughter. Marriage means life, the veil death.'

'Well, let it be death, and may death come quickly, Monsieur le Curé,' she said with a shocking eagerness.

'Death? But you have great obligations towards society to fulfil, Mademoiselle. Think of those poor creatures who regard themselves as your family, and look to you for warm clothes and firewood in winter and work in summer. Your great fortune is a loan which has to be paid back, and you have always accepted it as a sacred trust. To bury yourself in a convent would be selfish; and you ought not to live alone all your life. For one thing, how could you manage your vast fortune alone? You might easily lose it. In no time you would have innumerable lawsuits on your hands, and you might find yourself involved in inextricable difficulties. Take your pastor's word; a husband can be of use to you; you must preserve what God has given into your hands. I speak to you as a cherished member of my flock. You love God too sincerely not to achieve your salvation in the world, in spite of the world. You are one of its finest ornaments and provide it with a saintly example.'

At this point Madame des Grassins was announced. A thirst for revenge had brought her, and a profound despair.

'Mademoiselle ...,' she began. 'Oh! here's M. le Curé ... I won't say any more, then. I came to talk about some business with you, but I see you are deep in consultation.'

'I leave the field to you, Madame,' said the curé.

'Oh, Monsieur le Curé,' said Eugénie, 'please come back in a few minutes. I need your help very much just now.'

'Yes indeed, poor child!' said Madame des Grassins.

'What do you mean?' asked Mademoiselle Grandet and the curé, with one voice.

'Do you suppose I don't know about your cousin's coming back, and his marriage with Mademoiselle d'Aubrion? ... A woman doesn't go about with her wits in her pocket.'

A flush rose to Eugénie's cheeks and she was silent; but then and there she made up her mind to turn an impenetrable face to the world, as her father had done.

'Well, Madame,' she said dryly, 'I'm afraid I must have my wits in my pocket, for I don't understand you. What have you to say? You may speak freely before Monsieur le Curé; as you know, he is my director.'

'Well, Mademoiselle, see for yourself what des Grassins writes to me. Read this letter.'

This is what Eugénie read:

MY DEAR WIFE,

Charles Grandet has arrived back from the Indies. He has been in Paris for the last month ...

'The last month!' Eugénie said to herself, letting her hand fall to her side. Then she took up the letter again.

I had to dance attendance on him and await his pleasure before the future Comte d'Aubrion condescended to receive me, on my third call. Although all Paris is talking about his marriage, and the banns are published ...

'And he wrote to me after that?' Eugénie said to herself. She left the rest unspoken. She did not exclaim as a Parisian woman would have done 'the blackguard!' But her contempt, though unexpressed, was nevertheless complete.

... the marriage is not likely to take place soon; the Marquis d'Aubrion will not want to give his daughter to a bankrupt's son. I called to tell him of the trouble his uncle and I had taken over his father's affairs, and the clever dodges with which we have managed to keep the creditors quiet so far. Can you believe that the impudent young puppy had the face to say to me – to *me* who for five years have devoted myself night and day to the effort to serve his interests and save his credit – that *his father's affairs were not his*? A solicitor would have been entitled to claim a fee of thirty or forty thousand francs from him, at the rate of one per cent of the total debt; but, patience! twelve hundred thousand francs is strictly and legally due to the creditors, and I mean to declare his father bankrupt. I got involved in this business on the word of that old crocodile, Grandet, and I made promises in the name of the family. If M. le Comte d'Aubrion cares little about his honour, mine at least means a good deal to me; so I shall explain my position to the creditors. At the same time, I have too much respect for Mademoiselle Eugénie, with whom we hoped in happier times to have a closer connexion, to take any steps until you have spoken to her ...

Having read so far, Eugénie paused, and coldly handed the letter back to Madame des Grassins without finishing it.

'Thank you,' she said; '*we shall see ...*'

'That sounded exactly like your father!' exclaimed Madame des Grassins.

'Madame,' Nanon put in, holding out Charles's cheque, you have eight thousand francs to hand us over.'

'Quite so. Be so good as to come with me, Madame Cornoiller.'

'Monsieur le Curé,' Eugénie said, with a dignified composure induced by the thought of what she was about to say, 'would it be sinful to remain a virgin after marriage?'

'That is a question of conscience, and I don't know the answer to it. If you would care to hear what the celebrated Sanchez says about it in his great work *De Matrimonio* I could let you know tomorrow.'

The curé took his leave. Mademoiselle Grandet went upstairs to her father's strong-room and spent the day there alone, refusing to come down even to dinner, in spite of Nanon's urging. She appeared in the evening, when the usual company began to arrive. The Grandets' parlour had never been so full of people as it was that evening, for the whole town had heard the news of Charles's return and of his faithlessness and base ingratitude; but watch and listen as they might, the visitors' curiosity was not gratified. Eugénie was prepared for them, and let no trace of the bitter storm in her heart appear on her calm face. She was able to turn aside the compassionate words and looks of those who were anxious to demonstrate their interest, with a smile. Her unhappiness was concealed beneath a mask of politeness.

About nine o'clock the various rubbers came to an end and the players left their tables, settling their losses and discussing the play in the last hands as they joined the circle of those who had already finished and were sitting chatting. Then as the company made a general move in the direction of the door there came a dramatic turn to events which was to create a stir in Saumur and send a wave of excitement from

Saumur into the *arrondissement* and the four prefectures round about.

'Please stay, Monsieur le Président,' Eugénie said to M. de Bonfons, when she saw him take up his cane.

There was not a person in that crowd of people who did not feel a thrill of excitement at these words. The president turned quite pale, and was obliged to sit down.

'The millions go to the president,' said Mademoiselle de Gribeaucourt.

'Président de Bonfons is going to marry Mademoiselle Grandet – that's clear,' cried Madame d'Orsonval.

'It's the best trick of this evening's games,' said the abbé.

'A very pretty grand slam,' said the notary.

Everyone had his comment to make, his joke to cut: they all saw the heiress as a figure mounted on a pedestal made of bags of gold. This was the *dénouement* of the drama begun nine years before. To ask the president to stay in the face of the whole of Saumur, wasn't that as good as a declaration that she wished him to be her husband? In small towns the conventions are so strictly observed, that an infraction of them of that kind constitutes a most solemn promise.

'Monsieur le Président,' Eugénie began in an unsteady voice, as soon as they were alone, 'I am aware of what it is that you find attractive in me. Swear to leave me free till the end of my life, and never to remind me of the rights which marriage would give you over me, and I am ready to marry you. Oh!' she said, as she saw him about to fall on his knees, 'I haven't finished yet. I must tell you frankly that I cherish memories which time will never efface. All I have to offer my husband is friendship; and I am anxious neither to offend him nor to be disloyal to my own heart. But you can only have my hand and fortune at the price of a very great service which I want you to do me.'

'I am ready to do anything,' said the president.

'Here are fifteen hundred thousand francs, Monsieur le

Président,' she said, drawing a certificate for a hundred shares in the Banque de France from her bodice; 'will you set out for Paris at once? Don't put it off till tomorrow, don't put it off even for an hour, go now. You must go straight to M. des Grassins, get him to give you a list of all my uncle's creditors and call a meeting of them. Then you will settle all outstanding claims, both capital and interest at five per cent, from the day the debts were contracted to the day of repayment; and see that you get a receipt in every case, properly made out. You are a magistrate, and the only person I can entrust this matter to. You are a staunch friend and a man of honour, and you have given me your word: I will take your name as my protection and your word as my stout ship on the hazardous voyage through life. We will bear with one another. We have known each other so long that we are almost relatives, and you would not wish to make me unhappy, I am sure.'

The president fell at the rich heiress's feet in an agony of delight.

'I will be your slave!' he said.

'When you have all the receipts, Monsieur,' she went on, casting a cold look at him, 'you must take them, together with the bills, to my cousin Grandet, and give him this letter. When you come back, I will keep my word.'

The president understood perfectly well that he owed Mademoiselle Grandet's acceptance of him to a disappointment in love, and he made all the haste he could to carry out his orders for fear of some chance bringing about a reconciliation between the lovers. As soon as he had gone Eugénie sank into her chair and gave way to tears. Everything was arranged, and this was the end.

The president travelled post and reached Paris the following evening. Next morning he called on des Grassins, and the creditors were invited to a meeting in the office of the notary with whom the bills were deposited. Not a creditor failed to answer the summons. We must give even creditors their due; they were there to the minute at the appointed time.

Monsieur de Bonfons, in Mademoiselle Grandet's name, paid all the money owing, both principal and interest. The payment of the interest was the event of the century to the astonished business world of Paris. When the receipts had been duly registered, and des Grassins had been given fifty thousand francs for his services, as Eugénie had arranged, the president made his way to the Hôtel d'Aubrion; and there met Charles returning crushed from an interview with his future father-in-law. The old marquis had just informed him in no uncertain terms that his daughter's marriage with Charles would take place only when all Guillaume Grandet's creditors had been paid.

The president first of all handed Charles the following letter:

DEAR COUSIN,

M. le Président de Bonfons has undertaken to deliver to you personally this receipt for all the sums claimed against my uncle's estate, and a receipt acknowledging that I have received this money from you. I heard rumours of bankruptcy, and it occurred to me that with your late father bankrupt you might find difficulties in the way of your marriage with Mademoiselle d'Aubrion. Yes, cousin, you are quite right in the views you have formed about my tastes and manners: I have no doubt little in common with the world of fashion: its ways and its calculations are sealed books to me, and you would never find in my company the pleasures you look for in society. I hope you will be happy according to the social conventions to which you are sacrificing our early love. To make your happiness more complete the only thing that I can offer you is your father's good name. Good-bye. You will always find a faithful friend in your cousin,

EUGÉNIE.

The president smiled at the exclamation that burst from the ambitious young man, in spite of himself, when the receipts were put into his hands.

'We shall both have marriage announcements to make,' he said.

'Ah? You are marrying Eugénie? Well, I am very glad; she is a good-hearted girl. Why!' he exclaimed, as a bright thought suddenly struck him, 'she must be rich!'

'She had about nineteen millions four days ago,' replied the president, with a quizzical look; 'today she has only seventeen.'

Charles looked dazedly at the president.

'Seventeen ... mil–'

'Seventeen millions, yes. When we are married Mademoiselle Grandet and I will enjoy an income of seven hundred and fifty thousand livres a year between us.'

'My dear cousin,' said Charles, recovering some of his assurance, 'we shall be able to push each other on in the world.'

'Quite so,' said the president. 'There is one thing more,' he added, 'I have a little case here that I was to give only into your hands.' And he set down the box containing the dressing-case on the table.

'Well, my dear,' said Madame la Marquise d'Aubrion, sweeping into the room and entirely disregarding Cruchot, 'never mind what poor dear Monsieur d'Aubrion has just been saying to you; the Duchesse de Chaulieu has quite turned his head. I say it again, there is nothing to prevent your marriage ...'

'Nothing, Madame,' Charles answered. 'The three millions which my father owed were paid yesterday.'

'In money?' she asked.

'In full, interest and capital; I mean to have his good name re-established.'

'What nonsense!' cried his future mother-in-law. 'Who is

this person?' she whispered in Charles's ear, as she suddenly noticed Cruchot.

'My man of business,' he replied in a low voice. The Marquise bowed disdainfully in Monsieur de Bonfons' direction, and left the room.

'We are giving each other a helping hand already,' said the president, as he took up his hat. 'Good-bye, cousin.'

'That cockatoo from Saumur is jeering at me. I've a good mind to push six inches of steel down his throat,' Charles said to himself.

But the president had gone.

Three days later, in Saumur, Monsieur de Bonfons publicly announced his marriage with Eugénie. About six months later, he was appointed Councillor to the Court-Royal at Angers. But before they left Saumur Eugénie had the gold of the jewellery she had cherished so long melted down, and gave it, together with the eight thousand francs which her cousin had returned to her, to make a gold monstrance for the parish church in which she had so often prayed for him. From that time on her life was spent partly at Angers and partly at Saumur. Her husband, who had demonstrated his devotion to the Government in a political crisis, was first made President of the Chamber, and finally, a few years later, First President. He waited impatiently and expectantly for a general election, had visions of a peerage, and then ...

'And then the king will be his cousin, I suppose?' said Nanon, big Nanon, Madame Cornoiller, comfortable wife of a citizen of Saumur, when her mistress told her of the splendours in store.

Yet, after all, Monsieur le Président de Bonfons (he had finally dropped the patronymic Cruchot) was never to realize his ambitious dreams. He died a week after his appointment as deputy of Saumur. God who sees all and never strikes unjustly punished him, no doubt, for his calculation and the lawyer's cleverness with which, *accurante Cruchot*, he had drawn up his own marriage contract; in which husband and wife bequeathed to one another *in the event of there being no issue of the marriage all their property, both personalty and real estate, without exception or reservation, in full and absolute ownership, dispensing even with the formality of an inventory, provided that the omission of the said inventory should not injure their heirs and assigns, it being understood that this deed of gift, etc.* This clause may explain the profound respect which the president constantly showed for his wife's desire to live apart. Women called Monsieur le Premier Président the most delicate-minded and considerate of men, pitied him and blamed his wife, as they alone can blame one of their own sex, often going so far as to speak slightingly and with the cruellest insinuations about her sadness and her inability to forget her first love.

'Madame de Bonfons must be very poorly indeed if she has to leave her husband so much alone. Poor thing! Is her condition likely to improve soon? What's the matter with her, is it gastritis or cancer, or what? Why doesn't she do something about it, see doctors, go to Paris and visit some specialist? Her colour has been very bad for some time now. What reason can she have for not wanting a child? They say she is very fond of her husband; why can she not give him an heir, in his position? You know, it's really shocking, and if it's just because of some whim she has taken into her head she is very much to blame ... Poor president!'

Solitary people acquire a clear insight in their endless meditations, and an exquisite sensibility to the few things that touch them, and Eugénie had been taught by loneliness and sorrow and the sad lessons of the last few years to see and feel. She knew that the president wished for her death, that he wanted to be sole possessor of their colossal fortune, now still further increased by the deaths of his uncles the notary and the abbé, whom Heaven had seen fit to call from this world. Lonely as she was, and in a pitiful situation, she understood and pitied the president. He respected Eugénie's hopeless passion as the strongest guarantee of his own interests, for would giving life to a child not mean death to his egotistical dreams and delightful cherished ambitions? And Heaven exacted vengeance for such cold and cruel indifference and calculation on the part of a husband; but Eugénie was left, God's prisoner, and God poured quantities of gold into her lap, although gold meant nothing to her. She was to live, with all her hopes fixed on heaven and saintly thoughts for her companions, in goodness and religious faith, constantly employed in secret in succouring the distressed. Madame de Bonfons was left a widow at thirty-three years of age, with an income of eight hundred thousand livres.

She is beautiful still, but with the beauty now of a woman of nearly forty. Her face is pale, composed, and calm, her voice sweet but rather serious in tone, her manner unaffected. She has all the dignity that is acquired by suffering, and the saintliness of a person who has kept her soul unspotted by contact with the world, but she has all an old maid's rigidity too, and the penurious ways and narrow views of a small country town.

Although she has eight hundred thousand livres a year she stints herself as Eugénie Grandet was stinted long ago, lights her fire only on the days on which her father used to permit a fire in the parlour, and keeps all the regulations which were in force in her girlhood. She dresses as her mother did. The house at Saumur, cold, sunless, always overshadowed by the ramparts and gloomy, is like her life.

She looks carefully after her affairs, and sees her wealth accumulate from year to year; she might perhaps be called parsimonious if she did not disarm criticism by the noble use to which she puts her fortune. Various foundations for pious and charitable purposes, a home for the old, and schools for the young managed by the Church, a public library generously endowed, testify in turn as the years go by to the falseness of the charge of avarice which a few people bring against her.

The churches of Saumur, too, are indebted to her for certain improvements.

They sometimes call Madame de Bonfons *Mademoiselle* in joke, but everybody is very much in awe of her. Her tender heart, which always went out warmly to others, has been fated to find that others approach her only through motives of self-interest or calculation. The pale cold glitter of gold was destined to take the place of all warmth and colour in her innocent and blameless life, and lead a woman who was all feeling to look on any show of affection with mistrust.

'You are the only one who cares for me,' she often told Nanon.

Yet it is her hand that binds up the secret wounds in any household. Eugénie's way to heaven is marked by a succession of deeds of kindness. The true greatness of her soul lessens the effect of her narrow upbringing and the manner of her early life.

Such is the story of this woman, who is in the world but not of the world, who, made to be a magnificent wife and mother, has no husband, children or family. Lately there has been some talk of a new marriage for her. The tongues of the Saumur people are busy, linking her name with that of the Marquis de Froidfond; and indeed his family have begun to lay siege to the rich widow as the Cruchots did to Eugénie Grandet long ago. They say that Nanon and Cornoiller support the Marquis's party, but nothing could be more untrue. Neither big Nanon nor Cornoiller is sharp enough to understand the world's corruptions.

Paris, September 1833

PENGUIN CLASSICS

www.penguinclassics.com

- Details about every Penguin Classic

- Advanced information about forthcoming titles

- Hundreds of author biographies

- FREE resources including critical essays on the books and their historical background, reader's and teacher's guides.

- Links to other web resources for the Classics

- Discussion area

- Online review copy ordering for academics

- Competitions with prizes, and challenging Classics trivia quizzes

PENGUIN CLASSICS ONLINE

READ MORE IN PENGUIN

In every corner of the world, on every subject under the sun, Penguin represents quality and variety – the very best in publishing today.

For complete information about books available from Penguin – including Puffins, Penguin Classics and Arkana – and how to order them, write to us at the appropriate address below. Please note that for copyright reasons the selection of books varies from country to country.

In the United Kingdom: Please write to *Dept. EP, Penguin Books Ltd, Bath Road, Harmondsworth, West Drayton, Middlesex UB7 0DA*

In the United States: Please write to *Consumer Services, Penguin Putnam Inc., 405 Murray Hill Parkway, East Rutherford, New Jersey 07073-2136.* VISA and MasterCard holders call 1-800-631-8571 to order Penguin titles

In Canada: Please write to *Penguin Books Canada Ltd, 10 Alcorn Avenue, Suite 300, Toronto, Ontario M4V 3B2*

In Australia: Please write to *Penguin Books Australia Ltd, 487 Maroondah Highway, Ringwood, Victoria 3134*

In New Zealand: Please write to *Penguin Books (NZ) Ltd, Private Bag 102902, North Shore Mail Centre, Auckland 10*

In India: Please write to *Penguin Books India Pvt Ltd, 11 Community Centre, Panchsheel Park, New Delhi 110017*

In the Netherlands: Please write to *Penguin Books Netherlands bv, Postbus 3507, NL-1001 AH Amsterdam*

In Germany: Please write to *Penguin Books Deutschland GmbH, Metzlerstrasse 26, 60594 Frankfurt am Main*

In Spain: Please write to *Penguin Books S. A., Bravo Murillo 19, 1°B, 28015 Madrid*

In Italy: Please write to *Penguin Italia s.r.l., Via Vittorio Emanuele 45/a, 20094 Corsico, Milano*

In France: Please write to *Penguin France, 12, Rue Prosper Ferradou, 31700 Blagnac*

In Japan: Please write to *Penguin Books Japan Ltd, Iidabashi KM-Bldg, 2-23-9 Koraku, Bunkyo-Ku, Tokyo 112-0004*

In South Africa: Please write to *Penguin Books South Africa (Pty) Ltd, P.O. Box 751093, Gardenview, 2047 Johannesburg*

READ MORE IN PENGUIN

A CHOICE OF CLASSICS

Honoré de Balzac	**The Black Sheep**
	César Birotteau
	The Chouans
	Cousin Bette
	Cousin Pons
	Eugénie Grandet
	A Harlot High and Low
	History of the Thirteen
	Lost Illusions
	A Murky Business
	Old Goriot
	Selected Short Stories
	Ursule Mirouët
	The Wild Ass's Skin
J. A. Brillat-Savarin	**The Physiology of Taste**
Charles Baudelaire	**Baudelaire in English**
	Selected Poems
	Selected Writings on Art and Literature
Pierre Corneille	**The Cid/Cinna/The Theatrical Illusion**
Alphonse Daudet	**Letters from My Windmill**
Denis Diderot	**Jacques the Fatalist**
	The Nun
	Rameau's Nephew/D'Alembert's Dream
	Selected Writings on Art and Literature
Alexandre Dumas	**The Count of Monte Cristo**
	The Three Musketeers
Gustave Flaubert	**Bouvard and Pécuchet**
	Flaubert in Egypt
	Madame Bovary
	Salammbo
	Selected Letters
	Sentimental Education
	The Temptation of St Antony
	Three Tales
Victor Hugo	**Les Misérables**
	Notre-Dame of Paris
Laclos	**Les Liaisons Dangereuses**

READ MORE IN PENGUIN

A CHOICE OF CLASSICS

La Fontaine	**Selected Fables**
Madame de Lafayette	**The Princesse de Clèves**
Lautréamont	**Maldoror and Poems**
Molière	**The Misanthrope/The Sicilian/Tartuffe/A Doctor in Spite of Himself/The Imaginary Invalid**
	The Miser/The Would-be Gentleman/That Scoundrel Scapin/Love's the Best Doctor/ Don Juan
Michel de Montaigne	**An Apology for Raymond Sebond**
	Complete Essays
Blaise Pascal	**Pensées**
Abbé Prevost	**Manon Lescaut**
Rabelais	**The Histories of Gargantua and Pantagruel**
Racine	**Andromache/Britannicus/Berenice**
	Iphigenia/Phaedra/Athaliah
Arthur Rimbaud	**Collected Poems**
Jean-Jacques Rousseau	**The Confessions**
	A Discourse on Inequality
	Emile
	The Social Contract
Madame de Sevigné	**Selected Letters**
Stendhal	**The Life of Henry Brulard**
	Love
	Scarlet and Black
	The Charterhouse of Parma
Voltaire	**Candide**
	Letters on England
	Philosophical Dictionary
Emile Zola	**Zadig/L'Ingénu**
	L'Assomoir
	La Bête humaine
	The Debacle
	The Earth
	Germinal
	Nana
	Thérèse Raquin

READ MORE IN PENGUIN

A CHOICE OF CLASSICS

Leopoldo Alas	**La Regenta**
Leon B. Alberti	**On Painting**
Ludovico Ariosto	**Orlando Furioso** (in two volumes)
Giovanni Boccaccio	**The Decameron**
Baldassar Castiglione	**The Book of the Courtier**
Benvenuto Cellini	**Autobiography**
Miguel de Cervantes	**Don Quixote**
	Exemplary Stories
Dante	**The Divine Comedy** (in three volumes)
	La Vita Nuova
Machado de Assis	**Dom Casmurro**
Bernal Díaz	**The Conquest of New Spain**
Niccolò Machiavelli	**The Discourses**
	The Prince
Alessandro Manzoni	**The Betrothed**
Emilia Pardo Bazán	**The House of Ulloa**
Benito Pérez Galdós	**Fortunata and Jacinta**
Eça de Quierós	**The Maias**
Sor Juana Inés de la Cruz	**Poems, Protest and a Dream**
Giorgio Vasari	**Lives of the Artists** (in two volumes)

and

Five Italian Renaissance Comedies
  (Machiavelli/**The Mandragola**; Ariosto/**Lena**; Aretino/**The Stablemaster**; Gl'Intronati/**The Deceived**; Guarini/**The Faithful Shepherd**)
The Poem of the Cid
Two Spanish Picaresque Novels
  (Anon/**Lazarillo de Tormes**; de Quevedo/**The Swindler**)